Dear Reader,

This is the first of a trilogy of books about the children of Cole and Heather Everett from *Heather's Song*. It features Tanner, the mercenary from last year's novel, *Notorious*. The heroine, Anastasia, was named for Ingrid Bergman's character in the 1950s movie of the same name. However, Tanner's sister, Odalie, was named for a character in a novel written by my favourite historical author, Frank Yerby. The book was *The Foxes of Harrow*, which was published the year I was born, 1946, and made into a major motion picture (which gained an Oscar nomination) in 1947. He was the first African American to have a book purchased for a screen adaptation by a Hollywood studio. His list of honours is almost as long as his list of published novels, and the motion pictures they inspired. Although born in Georgia, he lived, and married, in Spain. George R. R. Martin lists him as one of the people who influenced his own writing. And Mr. Yerby certainly influenced mine!

When I started writing, before I sold my first book, I actually got up enough nerve to write to Mr. Yerby, who was a very famous author. He answered my letter. It was the thrill of my life. I had asked him for advice about getting published, and he was kind enough not only to advise me, but also to send me a copy of his newest hardcover novel, his masterpiece, *The Dahomean* (it still has pride of place in my library).

He is still my favourite historical author and, in my opinion, the finest historical author of all time. So I named Odalie for his heroine, in appreciation for the kind advice he gave me, and for taking time out of his busy life to write to an unknown author in a little town in Georgia. It was a privilege to know him, even from a distance.

I hope you like the book. I really had fun writing it.

Diana Palmer

THE LONER

DIANA PALMER

MILLS & BOON

Mills & Boon
An imprint of HarperCollins*Publishers* Ltd
1 London Bridge Street
London SE1 9GF

www.harpercollins.co.uk

HarperCollins*Publishers*
Macken House, 39/40 Mayor Street Upper,
Dublin 1, D01 C9W8, Ireland

This edition 2023

10 9 8 7 6 5 4 3 2 1

First published in Great Britain by Mills & Boon,
an imprint of HarperCollins*Publishers* Ltd 2023

Copyright © Diana Palmer 2023

Diana Palmer asserts the moral right to be
identified as the author of this work.
A catalogue record for this book is
available from the British Library.

ISBN: 978-1-84845-919-9

This book is produced from independently certified FSC™ paper
to ensure responsible forest management.

For more information visit: www.harpercollins.co.uk/green

Printed and Bound in the UK using 100% Renewable Electricity at
CPI Group (UK) Ltd

To all the wonderful doctors and nurses and aides in the Emergency Room and the old South Tower of the Northeast Georgia Medical Center in Gainesville, Georgia, who took such wonderful care of me in August of 2021 while I fought to survive COVID, and kept me alive so that I could write more books. And thank you to the doctors and nurses and aides who took care of my Jim during his final illness with COVID, in the same place. We were only about five rooms apart during that awful time. I came home. Jim didn't. During the writing of this book, I celebrated what would have been our 50th wedding anniversary. He was the best man I ever knew and my greatest love. And I miss him.

And thank you, my readers, for your wonderful cards and letters of sympathy both online and in writing. I wasn't kidding when I said that I read and saved every one of them. They are treasures, like all of you. I am still your biggest fan. Without you, there would be no Diana Palmer.

THE LONER

ONE

Anastasia Bolton, nicknamed Stasia, was nineteen today. She looked at herself critically in her bedroom mirror, making a face at her lack of beauty. She had a pretty mouth and big, soft brown eyes. Her cheekbones were high, her ears small. She was only medium height, but her figure was perfect. She had elegant long legs, just right for riding horses, which she did, a lot. She'd done barrel racing when she was younger, but art had taken over her leisure hours. She painted beautifully.

She was named after a semi-fictional character in a movie her romantic late mother had loved, *Anastasia*, which starred Yul Brynner and Ingrid Bergman. Her mother had loved the movie and named her only child after the unforgettable heroine. Stasia lived with her father, Glenn Bolton, on a huge beef ranch in Branntville, Texas. Her last living grandparents, her dad's parents, had died of a deadly virus the summer before her graduation from high school. Her mother had died tragically when Stasia was only thirteen. There was no other family left, just Stasia and Dad. They were close. Glenn Bolton was only fifty years old, but he had a very bad heart and he was in the final stages of heart failure. It was treatable, but he hadn't shared that knowledge with Stasia. He was terrified of the open-heart surgery treatment would require. He and the doctor had spoken privately the week before, and afterward, Glenn had been quieter than usual and he'd contacted his attorney. That had been a private conversation as well. Stasia worried about what was being discussed. She didn't want to think about what her life would be like without him. She had no family except him.

Well, there were the Everetts, who lived next door to her father's ranch on their own enormous ranch, the Big Spur. They were sort of like family, after all, since Stasia had known them all her life. Cole Everett and his youngest son, John, were frequent visitors. Glenn had the only groundwater suitable for ranching in the small community of Branntville, Texas. A river ran like a silver ribbon through his entire property, so he wasn't dependent on wells for watering his cattle, as other ranchers were. He approved of Cole and John. He wanted more than anything to see his daughter settled with one of the Everett sons, but she was only in love with one of them—with Tanner, the eldest, who was the cookie-cutter design of the spoiled rich kid.

Cole hadn't spoiled Tanner. That had been his wife, Heather, a former singing star and current songwriter. Their firstborn had been the light of her life. He was twenty-five now, a strong, incredibly handsome young man with dark hair and pale blue eyes, almost silver like his father's, and a Hollywood sort of physique. He liked variety in his women, but for the past year he'd had a girlfriend who enjoyed the jet-setting lifestyle that he favored.

Cole had given Tanner a Santa Gertrudis stud ranch that he'd bought when the owner went into a nursing home, hoping to settle down his wild son. It was a good property, adjoining his and the Bolton properties, but the water situation there was dire. There had been drought in the past year, and they'd had to drill wells to get enough water just to keep the livestock watered. The Bolton place had a river running through it, and many small streams that ran over into the Everetts' holdings. However, that water didn't belong to them so they were unable to divert it for any agricultural purposes.

For a long time, Cole had toyed with the idea of a merger with Glenn Bolton, but Glenn wouldn't hear of it. He found all sorts of reasons for his stubborn attitude. Cole saw right through him. Stasia was still living at home, and she was in love with Tanner. The fly in the ointment was that Tanner didn't like Stasia. He liked experienced, sophisticated women like Julienne Harper, his girlfriend. Tanner could have made an empire out of the ranch Cole had given him, but he wasn't home enough. He and Julienne were always on the go somewhere. Skiing in Colorado, parties on somebody's yacht off Monaco, summers in Nice. And so it went.

Stasia knew about Julienne. Everybody in Branntville did. It was a small community where gossip flourished. It was mostly kind gossip, because the people who lived there had known each other's families for generations. Tanner was one of them. But Julienne, who was sarcastic and condescending, was an outsider, a city woman who'd alienated just about everyone she came into contact with.

Tanner had a couple, Juan and Minnie Martinez, who ran the house and managed the ranch for him while he played around the world. They'd just threatened to quit because of

Julienne's last visit to Tanner's ranch. Cole had played peace-maker. The Martinezes were good at ranch management, and somebody had to keep the place going. Cole despaired of Tanner ever settling down to real work. He'd always had everything he wanted. Cole, who adored his wife of twenty-five years, hadn't had the heart to make her stop coddling Tanner, while there had still been time to knock some of the selfishness and snobby attitude out of him. Now, it was too late.

Stasia came into the living room where the men were talking with a tray of coffee and sliced pound cake. All three men stood up, an ancient custom in rural areas that still had the power to make her feel important. Her generation cared less about such things, as a rule, but Stasia was a throwback. Glenn had raised her the way his parents had raised him. She'd absorbed those conservative attitudes on the way of the modern world. She hated it. She hated it most because Tanner liked women who belonged to that sophisticated crowd.

John Everett looked like his mother, Heather, in coloring, at least. He was big and blond and drop-dead handsome, with his father's silver eyes. His young sister, Odalie, also looked like Heather, with pale blue eyes and blond hair. Tanner was the one who most resembled Cole, who was tall and still handsome. Tanner had the same thick, dark hair but with pale blue eyes that just missed being the silver of his father's.

John went forward and took the heavy tray from her. He grinned. "I love cake."

She laughed, a soft, breathy sound. "I know." She smiled at him with warm affection. He was like a cuddly big brother to her. He knew that and hid his disappointment.

"How's the art going?" Cole asked with a smile.

"I sold a painting!" she exclaimed happily. "There was a man passing through, from someplace back East, and he saw the landscape I painted in the local art shop. He said it was far too cheap for something that lovely, so he gave Mr. Dill, the owner, three times my asking price. I was just astonished."

"You paint beautifully," John said, his eyes brimming with love that she tried not to see. He indicated the landscapes on the walls of the Bolton home; one with running horses in a thunderstorm was entrancing.

"Thanks," she said, flushing a little. "Mr. Dill said the man looked Italian. He was big and muscular and he had these two other big guys with him. He was passing through on the way to San Antonio on business."

"Sounds ominous," John teased.

She laughed as she poured coffee all around and offered cake on saucers with sparkling clean forks. "He told Mr. Dill I should be selling those paintings up in New Jersey, where he was from, or even New York City, where he owned an art gallery and museum. He said he was going to talk to some people about me! He even took down Mr. Dill's number so he could get in touch." She sighed. "It was probably just one of those offhand remarks people make and then forget, but it was nice of him to say so."

"You really do have the talent, Stasia," Cole told her. "It would be nice if he could put you in touch with some people in the art world back East. If that's what you want to do with your life," he added gently.

She smiled at him. "I like to paint." She grimaced. "I'd like to marry and have a family, though."

"No reason you couldn't do both," John said. "And if you had to fly back East to talk to people, well, we have a share in a corporate jet, you know. You could let us know when you had business there and I could go with you."

She smiled sedately. "Thanks, John, but it's early days yet."

"How's Tanner?" Glenn asked.

Cole's light eyes grew glittery. "Off on another trip. To Italy, this time. My daughter's studying opera in Rome. He thought he'd stop by and see her on the way to Greece."

"Odalie has a beautiful voice," Stasia replied, hiding disappointment. She'd hoped Tanner might show up with his brother and father. "Does she want to sing at the Met eventually?"

"She does," Cole replied. He drew in a long breath and sipped coffee. "I'll hate having her so far from home. But you have to let kids grow up." He glanced at John with affection. "At least this one doesn't have itchy feet yet!"

"I'm a homebody," John said easily. "I love cattle. I love ranching. I don't want to leave home," he added, with a covert glance at Stasia.

"Good thing," Cole chuckled. "I have to leave the ranch to somebody when I'm gone."

"You're not going anywhere for years," Glenn chided. "The Everetts are a long-lived bunch. Your grandfather lived to be ninety."

"Yes, but my father died before he was sixty, and my mother died before I married Heather," Cole replied. His face tautened as he relived those days, when a lie split him apart from Heather, whom he'd loved with all his heart. It had been a torment, those months apart before he discovered that a jealous rival had told him lies about Heather's parentage and made it sound as if he and Heather were actually related. They weren't, but it was heartbreaking just to think it. Heather had been singing in nightclubs in those days. Cole had been cruel to her because her feelings for him were all too visible and he thought nothing could ever be allowed to happen between them. When he found out the truth, Heather had already backed out of his life. It had taken a long time to win her back.

He glanced at Stasia. She reminded him of Heather in her youth. She wasn't as beautiful as his wife, but she was sweet and gentle and she'd make someone a good wife and mother. He knew that it wasn't going to be Tanner. The boy had mentioned weeks ago that he hated having to talk to her father at all because Stasia would sit and stare at him as if he were a tub of kittens needing a home. He found her juvenile and dull. John, on the other hand, adored her. Cole grimaced as he processed the thought, because Stasia so obviously thought of John as the brotherly type.

"Now, about what I mentioned on the phone," Cole began as he finished his coffee and put it and the cup and saucer back on the tray.

"I know what you're going to say," Glenn broke in, with a smile. "But I'll never give you permission to dam the streams."

Cole sighed. "Only one stream, the one nearest my south pasture. The cattle are going to suffer for that decision," he told the older man. "We've drilled every well we can."

"I know that," Glenn told him. "I've got things in motion that will solve your problem. Don't bother asking; won't tell," he chuckled. "But you're worrying over something that's already fixed. Just a matter of time. Short time, at that," he added with a faraway look in his eyes.

Cole started to argue, realized it would do no good and just shrugged good-naturedly. "Okay. I'll rely on your conscience."

"Good place to put trust, since I do have one," Glenn replied. He scowled. "That boy of yours got himself into hot water in France, they say. It was on the front page of the tabloid those Lombard people back East publish."

"It wasn't Tanner who started the trouble," Cole replied curtly. "It was his…companion, Julienne Harper. She started a row in a high-ticket French restaurant with another woman, and her companion started cursing and threw a punch at Tanner when he intervened. Tanner had some explaining to do." He glanced at Glenn. "This time, I didn't interfere, and I wouldn't let Heather do it, either. The boy's got to grow up and take responsibility for his own actions."

"According to the tabloid, he made restitution for the victim's dress and paid the dentist to replace one of her date's front teeth." Glenn shook his head. "Reminds me of you, when you were that age," he added with twinkling eyes. "Got arrested for a bar brawl when you got home from the service, I believe…?"

Cole glared at him. "Some yahoo made a nasty joke about what soldiers did overseas. I took exception. The guy wasn't ever even in a good fight, what would he know about being a soldier?"

"Well, your dad kept him from suing, at least," Glenn said, and chuckled. "Most people around here were scared of your father anyway. He was a real hell-raiser."

Cole smiled sadly. "He was, and he died far too young."

Glenn knew some stories about Cole's father that he wasn't about to share. Some secrets, he reasoned, should be kept. "Your son was in black ops when he went in the military, wasn't he?" he asked suddenly.

Cole looked thunderous. "Yes, he was. I didn't find out until he was back home." He sighed. "I told him he had to get an education, so he joined the Army and got it that way. At least he finally decided that risking his life daily wasn't conducive to running a ranch. It's one reason I bought the old Banks property for him, to draw him back home." He leaned forward. "I thought if his income depended on ranching, he'd make better life decisions. At least he did get a degree in business, even if it was between assignments." He laughed shortly. "And then he met her." He shook his head.

Everybody knew what that meant. "Her." Julienne Harper. The fly in the ointment. She'd lured Tanner back into the jet-set lifestyle the military had purged him of, and now he was even less responsible than he'd been before.

"A bad woman can make a fool of a good man. And sometimes, the reverse," Glenn added. He didn't mention his late wife, but they all knew the tragic story. His wife had been suddenly and hopelessly attracted to a man straight out of prison who'd worked on the ranch. The tragic consequences were still being lived down, by Glenn and his daughter.

"She was a good woman," Glenn said stubbornly. "She was just impulsive and easily led."

"Which is how many good people end up in prison," John said sadly. "I'm hopeful that we can keep my big brother out of it."

Cole stood up with his son and clapped him on the back. "Something I'll never have to worry about with you," he said with obvious affection. "At least one of my kids turned out right."

He was referring to Odalie, who'd had a brush with the law in her teens, just as Tanner had—when going into the military was the only thing that saved him from serving time. Tanner had fallen in with a few ex-cons and gotten drunk with them. He passed out in the back seat just before they robbed a convenience store, but Cole had to get attorneys and pull a lot of strings to keep his son out of jail.

"Most kids turn out right eventually, even those who have a rough start," Glenn said with a smile.

"Yours turned out very well," Cole said, smiling gently at Stasia. "She reminds me of Heather at her age."

"And that's a compliment indeed," Glenn said, watching his daughter flush shyly.

"Well, we'd better get back home," Cole said. "We're getting ready for roundup. If you need any help over here, when you start, you know we'll do anything you need us for."

Glenn smiled and shook hands with both men. "Yes, I do know. I'll send my hands over if you need extras. We're waiting a week to start."

"We'd be grateful. No matter how many hands you have, a few more are always welcome."

"Done. Just say the word."

"I don't guess you'd like to take in a movie this weekend?" John asked Stasia on the way out the door.

She hesitated. She didn't want to hurt his feelings. She smiled gently. "I would, but I'm working on a landscape and I have a real incentive to finish it quickly now, just in case that nice man does give my name to somebody back East," she added with just the right touch of regret. She liked John, but she didn't want to encourage him. Nobody could replace Tanner in her heart.

"Okay," John said easily, hiding his disappointment. "Rain check?"

"Sure," she lied.

He grinned and they all went out onto the long, wide front porch to see the Everetts off.

Cole stared into the distance. "Good weather, for early spring," he said, admiring the grass that was just getting nice and green in the pastures beyond. "I hope it holds."

"So do I," Glenn replied.

"See you."

Glenn threw up a hand. Stasia waved.

The Everetts got into one of their top-of-the-line black ranch trucks and drove away.

"John's sweet on you," Glenn mentioned over supper that night.

"I know," she groaned. "I like him so much. He's like the

brother I never had. But he wants more than I can give him, Dad. It wouldn't be right to encourage him."

Glenn nodded. "I agree." He cocked his head at her. "It's still Tanner, isn't it?"

She grimaced and nodded. "I can't help it. I've been crazy about him since I was fifteen, and he can't see me for dust. It's such a shame that I'm not beautiful and rich and sophisticated," she added heavily.

"A man who loves you won't care what you are or what you've got," he said gently.

"I guess not." She poked at her salad with a fork. "Julienne's really beautiful. Of course, she doesn't talk to the peasants. I saw them together in Branntville just before they left for overseas. She looked me up and down and just laughed." Her face burned at the memory. "So did he, in fact. He thinks I'm a kid."

Glenn had a faraway look in his eyes. "That could change," he said, almost to himself. He turned his green eyes toward her, the same green eyes that he'd hoped she might inherit. But her brown ones were like his late wife's, he reflected, big and brown and beautiful. "You'll inherit this ranch," he added. "I hope you'll have the good sense to find a manager if you don't want the responsibility of running it yourself. And I hope you won't be taken in by any slick-talking young man who sees you as a meal ticket," he added worriedly, because she wasn't street-smart. "This property has been in our family for a hundred years. I'd hate to see it go to an amusement park for tourists."

She frowned. "Why would it go to someone like that?"

"Oh, this guy offered me a lot of money for the property just the other day, when I was at the bank renewing a couple of CDs. The bank president introduced us."

"You told him no, of course, right, Dad?" she asked.

He pursed his lips. He drew in a breath. "I told him I'd think about it." He didn't tell her that the ranch was mortgaged right up to the eaves of the house. His bad business decisions had led the place to ruin, something Cole Everett knew. It was why Cole was trying to get the ranch. But then, he'd have it soon, Glenn thought sadly. He couldn't let Stasia become a charity case, and the sale of the ranch wouldn't even cover the debts, as things stood.

"But it's right next door to the Everetts' new ranch, the one Tanner owns," she said worriedly. "Can you imagine how nervous purebred cattle would react to an amusement park next door?"

"I can," he said.

"Tanner could lose everything," she said. "His livelihood depends on the new ranch, especially since his dad has already split the inheritance at Big Spur between John and Odalie. He figured Tanner would have enough of a fortune with the Rocking C."

The Rocking C was the name of Tanner's ranch. The previous owner, an elderly Easterner, had called it his rocking chair spread. Hence the name.

"Well, Tanner might have to make a hard decision one day, when I'm gone," Glenn said, and smiled to himself.

"Are you plotting something, Dad?" she asked, worried.

"Me?" He contrived to look innocent. "Now what would I have to be plotting about?" He chuckled. "How about some of that apple pie you made? This new heart medicine my doctor put me on makes me hungrier, for some reason."

"You never did tell me what he said when you went to him last week," she mentioned.

"Same old same old. Take it easy, take my meds, don't do any heavy lifting," he answered, lying through his teeth. He was due to speak to a cardiologist soon, who would decide if the open-heart surgery Glenn was frightened of was required to keep him alive. A quadruple bypass, the doctor had recommended, and soon. Too many fats, too much cholesterol—despite Stasia's efforts to make him eat healthy food—a history of heart problems and not recognizing his limitations had placed Glenn in a bind. Glenn hadn't shared that information with his daughter. No need to worry her. Besides, he felt fine.

A few days later, just after his cardiologist's office had phoned with an early appointment to see the intervention cardiologist, he started up the steps into the house and fell down dead.

Tanner Everett was cursing at the top of his lungs, so loudly that Cole had to call him down before Heather heard her son.

"Go ahead. Rage," Cole snapped. "But the will can't be broken. Nobody in Branntville will agree that Glenn Bolton wasn't in his right mind when he made it."

"An amusement park! Next to my purebred herd!" Tanner whirled on his heel and glared at his parent. "And if I don't marry damned Stasia, that's my future."

Cole felt the resentment in the younger man. In his place, he'd have felt it as well. "It was a rotten thing to do," Cole agreed. "But we have to deal with what we've got, not what we wish we had."

"I'm twenty-five years old," Tanner raged. "I'm not ready to get married! Not for years yet!" He stared at his father. "You were older than me when you married Mother."

"Yes, I was. I played the field for years." He looked down at his boots. "I loved your mother. For a long time. But she had a rival who lied and said Heather and I were related by blood. She took years away from us."

Tanner knew the story. All the Everett kids did. It would have been a tragedy if Cole hadn't found out the truth in time.

"Heather was just about Stasia's age when I fell in love with her. She sang like a nightingale, just like Odalie does now. She was beautiful. She still is," he added softly.

Tanner, who'd never felt love for a woman, just stared at him without comprehension.

"There must be some way to dispute the will," Tanner said doggedly.

"Go ahead and look for one. But I'll tell you what our attorney told me: no way in hell. You marry Stasia or the property goes to the Blue Sky Management Properties. Stasia will get nothing."

"Bull! The ranch is worth millions," Tanner shot back.

"It was. Glenn was no rancher, even if his father was," Cole replied curtly. "The place is mortgaged to the hilt, and you can't tell Stasia that. She's got enough misery right now coping with her dad's death."

He grimaced. Even he was sorry for Stasia's situation. She couldn't help what she felt for him, he supposed. But he was never going to return it. She had to know that.

"Which leads to my suggestion. I'm giving you the Rocking Chair ranch, and merging Stasia's with Big Spur. We can pay off the debt by disposing of most of Glenn's beef cattle and replacing it with our purebred Santa Gerts. In other words," Cole added quietly, "either you make a go of your new ranch or you'll be out in the cold. I'm not changing my will, Tanner," he added firmly. "I'm sorry. But you could do worse. And it's about time you stayed home and managed your own damned ranch and stopped acting like some Eastern playboy."

"I hate dust and cattle," Tanner muttered. "You should have given this ranch to John. Then he could have married Stasia."

"She wouldn't have him," Cole said simply. "She doesn't love him."

He jammed his hands into his slacks pockets. "She doesn't

love me, or she wouldn't have encouraged her father to do this to me!"

"I don't think she had anything to do with it. Glenn had a bad heart and she had no other family."

"You could have adopted her," Tanner said with a sarcastic bite in his voice.

Cole's silver eyes narrowed and started to glitter.

Tanner cut his losses. "All right, damn it!" he muttered. "I'll do what I have to. But I'm not settling down to aprons and babies and white picket fences! Not for any woman!"

"Nobody's asking you to." Cole felt sorry for Stasia. She loved Tanner. Maybe, maybe love on one side would be enough. But he was worried. Tanner was like a stallion with a new rope around his neck. This wasn't going to end well.

Stasia was in shock. She sat at the kitchen table and made the funeral arrangements, relying on the funeral home and her father's attorney for clarity. She was penniless. Worse, her father had forced his attorney to put a clause in the will. Tanner married Stasia, or her father's property went to the amusement park man, who would turn it into a loud, cluttered nightmare for Cole's horses and cattle.

She'd heard the terms of her father's will from their attorney, Mr. Bellamy. She was shocked and miserable, especially when she recalled what her father had told her only days before, about the offer from the amusement park man. She'd thought she'd get at least enough to live on from the deal, but it wasn't like that at all. Her father had kept so much from her. The ranch was worthless, mortgaged and debt-ridden. There was no way she could run it for a profit, or even hire someone to run it. And if the amusement park man got it, it would destroy Cole's ranch as well as Tanner's. Neither of them could afford to tear down existing stables and barns and rebuild them in a safer location. In fact, there would be no safer location, with that overlit nightmare of noise and light nearby. Not for one minute did she think Tanner would give in to her father's subdued blackmail and marry her. She was ashamed that he'd even put that clause into his will. Tanner would probably think it was her idea.

When she finished the preliminaries, she went to her father's closet to look for his one good suit and his best pair of wing-tip shoes. The sight of the suit set her off. She dropped down onto the spotless paisley duvet on her father's bed and bawled until her eyes were red and her throat hurt.

That was probably why she didn't hear the knock at the front screen door, which wasn't locked. It was also probably why she wasn't aware that Tanner had come into the room and was standing in the doorway, just watching her.

He knew she loved her father. He was the only family she had left. It hurt him to watch her cry. He'd had no real feelings for her, except irritation that she was infatuated with him and let it show too much. But she was really hurting. He'd never lost anyone in his family. Both sets of his grandparents had been dead when he was born. He didn't know death except as an observer.

"Stasia?" he called quietly.

She jumped, startled, and lifted a wet face with red-lined eyes to his. She swallowed down the pincushion that seemed stuck there and swiped at her eyes with the tail of the bright yellow T-shirt she was wearing.

"It wasn't my idea, what he put in the will," she said, as if he'd already accused her of engineering it. Angry brown eyes warred with his pale blue ones. "He said the amusement park man would pay him millions for the land and in the next breath he said it had been in our family for over a century and we should hold onto it." She swallowed, hard.

"I didn't know we were bankrupt. I didn't even know how sick he was. He said he had new medicines and the doctor said he was...doing fine..."

Her voice trailed off. Tears fell like rain from her eyes. She averted them. She could feel the pity in him and she didn't want it. He didn't want her. She knew that without asking.

But he couldn't watch her cry. It touched something deep inside him that he didn't even know was there.

He moved closer, pulled her abruptly into his arms and folded her up close. "Let it out," he said in the softest tone he'd ever used to her. "Go on."

She did. Her father had never been physically affectionate with her. Neither had anyone, except Tanner's mother. It was so nice to be held and cuddled and told that everything was all right. Nothing was all right. But Tanner was strong and warm and he smelled of deliciously expensive male cologne. She melted into him, letting the tears fall.

Finally, she regained control of herself and moved shyly away. "Thanks," she choked.

He shrugged. "I've never really lost anyone," he confessed. "Buddies, when I was in the service, and in black ops. But nobody close."

She looked up at him. "I guess not. I'm really sorry. About the will." She swallowed, hard, and turned away. "I'll find another buyer," she said softly. Then she remembered that she couldn't sell it herself. Besides, it was bankrupt. "There must be a way..."

"There's no way to break the will," he returned. "My father spoke to our attorneys about it. Your father was in his right mind all the way," he added tersely.

She grimaced. Her pale blond hair was loose around her tanned shoulders, disheveled and wavy. In the tight jeans and

T-shirt she was very attractive. Tanner had never noticed how attractive before.

"Well, then, how about this?" she asked suddenly while he was still exploring her with new curiosity. "Suppose we get married and the next day we get it annulled?"

"No wedding night?" he asked with mock horror.

She just looked at him. "I don't want to sleep with you. I don't know where you've been," she said and forced a smile.

Humor flared in his pale blue eyes, despite his resentment at the situation they were in.

"Besides, I'm saving myself for my future husband," she added with faint hauteur.

"Most men like experience, not green girls, in bed," he returned.

"My husband will be an extraordinary man, with a good heart and brain, and he'll be grateful that I waited for him," she said.

"Of course. He'll be standing right next to the Easter Bunny, waiting."

She just stared at him. "Dad and I went to church every Sunday. My great-grandfather was a Methodist minister. He founded the church we go to. My great-grandmother had been a missionary in South America. You may live in the fast lane. Some of us still believe in fantastic things and we like a slower pace."

"Snail pace," he scoffed.

"Whatever." She turned away from him and pulled her father's suit and a clean, nicely pressed white shirt, and a tie, off the clothing rack. She picked up his immaculate black wing tips and put them beside the bed.

"What are you doing?"

"He has to have clothes to be…buried in." She almost faltered, but she took a deep breath and pulled a duffel bag out of her father's closet. "I'm going to take them to the funeral home and go over the arrangements with the director. Dad had insurance there that will pay for it all."

He was surprised at her efficiency, despite her obvious grief. He didn't know her well. In fact, he was convinced now that he'd never known her at all.

"Can I help?" he asked.

"Yes." She turned to look at him. "Go home."

Both eyebrows went up.

She cleared her throat. "I'm sorry. I don't mean to be snappy. I just want to be alone. I have to work through this by myself." Her eyes turned back up to his. "You never answered me. Can't we just get married long enough to fulfill the terms of the will and then get it annulled?" she asked.

"I honestly don't know," he replied. "But I can find out."

She nodded. "Then, would you do that?"

He stared at her with open curiosity. "You've followed me around like a puppy for years," he said absently, watching her flush. "For a woman with a monumental crush on me, you seem strangely reluctant to try and keep me."

"Most girls have crushes on totally unsuitable people," she said, fighting a scarlet blush. "They outgrow them."

"And you've outgrown yours?" he asked softly.

"Yes," she lied, averting her eyes. "Well, sort of. I mean, I just turned nineteen and I think I may have a future in art."

Sure she did, he thought to himself. She was talented, but a lot of women painted and never went past giving the canvases away as presents. His eyes went to a landscape on the wall of a windmill with a lone wolf sitting on a small grassy rise under a full moon. Beside it was a portrait of her father that was incredibly lifelike. He frowned. She really did have talent. Not that it would do her much good in this back-of-beyond place.

There was a knock at the front door. She stopped what she was doing, went around Tanner and went to the door. Two women from the church were there with casseroles and bags of food and even a cake.

"Oh, it's so kind," Stasia said, the tears returning as she hugged both women. "Thank you so much!"

"Your dad was a good man, honey," the eldest of the two said. "We all know where he'll end up."

"If you need anything at all, you just call. Or if you'd rather not be here alone at night…"

"I'll be fine," she said softly. "But thanks for the offer."

They said their goodbyes. She put up the food, aware that Tanner had come out of her father's room and was now lounging against the kitchen door.

"Small towns," he said, shaking his head. "And all the little idiosyncrasies that go with them, still amazes me. Nobody outside a rural community would bring food."

"It's a tradition here," she said quietly. "I've done my share of cooking to give to grieving families." She glanced at him. "But of course, that's not your style or Julienne's. You hate living here."

"I do. I've spent too much time in exotic places to settle for boring routine, even to please my father." He thought about Julienne with faint despair. She was great in bed. He'd never be able to replace her. She was already furious and threatening to leave him after being told about Bolton's will. "This isn't the lifestyle I want. The family ranch, a bunch of kids, a wife in the kitchen." He made a face. "I'd rather have Julienne in see-through black lace than all that put together."

"Fortunately for you, that's still possible. All we have to do is fulfill the conditions of my father's will and you can be off to the south of France, or Greece, or wherever you people go for fun."

He frowned. "What do you do for fun?"

Her eyebrows arched. "I paint."

"Besides that." He looked around. "It's just dirt and grass and mesquite and cattle."

"I like cattle. We have little white kittens in the barn," she said, and her face softened, like her brown eyes. "There's a family of rabbits out behind the barn. Dad had to fence them out of the kitchen garden." She stopped, swallowed hard, went back to storing away food. "I like to sit on the front porch in the evening, just at dusk, and listen to the dogs baying in the distance."

"God, how exciting!" he groaned.

She turned and looked at him. "You're older than me, but you don't know much about the way things really are, do you? You live in a fantasy world of artificial people and artificial places. I'd rather be who I am, where I am, doing what I'm doing."

"You'll rot here," he said shortly.

She just smiled. "Difference of opinion. I like my reality straight up. I don't need exotic stimulation to keep me going."

His eyes narrowed. "Meaning that I do?"

"You're not like your brother. John loves ranching," she said. "He doesn't even like to drive his Mercedes. He's more at home in a pickup truck or in the saddle. He's a realist, like me." She smiled sadly. "You're a dreamer. This is never going to be your kind of life." She said it with a hollow certainty that dulled her eyes. She loved him so much. But he didn't want her. He told her so with every word, every look. What he'd said about Julienne was like a knife through her poor heart.

"If I don't keep the ranch and make it pay, I'll lose everything and be stuck here in the mud like my brother," he said shortly.

"It's the end of the world as we know it!" she exclaimed in mock horror.

"What would you know about pretty clothes and party manners and sophisticated behavior?" he asked frankly, giving her a once-over with wise, sharp eyes. "I'd be embarrassed to take you anywhere in decent society."

"Did someone ask you to?" she asked reasonably and hid the pain that careless sentence dealt her pride.

"Just as well," he retorted. "Because if we can marry one day and annul it the next then, by God, we're doing it. I can't think of a worse fate than being tied to you for life."

"Thanks. I like you, too," she replied with a determined smile, mischief showing in her twinkling eyes. "You're sooooo sexy!" she breathed in her best femme fatale voice, puckering her lips at him.

Suddenly, it was just all too much for him. He was confused. She made him hungry, in a way even Julienne couldn't, and he was feeling trapped all over again. Damn her father!

He let out a rough curse and turned and walked out of the house. Only then did she give in to the misery she felt, when he could no longer see it.

TWO

Glenn Bolton was buried next to his wife and his parents in the big Bolton lot at the Branntville Methodist Church cemetery. The whole Everett family, except for Odalie, who was in Italy, attended. Just the same, Odalie sent a huge spray of flowers and called Stasia to tell her how sorry she was. Stasia and Odalie had been casual friends in school. In fact, Stasia was one of the few friends who stuck by her during all the problems Odalie had brought on herself back then. Despite being somewhat conceited and snobbish, Odalie felt close to Stasia. The feeling was mutual.

Tanner showed up at the ceremony, too. Julienne had reluctantly agreed to go, but Heather put her foot down. She was not sharing a pew with her son's call girl, as she put it. She ignored Tanner's outrage and Cole stepped in. He could do more with Tanner with a look than Heather could with outright indignation. Tanner went to the funeral with his parents and his brother. Without Julienne.

Stasia sat on the front pew and listened to the sermon, her face sad but resigned. Her father had been a good man. She would miss him terribly. But life did end. It was one of the absolutes that people just had to accept. Everybody died eventually.

She stopped on the way to the cemetery to speak to people she knew. At the cemetery there was a simple graveside service. Her father, a military veteran in his youth, had a flag and an honor escort from the local VFW post. It made her proud. When they handed her the flag that had covered his coffin, she couldn't hold back the tears.

"You're coming back home with us tonight," Heather told her when they were walking away from the cemetery. "You don't need to be alone."

"No, you don't," John agreed with a grin. "I'll show you my new calves!"

She smiled. "I'd like that."

Tanner glared at them all and went to his own car without a word and drove away.

"Tanner and I discussed Dad's will," Stasia told them later in their living room. "We're hoping that we can get married one day and have the marriage annulled the next," she added. "Then we'll both have what we want."

Cole ground his teeth together. He'd seen the will. He didn't want to tell her what he'd said to Tanner just two hours earlier. There was no room in the explicit language of the will for a loophole. They got married and they stayed married for at least a year. That was the deal. Stasia had been too upset to look at the will, but Cole and Tanner were allowed to see it, since it involved both Cole's ranch and the one he'd given Tanner. It was an airtight thing. Glenn must have anticipated Tanner's approach to marriage. It was a shame. But there was nothing even their fine attorneys could do to combat it. At least, not immediately. They were still looking for that one tiny hole in Glenn Bolton's document that would give Tanner and Stasia a way out. It was a long shot, but not impossible. They were great attorneys.

Cole dreaded telling Stasia about the reality of the will. For the time being, he put it on hold. There would be time to talk tomorrow, after the trauma of the funeral today.

Julienne was pacing the living room of Tanner's ultra-modern ranch when he got home. Her black hair curved in a pixie cut around her pretty face, but she was glaring for all she was worth.

"The Simpsons are waiting for us in Athens," she said angrily. "And we're stuck here while you nose around that stupid girl and her ranch!"

He stared at her with cold eyes. The only good thing about her was what she could do in bed. He'd never liked her. She was ice-cold with most people, and money was the only thing that mattered to her. She had no compassion for anyone.

"Not to mention your mother's attitude!" she went on. "What century does she think we're living in? I'm no call girl!"

"My parents and my siblings are conservative ranching people," he began.

"Well, I'm not hanging around here smothered in dust and smelly cattle. When can we leave?"

"My father and I went to see our attorneys this morning about the will. There's no provision to break it." He jerked off his tie and tossed it aside, dropping onto the couch. Nearby was a grand piano. He played, his mother considered, magnificently. She'd taught him from the age of three.

"What does that mean?" Julienne demanded.

"It means that if I don't marry Stasia, I lose the ranch."

"Oh, big deal, you can buy another one…"

"The ranch is where my inheritance is," he bit off. "No ranch, no money, Julie."

She stopped dead. "You mean…?"

"I mean that if I don't marry Stasia, her ranch has to be sold to the property developer and I'll have an amusement park for a neighbor. I'll lose the cattle because of the constant noise. No money. If I marry her, I keep the ranch, and the money."

"And what about me?" Julienne asked harshly.

"What about you?"

"You could marry me," she said, and smiled at him.

"The only money you have is mine. I'd be no better off," he pointed out. He got up and poured himself a stiff whisky. "And don't tell me you have scruples about sleeping with a married man," he said coldly, staring at her. "You don't have scruples."

She grimaced. He was right.

"So, what do we do?"

"You go to Greece. I'll marry Stasia and leave her here to take care of things. I'll be along in a week or so."

"Oh." She brightened.

"Did you think I had putting down roots in mind?" he asked, laughing. "Hell, I'm not family material, I never was. I did black ops when I was in the service. You learn not to value the things that normal people do." He finished the whisky. "This won't take long. I'll wrap it all up by next weekend. Get us a hotel on the beach. Somewhere ritzy."

"I'll do that very thing," she purred.

Tanner went looking for Stasia two days later. She was sitting on the porch of his father's ranch house with a cat in her lap, one of the white kittens from her barn that she'd given to John, who loved cats. She was wearing her ever-present jeans with a yellow pullover sweater because it was a nippy spring evening. Her hair was loose around her shoulders. She looked very sad. And very young.

He was surprised at his lack of antagonism for her. He thought that she'd talked her father into inserting that clause in the will. But the Everett attorneys said that wasn't the case at all. The old man was afraid that Stasia would be thrown on the street when he died, because the ranch was in such debt. She'd have stability, at least, with Tanner. They told Cole and Tanner one other thing as well. Stasia didn't know that the will had a clause that required a year of marriage. She hadn't even looked at the will.

She glanced up and saw him. Her face colored, just slightly, a response that she couldn't help. She hated seeing the irritation in his eyes as he approached her. He was hating this, hating her, and there was nothing she could do.

"Well?" she asked in a world-weary tone. "Is there a loophole? Can we get married and have it annulled right after?"

He sighed. "No."

She averted her gaze to the kitten in her lap. "I loved my father, and I miss him. But if I died today, I'd be looking for him with a big iron skillet and I'd lay his head open for leaving us in this mess!"

He shoved his big, lean hands into his jean pockets. "Pity he didn't try to leave you to John. He'd be down in Dallas buying rings by now."

"I know." She grimaced. "John is such a nice man."

Nice. It told him all he needed to know about her opinion of his younger brother. It was a damned shame that she couldn't love the other man.

"How long?" she asked, lifting her eyes to his.

Both dark brows lifted.

"How long do we have to stay married?" she asked, irritated.

He leaned against the railing of the porch steps. "A year."

She grimaced.

"Our attorneys couldn't find a single loophole that would avoid it, either," he added quietly.

"I guess Julienne has broken every piece of crockery in your house by now," she said idly.

"If she was over there, no doubt. She's gone to Athens. I'm going, too, next week."

She looked up at him with fire in her eyes. "Oh, I see. You're going to marry me so that you can keep your ranch, and then you're flying off to Greece to commit adultery the same day?"

His high cheekbones colored with anger. "I'm marrying you to keep a damned amusement park off my south border," he said shortly. "It's not going to be a traditional marriage."

She stood up, putting the kitten down very gently. She felt sick inside. She looked up at him. It was still a long way. "This town is still talking about my mother and what she did to Daddy," she said, trying to control her temper. "I've been the subject of gossip my whole life because of it. And now you're going to set the tongues wagging all over again by shaming me in the eyes of every decent person for miles around?"

"It's a paper marriage, not a real one," he said, his voice biting into her ears. "I don't want to marry you in the first place," he added, eyes blazing with bridled fury. "You're a little country hick with no sense of sophistication, you're barely educated and you're still living in the Victorian age! I couldn't tie myself to a worse woman if I looked for years!"

Her brown eyes glittered with feeling. Her small, pretty hands curled by her side. "Careful, cowboy," she said very softly. "I don't have to marry you."

He choked back another insult as he realized what she was saying. Of course she didn't have to marry him. She could sell the ranch and he couldn't do a thing to stop her. She'd have no money, having cut off her nose to spite her face, but she'd be revenged. And he and Cole would have a good chance of losing their respective ranches because the noise the amusement park would make would play merry hell with those purebred herds of Santa Gertrudis cattle, not to mention the quarter horses Cole also bred for sale.

"Hell and damnation!" he burst out.

She cocked her head and studied him. The pain those insults caused her was carefully camouflaged. You didn't show weakness in front of the enemy, ever. She'd learned that from her father.

"Go ahead," she invited. "Turn the air blue. Raise hell. And see if it does you one glimmer of good." She looked him up and down with forced indifference. "Like I want to tie myself to a man who uses women like a handkerchief."

She turned and started to walk away.

He had her before she went one step, her slender body suddenly riveted to the length of his in an embrace that set every nerve she had tingling with helpless pleasure.

"Brave words," he whispered at her mouth. "Pity I don't believe a word of it."

"I mean…!"

His mouth cut off the angry remark. She was soft and warm and her mouth tasted of iced tea and mint. He'd managed for years to keep his hands off her, because he was attracted to her, however reluctantly. Now, it was to his advantage to give in to those feelings. He needed her consent to the will's requirements as much as she needed him.

Heated, throbbing seconds later, he lifted his mouth just

above hers. "Pure bravado, was it?" he asked, his deep voice husky with arousal.

"I don't want to kiss you," she lied, but she wasn't moving away.

He smiled as he bent again. "Liar," he whispered, and it sounded almost like an endearment.

She sank against him, helpless to resist a kiss she'd ached for since her fifteenth birthday, when he'd refused to come to the birthday party with John and Odalie and broken her heart. It was the closest to heaven she'd ever been. She couldn't afford to give in to him, to allow herself to be manipulated this way. But, oh, it was sweet, to feel his arms closing around her, to feel the expert, demanding pressure of his mouth on hers. He wanted her. She wasn't so naïve that she didn't know what the sudden hardness of his body meant. He might resent the will, he might even resent her, but he wanted her. At least, there was that.

The sound of a car pulling up in the driveway brought him to his senses. He was so lost in her that he'd forgotten the will, Julienne, all of it. He looked down into drowning brown eyes in a flushed, yielded face utterly beautiful with fascination, wonder.

Her mouth was softly swollen. She was trembling. His big, lean hands smoothed down her arms and he smiled.

"I'm not marrying you," she managed.

He only chuckled, deep in his throat. "Yes, you are. My mother's already online looking at wedding gowns. You'll be prodded up to Neiman Marcus before you know it."

"I'm not playing second fiddle to your...!"

He bent and kissed her, very softly, enjoying the helpless response of her sweet little mouth. "I'll see you tomorrow. I have to go up to Dallas to see a man about a new stud bull." He kissed her one last time, smiling at her expression.

She looked loved. Fascinated. He hated the pleasure her expression gave him. She was still a virgin, he knew that from things her father had let drop. He'd never been with an innocent. It would be an adventure. As for Julienne, well, what this little sunflower didn't know wouldn't hurt her. He could be discreet.

"I don't want to marry your son," Stasia muttered while she tried on the wedding gown Heather had coaxed her toward. "He's only doing it to save his ranch, because of Daddy's will."

"A lot of men marry for the wrong reasons, and things end beautifully," Heather said softly, her pale blue eyes smiling at the younger woman as she tugged a piece of lace into place. "I had a particularly rough time getting to the altar."

"I know," Stasia said softly and smiled. "But everything turned out very well for you and your husband."

"Eventually," Heather said. "I was independent by then and certain that I wanted a singing career. Cole was equally determined that he came first." She sighed. "So we compromised. I taught music locally and wrote songs for various singing groups, including Desperado," she replied, naming one of the more famous rock bands.

"Didn't you mind giving it up?"

"I loved him," Heather said simply. "A career would have meant spending my life on the road. I couldn't raise a family that way, and I wanted children, oh, so much!" she added. "I wouldn't trade one second of my life for what I thought I wanted. And if I could live my whole life over, I wouldn't change a single thing."

Stasia smiled. "I love kids. I wouldn't mind having one of my own." She looked up at Heather. "Tanner doesn't love me, you know," she said abruptly. "His livelihood depends on keeping the ranch solvent. If Dad hadn't put that clause in the will, Tanner would never have considered me. He said I was an ignorant little country hick," she added, grimacing because the harsh words still stung.

"You aren't," Heather said quietly. "You're a talented artist. Very talented. Don't let him put you down."

"Oh, I don't," Stasia replied. She laughed. "I'm nobody's doormat. Not even his."

"No, you aren't," Heather agreed. "See that you remember that. He's always been stubborn and reckless. He and his father have gone head to head times without number because of it. He's too much like Cole."

"Was your husband like Tanner, when he was younger?"

"Exactly like him, doubled," Heather said flatly. "I'm still amazed that I didn't lay his head open with a baseball bat from time to time." She shook her head. "But he's like a rock when things get tough," she added. "I had a bad time giving birth to Tanner. I was in the hospital for over a week with complications, because they'd had to do a C-section. Cole never left me for a second. They put a cot in my room for him, and we stayed there, both of us, while I healed. Cole is an amazing person," she added softly.

Stasia smiled. "And you still love him, after twenty-five years of marriage," she marveled.

"Oh, yes," she agreed. "And you'll love Tanner just like that, after years of marriage and children."

"He doesn't want children," Stasia said sadly.

"Men don't know what they want," Heather said. "Give it time. He's been like a stallion all these years, free and wild. A bridle is a new thing to him."

"He said Julienne was in Athens waiting for him," Stasia confessed. "I told him that I'd had enough gossip in my life, without him rushing off to commit adultery on my wedding day."

"Well!" Heather exclaimed, and she hugged Stasia. "I was going to advise you, but I think you've got the situation well in hand."

Stasia hugged her back. "Thanks," she said, smiling. She looked at Heather with a sigh. "I'm only sorry it can't be John," she said softly. "I know how he feels, and it hurts me to see it. But I can't help what I feel for Tanner."

"John will find his own special woman one day," Heather said. "Pity is a sad excuse for a marriage."

Stasia nodded. "Yes, it is. But I wouldn't hurt John for the world."

"John will do just fine. Now. We need hose and shoes and a garter for you to toss!"

The wedding was the social event of Branntville. It had taken two weeks for the rushed preparations.

Julienne, sitting alone in Athens, had raged at Tanner over the phone, that it was just a paper marriage, so all the social things were unnecessary. To which Tanner had replied that Julienne could fly back and argue about them with his mother. Knowing how that lady felt about her, Julienne gave in with bad grace and hung up on him.

He mentioned the phone call to his father as he studied the new breeding bull in the barn at his ranch.

Cole gave him a steady glare. "You're being married by a minister," he pointed out.

He shrugged. "So?"

"So, marriage is a solemn vow," he replied. "You promise to be faithful to your partner."

"It's just words."

"Not to me," Cole said shortly. "Nor to your mother. We've been married for twenty-five years and I've never been tempted to stray. Neither has she."

Tanner eyed his father with surprise. "Never?"

Cole's silver eyes glittered. "Never. When I make a promise, I keep it."

"Well, it's different with me and Stasia," Tanner said curtly. "You got married voluntarily. I'm being forced to marry her."

"No, you're not," Cole said. "You can stop the wedding right now. Just go over to Stasia's place and tell her you're not going through with it."

Tanner grimaced. "Sure. And lose everything I own."

"For all the attention you pay to it, I can't imagine you'd miss it," came the surprising reply. "You're too busy hitting resorts all over the world with your professional escort."

Tanner's lips made a thin line. "You've been talking to Mom."

"You know how she feels about the woman."

"Julienne is my business."

"She'll be Stasia's business if you keep it up."

"I'll be discreet," Tanner told him. "But I'm not ready to settle down. Not even to keep an amusement park from moving in next door."

"Your choice," Cole said. He gave his son a steady look. "Don't disgrace the girl," he added in a soft, curt tone. "She's had enough of that."

He turned and walked off.

Tanner knew what he meant. Stasia and her dad had been forced to live down her mother's infamy, her affair, in a small community where everybody knew everybody else's business. It had been traumatic for Stasia, because she was still in school while it was going on. Worse, when her mother's paramour had suddenly turned his attention to a younger, richer woman, it had been Stasia who found her mother hanging on the back porch...

"Mr. Everett, there is a call for you," Minnie Martinez called from the back porch. Her voice was as cold as her demeanor. She didn't like her boss or his nasty girlfriend. Her husband was the full-time ranch manager. She kept the house immaculate and stood in for Tanner's secretary who worked two days a week in the office. Answering the phone was part of her responsibilities.

"Who is it?" he called back.

She made a face.

"Julienne?" He smiled as he turned and walked quickly up the steps and into the house, ignoring Minnie's angry glance.

"You should fire that stupid housekeeper," Julienne said, immediately going on the offensive. "She wouldn't call you to the phone because your father was with you. Is everybody afraid of him?"

"You've never seen him mad," he pointed out, "or you might have some sympathy for those of us who have."

"He's just a man," she scoffed.

"Sure." He sighed. "What do you want?"

"You! When are you coming over?"

"I'm getting married in two days."

"Then if you're not here in three days, I'm coming over there to pry you away from your wife," she replied. "Honestly, you don't have to sleep with her, do you?"

"Of course not," he lied, because just thinking about Stasia in his bed made him rigid with reluctant attraction.

"I'll make it worth your while," Julienne purred. "Do you miss me?"

"Yes, I miss you," he said. "And yes, I'll be there in three days."

"I'll hold you to that, lover," she said.

He went back outside to talk to Juan Martinez about the new bull. It was spring, too late to put him on the heifers, but he would be turned out with the other bulls in the fall, to produce a new crop of purebred Santa Gertrudis bulls and heifers next spring.

Stasia was getting dressed for her wedding with Odalie Everett helping in the bedroom of the Bolton home.

"I'll trip over my train and go headfirst into the minister," Stasia moaned as Odalie fastened the last button on top of her wedding gown and twitched the fingertip veil carefully in place on the upswept, artistic hairdo with its pearl hairpins.

"You won't," Odalie said, smiling. She was beautiful, as Stasia wasn't. A lot of people didn't like her, because she could be arrogant and cruel. But she was kind to Stasia because Stasia had been her staunch friend during Odalie's brush with the law in high school. Odalie never forgot a favor, and she was fond of Stasia even without their shared past. There was one other reason for her affection: John loved Stasia and she loved her brother. Odalie and Tanner didn't get along, except for brief periods. Like the rest of her family, Odalie had no use for Julienne and said so, frequently.

"I wish I looked as good as you do," Stasia sighed, because Odalie was a picture in blue chiffon, with her pale blond hair looped in braids on top of her head, her pale blue eyes in a face as beautiful as a fairy's.

"You look just fine," Odalie teased.

"And I wish I could sing like you. Honestly, you had me in tears when you sang 'Jerusalem' in church last Sunday!"

"I inherited that from Mom," Odalie said with a smile. "She could have been famous, but she just wanted to marry Dad and have kids."

"That's what I'd like to do. Have kids." Stasia made a face. "Fat chance. Tanner doesn't want kids. He's made that very clear. Which reminds me, I have to start taking a pill today."

"You didn't take the shot?" Odalie asked.

"I'm afraid of it. Some women get terrible weight gain. I like being slender. And how do you know about birth control?" she chided.

Odalie laughed. "Not for the reason you're thinking. I'm not shacking up with anybody until my wedding night. I've lived for a chance at the Metropolitan Opera all my life. But after I do that, if I can, I want the sort of marriage my parents have."

"I envy them," Stasia said.

"Me, too." She stood back and gave Stasia a nod. "You look super. And to allay your suspicions, I was having trouble with my periods, so my doctor put me on birth control just long enough to get them regulated again. Not for other purposes. As you might have noticed, my family doesn't move with the times."

"Well, most of it doesn't," Stasia corrected.

"Yes, I know, Tanner's private life is a trial to us all. Mom and Dad hate that woman he's with, but he won't give her up and he doesn't care what people say. Well, he will now, because Dad's made threats."

"He has?" Stasia was fascinated.

"You see," Odalie said as she started to put on the pretty wide-brimmed blue hat that went with her dress, because she was maid of honor, "Tanner doesn't actually own the ranch outright. Dad has controlling interest in it, along with a provision that allows him to buy back Tanner's interest in it any time he pleases."

"But he wouldn't do that," Stasia protested. "He'd leave Tanner penniless, especially since your dad has already split the Big Spur between you and John."

"Dad won't do it unless he's pushed," Odalie corrected, adjusting the tilt of her hat. She turned, smiling, a picture in her dressy outfit. "But Tanner won't push him. He's getting married today. And I expect Tanner will find marriage so sweet that he may never leave town again," she teased.

Stasia blushed. "On the other hand, he may light a shuck out of town immediately after the ceremony."

"Don't be silly. Okay, it's almost time. I'll leave you to drive over to the church with John."

Stasia hugged her. "Thanks, for everything."

"You're going to be my sister." She grinned. "I always wanted one. See you later."

Stasia watched her leave. Big, handsome John Everett, his brother's best man, paused in the doorway to look at Stasia with eyes that ate her from head to toe. He adored her. He knew that he'd never replace Tanner in her eyes, but he never gave up hope.

He towered over his father and his brother, a giant of a man with thick blond hair, and silver eyes like his father. In his fancy suit, he looked good enough to eat.

Stasia didn't love him, not the way she loved Tanner, but she did adore him. She grinned at him. "Nice of you to give me a ride."

"No problem. Old Mr. Sartain, who's giving you away, can't drive anymore because he refuses to get his cataracts removed." He sighed. "I hope he won't walk you into the minister at the church."

She laughed. "I'll keep him pointed in the right direction. Shall we go?"

John put her in the car, very carefully because of her voluminous dress, and then climbed in beside her.

"The church is full," he remarked. "I didn't realize we knew so many people."

"Your mother said that a lot of them came from out of town."

"Yes, they did, including a friend of Tanner's from some-place called Jacobsville, down south of San Antonio." He leaned down. "They say he's a merc!"

Her eyes widened. "A professional soldier?"

"Worse. He owns an anti-terrorism school. He spent years in the profession himself. Now he trains younger men in anti-terrorism tactics. His name's Eb Scott."

"Tanner seems to know a lot of unorthodox people," she pointed out. "Remember what a stir he caused last year when one of his former black ops friends from England came to town? I thought Odalie was going to swoon, just to get his attention."

"Oh, he was off women," John replied drolly. "And he must have been a eunuch, to resist my sister." He shook his head. "Honestly, even if she is my sister, she's a dish!"

"Yes, she is," she agreed. "I didn't dare ask her, but is she still mourning your friend Cort?"

Cort Brannt was John's best friend, the son of King Brannt and his wife Shelby. They had a daughter as well, Morie, who was married to one of the Kirk brothers of ranching fame up in Wyoming.

"Not really," John said. "She didn't love him. She was only jealous when he started paying attention to his new wife, before she was his wife. And that's a story that ended with Odalie turning into the sweetheart she is now. Meanwhile she has those opera cravings. She wants to sing in the Met one day, so she's pressuring Mom and Dad to let her extend her studies in Italy. I think they'll give in. Mom could have done that, you know. She really has the voice for it."

"I know. Even Tanner is musical," she recalled. "He plays the piano with a gift."

"While the only thing I can play is the radio," John lamented as they pulled up in front of the church.

"And that's a fib," she teased. "You play classical guitar with a gift of your own."

"Mom gave up on me with the piano. I wanted to play baseball from morning to night, not sit at a piano." He glanced at her with a grin. "Guitars are portable. I could practice anywhere. And I was invited to. Anywhere *not* in the house," he added, and she laughed with him.

He parked his luxury car at the door of the sparkling white Methodist church with its towering steeple and went around to help Stasia out in the extravagant folds of her lovely wedding gown.

He paused and looked down at her with eyes that agonized, a look he quickly erased when she turned her gaze upward and smiled at him.

"Be happy," he said softly.

"Thanks."

He escorted her to the door, handed her over to Mr. Sartain, a family friend of hers and the Everetts' for many years, and took his place at the altar beside his irritated brother.

Tanner faced front, even when the music started and Stasia came down the aisle. For two cents, he told himself, he'd turn around and march past Stasia right out the front door. And what would that accomplish? He'd lose the ranch and his inheritance and be forced to work for a meager living for the rest of his life. Well, he'd have the legacy his grandmother had given Heather, which she'd given to him on his twenty-first birthday, and it would keep him for a while. But it wouldn't accommodate the jet-set lifestyle he and Julienne were accustomed to.

No, better to tough it out and do what he had to do. After all, Stasia meant nothing to him, really, and what he was doing would save the ranch. Stasia could stay here with her painting and he could go to Athens with Julienne. It was only for a year. A lot could happen in that length of time. Stasia might actually fall in love with his suffering brother John, divorce him and marry John. He frowned. Odd, how little that appealed to him, all at once.

The music was playing. The "Wedding March." He had the sheet music, in a book of similar compositions, but he'd never played it. The organist missed a note and he grimaced inwardly. But there was no time to process the thought.

Stasia was standing beside him, her head barely topping his shoulder. He looked down at her upturned face and almost caught his breath at her innocent beauty. He'd never really paid that much attention to her over the years. She was just Stasia, mostly a nuisance he had to put up with to see her father. But now...

"Dearly beloved," the minister began.

And Tanner took a deep breath.

THREE

The service seemed to fly by. Tanner slid a simple gold wedding ring onto Stasia's finger, and she put a similar one on his. The rings had already been purchased before she could pick out something she liked. He hadn't been forthcoming about an engagement ring and she'd been too proud to ask, especially after he'd bulldozed ahead with the wedding bands.

At least he'd gotten the size right, she thought, even if he hadn't asked what hers was. It was just one more indication that he had nothing invested in this wedding.

The reception was held at the church's fellowship hall, after the bride and groom had posed for wedding photographs. After noting Tanner's bored expression, Stasia was certain that she'd never want to look at them again. He made sure that everyone knew this was a forced marriage, that he had no interest in either it or his bride. He was doing it because

Stasia's father had made it a condition of his will. Everybody knew that, it being a small community.

It didn't help Stasia's lacerated feelings one bit, and she wished that she'd refused to go through with it. Her own weakness for Tanner had been her worst enemy. She loved him too much to refuse the marriage. But she should have refused. How was it going to be, with him off partying with another woman and the whole world knowing about it, guessing even if they weren't certain? Tanner Everett wasn't a man to be forced into anything. It would be like a bull yearling with his head in a noose and a cowboy on the other end. He'd fight, and keep on fighting, to throw it off.

She'd hoped against hope that he might give in, might actually learn to love her in time. But he was making it clear, without saying a word, that he didn't want Stasia. Looking around her, she noted the looks of sympathy she was getting from older people in the community. They knew. They all knew, and pitied her.

She cut the cake in the fellowship hall, Tanner's cool hand only briefly over hers as the photographer snapped his picture.

"And that's another one I'll never look at," she said under her breath as the photographer moved around the room.

"Excuse me?" Tanner asked, surprised.

She looked up at him with actual distaste. "The photographs. It must be like taking pictures at a wake. Nobody except your family is ever even going to see them."

He felt a surge of shame as she said that. He felt guilty for a lot of things. This was just the latest one. He was surprised at that, because shame was new to him.

He started to speak, but Stasia had already moved away, leaving her untouched cake behind, to speak to a friend of her father's.

★ ★ ★

It was a long afternoon, because the bride and groom weren't anxious to leave, and the gathering was a good excuse for some gossip and a lot of catching up on the part of local people. Stasia, standing with Heather Everett, watched it with interest.

"There's old Miss Barnes with old Mr. Jackson," she whispered to Heather, in a joyful undertone. "Both old, both single, and she's keen on him. He lost his wife last year and she's never been married!"

"Matchmaker," Heather chuckled as she sipped coffee.

"I like to see people happy," Stasia said simply, smiling.

"I wish you were, sweetheart," Heather said softly.

Stasia looked up at her with wide, resolved brown eyes. "I can still go stay at my own house when I like, your husband said so. It was nice of you both to offer to pay it off, much less keep it up."

"Everybody needs a place to go when they want some privacy," Heather said. "Besides, and I have to apologize for saying it, acquiring your father's ranch solves our water problems for many years to come."

"I did notice that," Stasia teased. She sipped her own coffee. "I'm just glad that it stays in the family, so to speak," she added. "It's been in our family for generations. It's home."

Heather touched her veil, pushed back over her pretty long, waving light blond hair since Tanner had lifted it and kissed her, quite coldly, during the ceremony. "The gown is beautiful. I noticed the photographer got a lot of candid shots."

"Oh, yes," Stasia said enthusiastically. "He got one of Tanner being bored during the ceremony, and one of Tanner being bored while cutting the cake. Look, there he is getting one of Tanner being bored drinking coffee…!" She stopped at the sight of Heather's expression. "Sorry. I got carried away."

"I'm sorry, that things have turned out like this," Heather replied. "You know you've always been my first choice of possible daughters-in-law."

"I do know that, and I'm sorry, too." She drew in a breath and looked toward John, who was sipping punch with a morose expression. "Why couldn't it have been John?" she wondered sadly.

"That's a question for the philosophers. And it's going on five o'clock. If you and Tanner stay here much longer, there's going to be even more gossip, I'm afraid."

"Good point. I'll turn in my coffee cup and announce it to him. He'll be thrilled. I'll have to alert the photographer," she added pertly.

Heather just shook her head.

Stasia put the coffee cup back on the table and thanked the caterers at the same time. Then she went in search of Tanner.

He was standing by a window, looking out, both hands in his pockets.

"Your mother says that if we don't leave soon, people will start to talk about us," she told him.

He seemed to brighten.

Stasia motioned to the photographer. "Quick," she said, "get a shot of him right now!"

The photographer, not in the know but obliging, took a quick picture of the two of them, Stasia with a sparkle in her eyes and a smile on her pretty mouth, and the surprised but amused look on Tanner's face.

"Be careful with that one," she told the photographer. "It's sure to be a family favorite."

He chuckled. "Yes, ma'am."

"We're about to leave," she added, "so you might get shots of the car that a few of the local boys have been…adorning."

"Yes, I, uh, did notice soap and cans and string…"

She grinned as he left.

"What did you mean, about the photo being a family favorite?" Tanner asked.

"It's going to be the only one the man gets that shows you with anything except a bored expression, of course," she replied. "Don't mind my feelings, I don't have any. They've all been sheared off by the will and its aftermath. This isn't a day I want to remember, either, Tanner, in case you wondered," she added, and she turned around. "Thank you all so much for coming!" she called to the people, most of whom she knew. "We're going home now."

There were some knowing looks and a few chuckles as she started toward the front of the fellowship hall with Tanner trailing behind. He stopped to talk to a tall man with blond-streaked brown hair, a little silver mixed in. He shook hands with him before rejoining Stasia. He didn't offer to introduce his visitor.

Stasia didn't care. She was tired and sick of the whole business. Seeing John standing to one side with agony in the eyes he averted, she felt even sicker.

She went to him, compassion forcing her actions. "You have to come and stand with the others, because I'm throwing the bouquet right to you," she teased.

He forced a smile. "Throw it to somebody who has a chance of getting married."

She wiggled her eyebrows. "I am!" She leaned up and kissed his tanned cheek and then went back to Tanner.

He was suddenly irritated, and it showed. "What was that all about?" he asked curtly.

"Nothing you need to know," she said with a cool smile. She turned and lifted the bouquet, with people lining the sidewalk on both sides. "Okay. Here goes!" And she threw the bouquet, just as she'd threatened, right into John's hands with the accuracy she'd always managed when playing sand-lot baseball with her friends as a child. Sadly, most of those friends had moved to the city for better opportunities, or married. They kept touch, but lightly. Small towns had little to offer in the way of high-tech opportunities.

The chauffeur held the door to the limo open, with the photographer hovering.

"We might as well make a traditional exit," Tanner muttered under his breath. Before Stasia could react, he pulled her into his arms, bent, and kissed her as if he were going to war on a sailing ship and would never see land again.

She went under like a drowning victim. She never could resist him. She loved him too much. She stifled a moan as the kiss deepened into layers of pleasure she hadn't dreamed of. Just when she thought she might actually pass out from it, he twirled her back up into a standing position and eased her into the car.

"That should solve two dilemmas," he said shortly as the chauffeur closed the back door.

"What…dilemmas?" she managed in a high-pitched, shivery tone.

"Your need for proper photos, and my brother's to keep his hands off you."

She gaped at him.

He averted his eyes. That had popped out from nowhere. It hadn't been on his mind. Or had it? He hadn't liked Stasia kissing John, even on the cheek. That had made him angry. And guilt had ridden him hard, because he'd cared nothing for Stasia's feelings as he proceeded to turn a wedding into a wake.

He was confused and mad and unsettled. It wasn't a normal condition. He'd stopped to thank Eb Scott for showing up, but he hadn't wanted to introduce his friend to Stasia. He didn't want any part of his life, past or present, to be entangled with hers. He wanted freedom. He wanted Julienne. Yes. He had to remember that. He wanted Julienne. Perhaps he could write it on his palm and refer to it often, because when he'd been kissing Stasia, Julienne had never existed. That was a surprise. His attraction to his new wife was an unwanted, unneeded obstacle. His life was planned. Stasia had no part in it, now or ever.

Before he'd settled that in his mind, they were at the ranch. He paid the chauffeur, thanked him and followed Stasia into his house.

The Martinezes were enthusing over her dress.

"Everything is prepared, just so," Minnie said quickly. "The master bedroom, and the food only needs to be heated. Most of it is cold cuts, too. There is wine and champagne in the refrigerator. And flowers everywhere!" she added, indicating vases full of them. One was filled with Stasia's favorite, sunflowers. She went close to sniff them, smiling.

"Those are from Mrs. Everett," Minnie said. "She loves them, too."

"It's my father's nickname for her," Tanner volunteered. "Sunflower."

"We must go. It is my brother's birthday, so Juan and I are leaving. If you need us, Señor Everett, you have our cell phone numbers," Minnie concluded.

"Sure. Have fun," he said.

Juan congratulated them also but avoided speaking directly to Tanner. He had only contempt for a man who kept mistresses. He was very conventional. Like Minnie.

"Are you hungry?" Stasia asked, looking in the fridge. "There's a whole tray of cold cuts, cheese and salami and even prosciutto!" she exclaimed. "And black olives, my favorite, Edam and Gouda and Havarti cheese...!"

Her enthusiasm made him smile. "Okay. It sounds good. Breakfast was a long time ago."

"Yes, it was, and I didn't have any. I was too nervous to eat anything," she confessed. "I'll just change…oh, my gosh!"

He laughed at her expression. "What's wrong now?"

"My clothes!" she said. "I don't have any!"

He gave her a long look. He was still fascinated with his reaction to her at the church, and churning inside with unexpected desire that hadn't lessened even a fraction since their arrival here. "I expect if you check the bedroom, my mother will have packed a suitcase for you."

She let out a sigh. "Of course. I didn't even think… I'll be right back!"

She went out of the room at a fast clip, her mind entirely on finding the suitcase. That was why she didn't notice that Tanner was close behind her. She moved into the master bedroom and it wasn't until she heard the door close, and then lock, that she realized she wasn't alone…

She turned around and he was moving toward her, his eyes blazing with hunger. She caught her breath.

"What, cold feet?" he chided. "When we both know how you feel about me."

"I'm hungry," she procrastinated, trying to move back. "We could have some cold cuts."

"While you work up an appetite?" he mused. His hands circled her tiny waist and his mouth went to her neck. "I already have one, thanks."

"Tanner, this isn't a good idea," she faltered, her breath coming in tiny jerks as her cold hands rested on his broad, muscular chest.

"Why not?"

"I can think of a whole bunch of reasons," she said, but

her eyes were closing, her body was arching toward him, her senses were exploding in sensuality.

"Me, too," he whispered at her mouth. "We can discuss them later."

And while his mouth covered hers, suddenly demanding, he carried her to the bed.

She knew about men and women. Her classes in school had been moderately shocking. But what Tanner did to her was completely out of her experience, even beyond what she'd read in the passionate romance novels she loved to read.

Well, some of it was like that. But reading wasn't like doing. When you were reading, you couldn't feel the soft abrasion of a man's skin sliding against yours, or feel the sensations his big, lean hands aroused when they slid to the inside of your thighs and around them, or the ache that came from feeling a man's mouth on your bare breasts.

Her short nails bit into his back as he moved on her, her wedding gown on the floor beside the bed, along with his suit, as one intimacy led to an even greater one. The window was open next to the bed, and the curtains blew back and forth, echoing the motion of the lean body moving on Stasia's.

The first quick thrust had first shocked and then caused a burning pain. But his mouth had erased the pain very efficiently as it moved to her breasts. His hands went between them and aroused a sudden stab of pleasure that made her eyes roll back in her head. She felt like flame, burning and reaching up even to the stars in a mad bubble of ecstasy that arched her tortured body and let out a shuddering, alien moan from her mouth until his covered it.

She went from one plateau to another, mindless and fluid, a prisoner of his desire and her ache to assuage it. She gloried in his own satisfaction when it finally came, feeling him shudder endlessly, hearing his tormented moan at her ear as he clutched the sheet on either side of her head and arched down into her in an agony of fulfillment.

She'd wanted to look, but she was too shy. She hid her red face in his neck and held on while they shivered and sweated in the lazy aftermath of an unexpected mutual satisfaction.

Stasia had read that virgins almost never enjoyed their first time, that it was embarrassing and painful. At least, that's what her girlfriends had told her. It hadn't been that way for her. Tanner was dynamite in bed. No wonder Julienne stayed with him so long.

Julienne. Her body cooled. She was a body in bed. Had he been thinking of Julienne during that long evening of pleasure? Had she been standing in for the woman? It was like a stab in the heart.

And there was something else. She hadn't taken the first of the pills that would prevent pregnancy. If she turned up with a child, she'd have to fight Tanner tooth and nail, because he'd demand a termination. In fact, he'd probably be standing over her in the morning with that pill they gave after the fact. If he knew. If. He. Knew.

She hated herself for the thought. She couldn't hide a pregnancy, much less a child. He'd know as soon as his family knew, and he'd hate her.

But this hadn't been her idea. She hadn't asked for it. Had she?

He moved away from her, aware of guilty pleasure and shock. He hadn't meant that to happen. He'd been missing Julienne. No. That was a lie. He'd gone hungry for Stasia from the first time he'd kissed her. The hunger had only grown. Today, it had reached flash point. The issue was that one time hadn't satisfied him. He'd had her, how many times? Twice, three times? Well, at least she was on the pill. He didn't have that to worry about. He'd actually phoned the pharmacist, whom he knew, to make sure she'd picked up the prescription.

So what did they do now? He'd done something he couldn't take back. It was a low thing, to seduce a woman he didn't plan to stay married to, to give her false hope that he was beginning to care. He wasn't, of course. She was sweet and kind and good-natured, and surprisingly passionate in bed. Not that it mattered, when Julienne was waiting for him in Greece, of course.

He swung out of the bed without a word and walked, nude, down the hall to his own room. He pulled clean clothes out of his closet and went to take a shower. Maybe it would wash off the lingering scent of that light, floral perfume that Stasia favored.

Stasia lay where he'd left her, in a jumble of emotions, the foremost of which was exhausted pleasure. But she'd better not dwell on that. Of course he'd enjoyed her, he was a man. They could enjoy anything feminine, anytime, she knew that.

When he was gone, she got up and found her suitcase, hurriedly dragging out jeans and underthings and a T-shirt with a sunflower on it.

She rushed into the shower and soaped away the smell of her reluctant husband. She washed her hair as well. It was so baby-fine that it would air dry, and the waves would fall naturally into it.

When she was clean, she hung up her wedding finery and went off into the kitchen to fix lunch. She glanced at the clock and grimaced. Supper.

She had food on the table when Tanner came back. She avoided looking directly at him, but she couldn't help the scarlet blush.

"I didn't know what you wanted to drink. I made coffee, because that's what I usually have with supper."

"Dinner," he said, going to the refrigerator. "Supper is colloquial."

"Okay, go ahead, throw your exotic references at me to point out that I'm just a stupid country girl with no education," she said merrily. "I don't care." She lifted the glass of white wine she'd poured herself to her lips and took a big, long swallow.

He turned, not certain he'd heard her right.

She looked back at him with raised eyebrows. "Oh, shouldn't I have said that? You've started early, you know. Correcting my grammar. Next you'll be on about my accent, and then you'll start on my clothes."

He glared at her, looked back in the fridge and frowned. "I thought there was a bottle of Riesling in here."

She picked up the half-empty bottle and read the letters to him. "R.I.E.S.L.I.N.G. Is this it? If you want some of it, you'd better hurry." She showed him the bottle. "It's going fast."

He scowled at her as he closed the refrigerator. "You don't drink."

She held up her glass and sloshed it at him.

"You didn't drink," he corrected. He took the bottle from her and poured himself a large glass before putting the stopper back in it. "There was a nice merlot in there also."

"Was that the dark wine?" she asked, and he nodded. "I can't drink dark wine. It has tannin in it."

"So?" he asked.

"I get violent migraines from tannins."

He sipped his wine. "My mother has them. So does John."

"I know. Your mother talked to my doctor about a preventative. I take it. But I still get them sometimes."

"I never get headaches."

While they talked, they filled their plates.

"How do you know about prosciutto?" he wondered while they ate.

"Daddy took me to this really elegant restaurant in San Antonio once, so I'd know what they were like. We had all sorts of expensive dishes, including this lovely ham." She took a bite of it and closed her eyes with delight. "I could eat my weight in it."

He studied her under his eyelids. She was pretty, like that, with her hair curling down around her shoulders, no makeup on. She looked natural, real. Nothing like the over-painted women he'd spent most of his adult life around.

He looked back down at his plate.

"When do you leave?" she asked, and took another sip of wine.

He looked at her with his glass suspended between his mouth and his hand. "What?"

"It's a simple question. When do you leave for Greece?"

He scowled. "Why do you want to know?"

She sighed and finished her wine. "Because when you leave, I'm moving back home," she said simply. "I have a canvas to finish."

"The will says that you live here," he pointed out.

"Wills can't read," she retorted.

"People can, and it will be noted. Your father's attorney will be watching, Stasia," he added curtly. "So will the prospective buyer's attorney, who's still in town, hoping for a chance to get his hands on your ranch."

"Oh, bother," she muttered. "If my father hadn't interfered, I could have sold the ranch to your father, you could have your kept woman, and I could go home and finish my canvas!"

He stared at her with icy pale blue eyes. "My kept woman?"

She blinked, half-lit. "If she isn't independently wealthy,

and you pay all her bills, that means you keep her, doesn't it?" she asked simply.

"You make it sound raunchy."

"I haven't given an opinion."

"My mother has. Several. Repeatedly," he muttered.

"Your mother is a conventional woman with a wonderful marriage."

"Conventional," he agreed, irritated. "Unlike your own mother, yes?" he added, hitting where he knew it would hurt.

She was too tipsy to care what he said. She just looked at him, with eyes as old as the earth in a face gone quiet and pale with misery.

"God, I'm sorry!" he said shortly. "I didn't mean that."

"Sure you did, Tanner," she replied, sitting back in her chair. "You're here under protest because my father forced you to marry me, and all you want is to be free. Well, be my guest," she said, waving a hand in the air. "I'll stay here and paint while you sail around the world with your…" She stopped and laughed drunkenly. "I was going to say, your kept woman, but you don't like that. So how about your dependent? No? Your harlot…oh, no, excuse me, that was a very low blow, wasn't it?" She burst out laughing as his face hardened. "We don't have harlots in the modern world. There is no right and wrong. Everything's good, no matter how sordid. The world's turned upside down, and I'm living on the wrong side." She sighed, reaching for the bottle again.

"No." He took it away from her, got up and filled two cups with coffee. He was vaguely ashamed of himself. He didn't like the feeling. But that was no excuse for savaging Stasia, who'd also been forced into marriage. She loved him. He ground down on that thought, because it hurt him even more.

He put the coffee in front of her. "Drink that," he said firmly.

"No," she said belligerently, and glared up at him. "I'm happy. If I drink that, I'll remember this day, and I'll be looking for a dagger to do myself in with!"

"Join the club," he muttered, sitting back down.

"I hate you!" she blurted out.

"That'll be the day," he said curtly.

"I wish I hated you," she corrected. She glared at him. "You didn't have to sleep with me!"

"We didn't sleep," he pointed out.

She flushed. "You know what I mean!"

He gave her a long, appraising look. "A marriage on paper isn't legally binding without consummation." It was the truth. And it wasn't. He could have left her innocent. But that kiss on John's cheek still rankled, for reasons he couldn't understand. He hadn't wanted to take a chance that John might poach on his preserves while he was off in Greece with Julienne.

Put that way, it sounded cruel. Attached to one woman, married to another. Adultery or bigamy? But then, he didn't want Julienne for keeps. She was too cold, too heartless. She was like him, he thought, surprised. He was cold and heartless, too, for putting money above compassion. He'd let himself be forced into marriage with Stasia, discounting her feelings for him, walking all over them, in fact. Her wedding day and he'd spoiled it for her. He'd taken the joy out of it. Likely she'd never marry again. This would be her only memory of what should have been a joyful occasion. As she'd said, even the photographs would be a sad memoir of a sad day.

"I'm leaving tonight," he said curtly, and got up.

She just looked at him, pleasantly drunk and uncaring. "Shall I pack for you?" she asked airily. "I read that in one of my books. It sounded so...married," she added, and laughed.

"You're drunk," he pointed out.

She grinned. "And you're lucky. Because if I wasn't drunk,

I'd be looking for the biggest baseball bat I could find, and then I'd go looking for you."

She probably would have. He remembered her playing baseball with all of them and a few other ranching kids after they'd branded calves and were enjoying home-cooked bar-beque outside the barn.

She'd been a scrawny little thing, but she had grit. She'd outrun half the boys and outfought them as well. She never gave up, never gave in. She was pretty, even if not in the same class with Julienne, and she was loyal to the people she cared about. She had many good qualities. They could leave out the drinking one. He laughed to himself as he packed. Even drunk, he couldn't sink her.

He was sorry for that remark he'd made about her mother. He remembered the harsh gossip she and her father had endured after her mother's suicide. She'd found her mother, hanging from a rope on the back porch, after she got home on the school bus. Glenn had been out of town for two days. So Stasia had made the discovery all alone. She'd phoned the Everett home in hysterics. It was Tanner who'd answered the phone, who'd left a trail of fire getting to her house to hold her and comfort her, and then to call for help.

How could he have forgotten that? He'd been home on leave from the military at the time. Stasia had been, how old then, six years ago? Thirteen. A scrawny, leggy thirteen, but with that odd vulnerability over a core of steel that still hall-marked her personality. She'd straightened up very quickly from the shock and gotten on with the nuts and bolts of no-tifying her father and helping him through the grief.

She was an odd person, he thought as he finished pack-ing. Vulnerable and soft on the surface, pure rock underneath when she needed to be. And in bed, a sensual dream of per-fection, he thought, and then smothered the thought. That was the way to hell, paved with his good intentions. He didn't want to be a ranching husband with a brood of children. That was Stasia's dream, and he hoped she'd find a man who shared her hunger. Just not his brother John, he amended, and then stopped and glared at himself in the mirror. Where the hell had that thought come from?

He walked back into the dining room to find Stasia almost comatose at the table, her hair all over the place, her head down on her hands.

"You're going to have the great-grandmother of headaches when you wake up in the morning," he assured her.

"Go away. I'm sleeping."

He sighed. He put down the suitcase, swung her up into his arms and started for the master bedroom.

"I can walk," she protested.

"I could let you prove that," he threatened.

She relaxed against him, provoking more unwanted and unwelcome sensations that made his feet tingle.

"Go away, then, I don't care," she murmured drowsily. "I'll just paint until you're a distant memory."

"Good luck with that."

She made a rude sound and sighed. "I hate you."

"You said that."

"Oh. Okay. Just so you know."

He put her down on the bed, grimacing as he recalled the pleasure they'd shared on it so recently. He took off her sandals and pulled the cover over her.

"You will hate yourself in the morning," he predicted.

"I hate myself now," she murmured.

"Good. If you can't hold your liquor, don't drink."

She made a sound and then fell asleep.

He stood looking at her for a long time before he finally turned away, closing the door behind him. He felt as if he'd just made a monumental mistake, but he didn't know why.

FOUR

Juan and Minnie came home late in the evening to a table still laden with the remains of supper and two wineglasses, both empty.

They exchanged knowing smiles. At least, until Minnie's sharp eyes spotted the note pinned to the refrigerator with a magnet.

She pulled it off. It was terse. *Gone to Greece. Take care of Stasia.* And there was a big *T* in script.

She handed it to Juan.

"So the streetwalker wins," Juan said heavily. "I had hoped."

"Yes, so had I," she replied. "Well, we must take care of Stasia. As if we wouldn't already. Such a sweet child. No guile, no vices. And he takes up with a woman who makes a *bruja* look civilized." She sighed. "So much for happily ever after."

"Fairy tales take much work before the ever after part," he teased. "I will take care of the dishes, *mi amor*. You might see about our baby chick. She does not drink, but I think that is not the case tonight."

She kissed him warmly. "I think you may be right."

★ ★ ★

Stasia woke with nausea welling up in her throat. She barely made it to the bathroom in time. Minnie, standing at the bedroom door, grimaced and went back to the kitchen to make coffee.

Eventually, Stasia made her way to the dining room and sat down at the table with her head in her hands. Juan had finished the dishes and gone out to see to the duties of the cowboys.

"Ah, the wine," Minnie said at once when Stasia lifted her throbbing head long enough to look at her.

Stasia nodded and then groaned. "And I don't have my headache medicine," she moaned.

"But you do," Minnie replied surprisingly. "Your new mother-in-law sent it, along with your suitcase. She anticipated a difficult evening, I believe."

"He went to Greece, didn't he?" she asked without moving.

"Yes."

She sighed. "And that was just what I expected."

It wasn't what Minnie had expected at all. She'd had high hopes. Those were gone, of course.

"You should take your medicine and lie down again while it takes effect," Minnie said. "And I made strong coffee. I will give you a cup to take with you."

"Okay. That sounds lovely."

Minnie gave the pill bottle to Stasia and made sure she took the correct dosage. Then she put up the bottle and poured the wan girl a cup of strong coffee. "This will help," she said with an affectionate smile.

Stasia got up from the table and picked up the mug. She studied Minnie, who probably could guess what sort of wedding night the poor child had. "Thanks again," she added gently.

"It is no problem. None at all. Niña, can you use your room while I tidy Tanner's?"

"Sure, I can," Stasia mumbled.

"If you need me, you just call. Leave the door open."

"I will."

It wasn't until she slept, and then woke, that she remembered Minnie was going to tidy up the master bedroom. That would include changing the bed linen. The sheets. Her sharp eyes would notice something embarrassing. Stasia ground her teeth together as she pictured that. But, then, Minnie was a married woman, too. Nothing would shock her. Especially not after having Julienne around.

Julienne! Tanner was with her by now, probably enjoying more of what he'd introduced Stasia to the day before! Her cheeks flamed with anger. She wanted to lay into him with that baseball bat she'd mentioned. Sadly, it wouldn't change a thing. He wasn't going to rush back home and want to start a family.

She moaned silently. He hadn't given her a chance to mention that she had no sort of protection. She was supposed to start the birth control pills today, but it was too late. There was a morning after pill, but how could she walk into the little pharmacy she'd used all her life, where she was known, and buy one? What a sensation that would cause! She'd have to go all the way into San Antonio, and that was a long drive.

Besides, it was unlikely. She wasn't halfway between periods and she was regular. She didn't need to start worrying about possibilities. She wished she could stop remembering that long, leisurely delight in bed that Tanner had introduced her to. She wished she could go back to her innocent state, so that she wouldn't know what it felt like to be loved. Well, physically loved, if not emotionally. Now she felt a hunger unlike anything she'd ever experienced. She wanted Tanner. Wanted him obsessively. And he was over in Greece, with his kept woman. And Stasia was here, miserable.

Ah, well. She still had her painting. She found an unused room and called one of the ranch hands to come get her. She packed up her painting supplies, complete with easel and tarps and paints, and took one of the ranch pickups back over to Tanner's place. If she had to live in his house, she was going to have her things with her.

So she packed up her giant stuffed Totoro from the anime movie she loved and took him with her as well. He slept with her at home. So she'd have a companion here at night as well.

She was just finishing a portrait of two little girls, children that belonged to the Everetts' cattle foreman, when Minnie called her to the phone.

She recognized the voice at once. It was Mr. Dill, who owned the art supply store in town.

"I have some rather exciting news," he enthused. "You recall the gentleman from back East who was so interested in your paintings?"

"Oh, yes, I do!" she replied.

"Well, he called me this morning and asked if you might be interested in doing a commission for a friend of his, an associate, I believe he said. He would like for you to do a portrait of the man."

"Yes, I'd love to, but would I have to go there to do it?" she asked worriedly. "I've never even been out of Texas, Mr. Dill. My dad hated to travel, even when he had to do it for business."

"I recall that. I told the gentleman that I thought you might be reluctant to go so far, and alone. He said that you could work from photographs, and he can send you a brief video of the subject, so that you can see how he moves and smiles, that sort of thing." He paused. "Stasia, he's offering you ten thousand dollars to do it."

To a woman whose fortunes were on the rocks, that was an exciting figure. "So much?" she exclaimed.

"He says your work is worth it, and that you don't charge enough for the wonderful work you do. He'd like you to start next week, if that's agreeable."

She caught her breath. "I'd love to!"

He chuckled. "I thought you might. He was rather secretive about the reason for the portrait, but he intimated that it might lead to surprising things for you."

She sat down, still holding the phone. Her eyes were full of dreams. She'd always just been her father's child, living on a cattle ranch in Texas. She had good clothes, the best food, expensive cars, all that. But it was her father's accomplishment, not her own, and when he died the ranch was mortgaged to the hilt. She couldn't have kept it if Cole Everett hadn't wanted it for the water rights, not to mention protecting both men's cattle herds from an amusement park next door. She'd be living on the street by now. And even married to Tanner, she had no security whatsoever, no way to support herself. She'd longed for something to do that would be hers alone, that would define her. Especially now, with a husband who didn't want to be one, who was even now off with his mistress.

"It would be an exciting project," she told Mr. Dill. "I love painting. I'd love to be able to make a living at it. And I'd like to be independent." She caught her breath as that slipped out. It was a strange thing for a newly married woman to say, but Mr. Dill wasn't paying attention, because he didn't catch it.

"Then this is your chance, to make a name for yourself in art," Mr. Dill said. "Grab it with both hands."

"That, I'll do! When is he sending the photographs and the video?"

He laughed softly. "I'm texting them to your cell phone as we speak," he said. "I told him to go ahead and send them. I had a feeling you'd want to do it."

"Thank you so much!" she said.

"You hit the big time, young lady," he said, "and make our little town famous. We can put up a sign at the city limits of Branntville, with your name on it, and lettering that says this is where it all started for you!"

She laughed. "Well, that might take some time, and a lot of work. But every journey begins with a single step, as they say."

"It does. I'll be in touch."

He hung up and Stasia went to find her cell phone. She groaned when she noticed that she'd forgotten to charge it. Well, in her defense, her wedding day had been rather traumatic, for several reasons. She blushed thinking about one of them.

She was married. Her wedding had been the day before. She looked at the simple gold band on her hand, the one Tanner had bought without even asking what kind of gold she wanted.

She hated white gold. But by some odd chance, this one was yellow gold, her favorite. It looked good on her hand. But it had no meaning, not when her husband was determined to have nothing to do with her for a whole year.

A year! How could she live in his house for that long and stay sane? Although, she was pretty sure that Tanner wouldn't be living here with her. He'd already said that he didn't consider the marriage binding.

Living in a small town was both a blessing and a curse. The curse part was that everybody knew Tanner had left his new wife the day after the wedding and taken off with his mistress. It was something that Stasia would have to live down.

Not that Tanner would care. He'd never cared about any-body's opinion but his own.

She plugged in her cell phone charger, connected the phone, and went off to find Minnie and ask for coffee. She'd need something to knock her out of this miserable lethargy so that she could start on the portrait.

"Minnie?" she called when she got to the kitchen.

Minnie stuck her head around the door and black eyes in a face framed by short, curly silver hair twinkled at her. "There's a whole pot of strong black coffee I just made, on the counter. Head better?"

She nodded. "Oh, yes, thank you. But strong caffeine will help keep it from coming back. I've got a commission!" she added excitedly. "This man back East wants me to do a por-trait of an acquaintance of his and he's going to pay me ten thousand dollars for it!"

Minnie whistled. "My goodness!"

"Isn't it incredible?" she asked, sighing. "I mean, here I am, mostly penniless. I'm married, but my husband isn't, and I'm dependent on him right now for the very food that goes into my mouth." Her brown eyes took on a glitter. "Well, I'll show him," she said under her breath. "I can make my own way in the world if I get the chance, and I just got it. No way am I going to sit here on my tuffet waiting for him to come home, if he ever does."

Minnie watched Stasia pour black coffee into a mug. "I know that things look very dark right now," she said gently. "But many good marriages start out this way, with one part-ner running from the responsibility."

She turned with the cup held in both hands. "He never wanted to marry me," she said quietly. "John did. But I don't love John." She looked up. "I feel so sorry for him. John is the loneliest man I've ever known. He could just crook his finger and ten beautiful women would come running. But he wants me, and I love him like a brother. It's such a shame!"

"It would be more of a shame if he married you," Minnie returned. "He would resent you, and blame you, even if it wasn't consciously. In time, he might come to hate you for your lack of feeling for him."

She nodded. "I know that. It's why I never encouraged him. He's such a sweet man."

"Yes, he is."

"But Tanner…"

"Tanner is cut out of sharp cloth," Minnie replied. "He doesn't know who he is," she added surprisingly. "Until he does, he is not fit to be anyone's husband."

Stasia stared at Minnie and frowned, concentrating. "He's always so certain about things, so focused," she began.

"About business, of a certainty, and he knows his way around guns and bad people," she added.

"What do you mean?" Stasia asked gently. "He's been out of the military for a while now, and Cole says he's never mentioned going back."

"Did you notice the man with him yesterday, the one with blond-streaked brown hair, very tall?"

"Yes. I wondered who he was."

"His name is Eb Scott. He runs a counterterrorism school in a little town near San Antonio," Minnie said.

"That was Eb Scott?" Stasia exclaimed. "I knew about him, but I'd never seen a picture of him."

"He was a professional mercenary when he was younger. He went on missions with two other men who now live near him," Minnie said. "Now, he only trains others to do what he did. The school is famous all over the world. They teach everything from guns to handling cars in kidnapping situations. It's very hush-hush. And very expensive."

"Tanner must think a lot of him, to invite him to the wedding," Stasia said. She put a hand to her temple and groaned softly. "I thought I'd licked the migraine. It's coming back."

"You should drink that coffee and then go and lie down," Minnie said. "You look very pale."

Stasia smiled. "I guess I should lie down. The headache isn't slowing down. Too much excitement," she added with a short laugh.

"And a weather system moving in," Minnie added. "Storms always make those headaches worse."

"How do you know that?" she asked.

"My mother had them," she said. "I've been lucky. They never showed up at my door. But they tend to run in families."

Stasia scowled. "My mother had them," she said slowly. "I remember Dad mentioning that once. And her mother had them. Well, my goodness! I never thought about that before."

"Life is all lessons," Minnie chuckled. "We learn more every day." She took the empty cup to the sink. "Now you go lie down and sleep for a while. It will help."

"I wanted to get started on the portrait."

"Time enough to do that when you can see what you're doing," the older woman teased.

Stasia just smiled at her. It was a good idea. Her head was pounding again. She could hardly get over her good fortune. And it had dropped right in her lap!

"I still don't understand why you had to marry her in the first place," Julienne was raging in their hotel room in Greece. She was tossing clothes aside while she searched for the right blouse to go with her outlandishly colorful leggings.

"I told you why," Tanner said curtly.

She glanced at him with visible irritation. "And what are you going to do if she contests the divorce?" she asked.

"She won't," he said carelessly.

"She lost everything when her father died, you said. So how will she support herself? She's never even had a job, has she?"

"She never needed one. Her father's ranch was very successful, until his heart started playing up and he delegated too much of the responsibility. Many of the methods he used in his youth have been adopted by other ranchers, things like reduced use of pesticides and antibiotics…"

"Please," she muttered, holding up a hand. "When I want lessons in economics, I'll date a college professor."

Once, he would have found that funny. But his situation had upset him too much for humor. He was trying to forget the feel of Stasia in his arms, without much luck. The wedding ring on his finger was making him very uncomfortable as well.

He'd never given much thought to professions of faith, to vows and promises, although his father and mother were big on such things. Now, he was looking at the world in a different way. It was already interfering with his sense of freedom.

He jammed his hands into his slacks pockets and looked out the window at the people milling below on the beach. He wondered if any of them were as conflicted as he was.

"Found it," she said triumphantly, and pulled out a smock blouse in a nauseating shade of yellow. "It just matches my leggings, too!" She pulled off her T-shirt and slid the blouse over her pert black lacy bra. "There! How do I look?" she asked.

He turned and just stared at her.

"Well?" she prompted irritably.

"You need big floppy shoes and a wig with red hair that sticks out both sides."

She stood staring at him in blatant disbelief.

"What do you think you look like?" he asked curtly, as his eyes slid over her body. Odd how little it appealed to him now.

"It's very fashionable," she shot back.

"To whom, circus clowns?" he asked reasonably.

"Thank you very much," she muttered, slamming clothes back into her suitcase.

He checked his watch. "I'm hungry. Do you want to get something to eat?"

"Yes, if there's a restaurant that serves American food. I'm not eating goats or whatever they eat over here," she said irritably.

He stared at her. "Most people like to sample native dishes."

"I'm not most people. I should have stayed in London," she added, glaring at him. "I could sleep by myself there, too. What's wrong with you? Did you have a wild sex orgy with your new bride and lose your taste for somebody more so-phisticated?" she taunted.

"Don't be absurd," he said. "If that were the case, I'd still be in Big Spur."

She stared at him for a few seconds, apparently satisfied with his bland expression. "All right, then," she said.

He moved closer, but he didn't take his hands out of his pockets. "My father and I are working on some improvements to the new ranch property, and I'm still overwhelmed by a marriage I didn't want. Give me some space."

She sighed half-angrily. "All right. But not too much." Her eyes were wary and suspicious. "I'm not sharing you with the little ranch groupie," she added.

"I'll remind you that I make my living as a rancher," he said, his voice unusually soft. "It pays the bills, including your couture gowns and jewelry."

She tossed her hair back. "Nasty, dirty things, polluting the planet," she muttered. "I don't eat meat. Nobody should…"

"Stop right there." He didn't raise his voice, but she heard the inflection in it, and she stopped dead. It began to occur to her that he was drawing a line in the sand. Yes, she could find another rich man to keep her. But she liked this one well enough, and he didn't have as many annoying appendages as some of her other acquaintances did. There was his family, of course, the ones that didn't approve of her. But, then, they were usually somewhere else, so she didn't have to put up with them. And certainly there was no question of marriage.

She frowned as her eyes went to his left hand. "Why are you wearing a wedding ring?" she asked. "I don't believe it!"

He took the ring off, opened a drawer in the dresser and tossed it in, closing it back with terse subdued violence. "I forgot I had it on."

She moved toward him and curled herself up around him, her hands finding his muscular chest and caressing it. "Do you really want to go get something to eat?" she purred. "I can think of something much better to do…"

He put her away. "I told you, I'm not in the mood," he cut her off. "If you're coming, let's go."

He held the door open. She grabbed up her purse and glared at him. He was acting very oddly. She felt a twinge of fear. He was very generous and she didn't want to have to start searching for someone else. Not unprepared, certainly. It wouldn't hurt to play along with him. She knew he didn't want to marry that silly girl back home, and the fact that he was here instead of with his bride spoke volumes about his preferences.

It would be all right, she told herself, relaxing. He was just uptight about being forced to marry the girl. When his anger abated, there would be plenty of time for Julienne to regain the advantage she'd temporarily lost.

Stasia just stared at the photographs for a long time without saying a word, while an interested Minnie stood just inside the room Stasia had appropriated for her painting.

"He looks…well, not like people from around here," Minnie said finally.

"I did notice that," came the amused reply. She sighed. "He's not bad-looking," she added. "But there's something very menacing about him."

"Not a man you'd want to run across in a blind alley at midnight," Minnie mused.

"Exactly." She cocked her head. "So why is a portrait of him worth so much money?"

"Unless you really, really need to know," Minnie advised, tongue in cheek, "paint the picture, take the money and run. No need to agonize over reasons you'll probably never know."

"Sound advice," Stasia sighed. "Well, I'll start sketching."

"I'll go make another pot of coffee," Minnie said.

"That's a great idea," came the teasing reply. "And while you do that, I'll immortalize our subject here." She frowned and pursed her lips. "Let me see. I'll do a statue in the background, something somber and dignified. And maybe some ancient tomes lying around…"

Minnie left her to it.

A pot of coffee later, Stasia had the subject roughed out on a huge canvas.

Minnie stood behind her, surveying it. She had her arms folded, and she was shaking her head. "I don't know how you do it," she said softly. "But you really do have genius in your fingers. This is going to be magnificent."

"I hope so, for what the nice man is paying me for it," Stasia enthused. "Goodness, I still can't believe a piece of canvas with paint on it is worth that much money. Although I'm very glad it is," she added. "I've worried a lot about how I was going to make it, with Daddy gone." She drew in a breath. "Tanner doesn't want me, and I can't spend the rest of my life sponging off him. I have to earn my own living. I had no idea what I'd be able to do. And then, this happened."

Minnie smiled at her. "Life is full of surprises. This is one of the nicer ones."

"It certainly is." She put down her coffee cup. "I suppose Tanner's out on the town with his companion by now. He thinks glitter is the answer to everything." She turned and looked at Minnie. "And that's not true. The only thing in the world that really matters is to have people who love you. And to love them back."

"Darlin', you have learned a powerful lesson very early in life," the older woman said softly. "In the end, family is all that matters."

Stasia just smiled.

Stasia slept badly. She was still hung up on her reluctant husband, regardless of how fictional her marriage really was. She couldn't forget the feast of passion he'd introduced her to, before he walked out of her life. He could have spared her that, she thought miserably. She'd been blissfully ignorant to the hungers of the flesh until her wedding night. But now, she knew what passion was, and she was starving for a man who couldn't see her for dust. When she thought about Tanner in bed with Julienne, she wanted to scream and throw things. He'd taken the same vow she had, forsaking all others, but he had no thought of forsaking his mistress.

It was taking a toll on Stasia as she painted. She was unhappy, but it was more than that. Her appetite had suffered. She was nauseous from time to time, and so tired that she could hardly stay awake past seven at night. Worse, she was gaining weight. She'd had to leave her jeans unbuttoned at the top, because she couldn't fasten them. She laughed to herself. Her father had always said she was too thin. Now, maybe, she'd put on some weight and look better!

"You need to see a doctor," Minnie grumbled as Stasia left

most of her breakfast on the table. "You aren't eating enough to keep a cricket alive."

"I'm just not hungry," came the plaintive reply. "It's so hot, even with the air conditioner going full tilt. Nobody has much appetite. Not even you."

"Well, I guess that's true enough," Minnie had to admit.

"And I'm not losing weight. If anything, I'm gaining more," Stasia muttered, fiddling with the button at her waist.

Minnie was just staring at her while wheels turned in her head. It was almost a month since Stasia had married Tanner, and she knew without a doubt that there had been intimacy between them. What she didn't know was whether or not Stasia was on birth control. She wanted to ask, but Stasia was such a private little person. She didn't volunteer any intimate details about herself to people. But Minnie wondered if she could be pregnant.

"You should see a doctor anyway," Minnie persisted. "Just in case. He could give you something to improve your appetite."

"Well, there is that," she had to admit. "I guess I should."

"Good. Go make an appointment right now, before you talk yourself out of it," Minnie said firmly. She smiled gently. "Go on. I worry about you."

Stasia fought tears. "Gee, that's nice," she said.

"You poor kid." Minnie took her in her arms and rocked her while Stasia cried. "It's all right. Life evens things out. You'll see."

Stasia just smiled. Since her mother's death, even before, she'd gone without hugs and affection. Her mother had loved her, but in a lukewarm way. Her father had loved her, but he never touched her. It was nice to be hugged, to have somebody care about you.

She sighed. "Nobody ever hugged me at home," she murmured into Minnie's ample shoulder. "It's nice."

Minnie chuckled. "Sometimes, all you need is a hug."

"So true!"

Minnie drew back. "Now dry those tears and make that phone call."

"Okay."

"It's probably just the heat, but it never hurts to be sure," Minnie said.

"I guess so. I'm pretty healthy usually." She took a last look at the painting. "What do you think? Will he like it?"

"He'll love it," she predicted.

Stasia grinned from ear to ear.

When Mr. Dill got a good look at the painting, he was speechless. "I knew you had talent, but I never realized how much," he said, shaking his head. "Stasia, this is truly magnificent!"

Stasia beamed. "Thank you, Mr. Dill."

"I'll call my client this afternoon. He said he'd probably have me FedEx it up to him, and he'd arrange for packing and shipping and so forth. He'll be delighted! I've rarely seen such talent!"

"You're giving me a big head," Stasia protested. "I can't live up to the hype!"

"Sure you can," he replied. "This may lead to something… well, something very, very big!" he said. "I can't wait to see what develops."

"Honestly, neither can I," Stasia said, her brown eyes twinkling with delight. "You'll let me know what he thinks?"

"Of course I will! The minute I hear from him, I promise you!"

Stasia drew in a contented breath. "Thanks a million, Mr. Dill. Especially, thanks for putting that other painting in your shop. If you hadn't, that nice man would never have seen it and offered me an insane amount of money for another painting. I can never thank you enough!"

"I'm happy about it, too," he replied with a smile. "Living where we do, out of touch with the world, it's logical to think such chances never happen to us. But fate steps in from time to time."

"I'm very grateful that fate took a step in this direction," Stasia said.

Mr. Dill smiled. "So am I, Stasia. I'll keep you in the loop!"

Stasia started on yet another canvas, this one of Minnie and Juan, for their thirtieth wedding anniversary. It was getting harder for her to work. The nausea was increasing and she could only keep milkshakes down. She was so tired that she could hardly function, despite the addition of a multivitamin to her daily regimen.

The doctor's appointment was for the following week, and she was dreading it. What if she had some profound illness? What if it was cancer? She almost panicked, thinking about the possibilities.

"Stop," Minnie teased. "I can hear you thinking all the way in the kitchen. You aren't dying. Honest. Just take one day at a time. The doctor will have some answers."

"I hope they'll be good ones," she sighed.

"They will be," Minnie promised.

Julienne was barely speaking to Tanner. He hadn't touched her since he'd come hotfoot from his marriage bed to Greece. She was having suspicions that boiled over, all at once.

"You slept with that skinny little blonde, didn't you?" Julienne accused angrily. "I can just hear her telling you all about the sanctity of marriage, and keeping a holy vow, and all that silly middle-class morality that's just hypocrisy!"

Tanner glared at her.

She glared back.

He was thinking, and very hard, about those vows he'd taken so lightly. He turned and walked out of the room.

FIVE

There was a beautiful tiled swimming pool around back of the ranch house at Tanner's place. Stasia, in a patterned pale-yellow bikini, was enjoying the warmth of the sun on her body as she lay on one of the chaise lounges by the pool. Minnie had brought her some sweetened iced tea with mint, which helped the ongoing nausea. The sun seemed to help as well.

She heard voices, but she was drowsy from lack of sleep, and almost dozed off when one of the voices sounded vaguely familiar.

She sat up and looked toward the corner of the house. And there she was. Odalie, Tanner's sister. She looked like their mother, with pale blue eyes and almost platinum-blond hair, worn in a complicated braid. She was dressed in blue chiffon. She looked beautiful and rich and as if she owned the world.

"Odalie?" Stasia exclaimed.

Odalie laughed, her voice sweet and clear when she spoke.

"Yes, it's me. I wanted to come home for a few weeks. Frankly, my voice teacher and I are pretty sick of each other. It's my fault, I'm sure." She hugged Stasia. "You look great! Imagine you, marrying my big brother! Honestly, I thought it would be John."

Stasia grimaced. "He's a great guy and I love him like a brother. But that's all it would ever be, even if I lived to be a hundred," she said with sad tenderness in her voice.

"We never love where we ought, do we?" Odalie asked on a sigh. "I don't think I've ever been in love. Not really. I've had crushes, but that's all. It's been opera since I was old enough to sing, and it still is. I'm obsessed with it. I want to sing at the Met."

"And you will," Stasia said solemnly. "I know you will."

"You're sweet," came the soft reply. She looked around. "Tanner's not here, of course."

"Nope. He's in Greece with that horrible woman," Stasia said through her teeth. "I get pitying looks in every store in town. It's an open secret."

"I could kick him!"

"Please do," Stasia said enthusiastically. "I'll loan you my steel-toed boots."

Odalie couldn't help it. She laughed. "Well, is he coming home anytime soon?"

Stasia picked up a folded tabloid beside the chaise, on the pavement, and handed it to her friend.

There was a bold headline on the second page. Ranching Magnate and Friend Relax in Greece While Wife Sits Home Alone.

Stasia lifted an eyebrow. "So now, it's sort of an open international secret," she mused. She sighed. "Maybe I could offer interviews to interested paparazzi?" she wondered aloud. "Or offer to pose for pictures in a granny dress?"

Odalie's eyes twinkled. "Well, at least you haven't lost your sense of humor," she said, dropping down on the chaise next to Stasia's. "How are you?"

"Okay," came the reply. "I don't have an appetite and I'm gaining weight just the same, so Minnie says I have to see a doctor."

"Good idea," Odalie replied, and she was serious. "How long has that been going on?"

"A couple of weeks," Stasia said. "Maybe a little longer. I've only paid attention to it recently." She made a face. "I've convinced myself that it's cancer."

"Probably the heat," Odalie returned. "Heavens, our foreman says the cattle are sweating, can you believe it?" And she laughed.

Stasia laughed, too. "I wouldn't be surprised. The heat is awful here. If we didn't have air-conditioning, I think I'd move into the swimming pool. I love it here. Those tiles are so beautiful!"

"Beautiful and dangerous," Minnie muttered. "There was a party here last year. One of the guests, a young one at that, slipped on those tiles where they were slick with water, and broke her back!"

"It might not be a bad idea to have them replaced with a big rubber mat," Odalie teased.

"Tanner would never hear of it," Minnie sighed. "He says beauty is often dangerous and we just have to be very careful."

"That sounds just like my big brother," Odalie replied. "I almost passed out when I heard about the marriage. Tanner has been vocal for years about never wanting to get married."

"He's still vocal about it," Stasia assured her. "But my father left an airtight will, and Tanner and I had no choice. Your family's holdings were all at stake."

"Everything boils down to money, doesn't it?" Odalie asked sadly.

"In this case, certainly. Tanner's inheritance would have gone down the drain if we hadn't married, and I'd be flat broke. Dad had mortgaged the property to the hilt." She shook her head. "I had no idea what he'd done until the will was read. If he'd only told me…!"

"Your dad was looking out for you," Odalie said gently. "He wanted you to be looked after."

"Gosh, that sounds like I'm somebody with a huge head injury," Stasia teased. "Yes, he was, I suppose. But I won't need looking after now! I've got a commission! Ten thousand dollars, just to do a portrait!"

Odalie reached over and touched Stasia's forehead. "No fever," she mused.

"I'm not joking! Minnie, tell her." Stasia enlisted the housekeeper as she came out with a tray of coffee and cookies. "Tell her about the painting!"

"She did one for this guy back East," Minnie said obligingly. "He came through a few weeks ago and saw one of Stasia's paintings at Mr. Dill's art supply store in town," she added. "He said he'd be in touch about getting a portrait done. We all thought he was kidding. He wasn't."

"Imagine that," Odalie said, impressed. "Not a lot of people keep their word these days."

"So true," Stasia sighed. She smiled. "So I made a lot of money. I'll put it in the bank and go to see an investment counselor, so I can grow my nest egg before Tanner puts me out on the sidewalk!"

"He'd never do that," Odalie said airily. "Not that he'd mind the gossip, but in spite of everything, he's fond of you."

"I'm fond of chocolate cake," Stasia said with a sigh. "I wanted to be swept off my feet, like the women in those romance novels I read. What I got was knocked off my feet by a will I never expected my dad to leave."

"Women don't get swept off their feet anymore," Odalie said gently. "The kind of man who featured in those older novels doesn't exist anymore. He was bludgeoned to death by political correctness."

Stasia made a face. "So now we have the tofu men eating mock meat and dyeing their hair green."

"Not all of them," Odalie said. "I can't see either of my brothers in that sort of mood."

"Honestly, neither can I," she replied with a grin.

"John is still mourning," Odalie said.

Stasia sighed heavily. "I feel so bad for him," she said. "He's the nicest man I know. I wish things could be different. He wouldn't run off to Greece with another woman!"

"No. John's very conventional. Tanner... Tanner is a free spirit," Odalie replied. "He's always been difficult. He and Dad argue so much. I don't think they have one point of agreement in common."

"He doesn't know who he is," Stasia said, repeating something she'd heard from Minnie.

Odalie's blond brows met in the middle of her forehead. "That's exactly what my mother says about him."

She smiled. "Your mother is a card. I love her. I especially love her music! How many Grammys is it to date...?"

Odalie laughed. "Only two."

"Only." Stasia shook her head. "Heather could have been at the Met if she'd wanted to, or even a famous pop singer. But she threw it all up to marry your father and have kids."

"That's all she ever really wanted. She loved my dad when she was still a teenager. They had a rocky path to marriage. But now, they're so involved with each other. Sometimes I think they even forget they have kids. It's like they can just drift off into a world where only the two of them exist. They're still madly in love."

Stasia's eyes twinkled. "That's the sort of marriage I wanted. One that was romantic and sweet, but settled. I've always wanted a family. At least two children, maybe more. And I'm married to a man who thinks children are a figment."

Odalie shook her head. "I'll have to remember that one."

"Don't you want to marry and have a family?" Stasia asked.

"Oh, yes. But first I want to sing at the Met. And it's a long, slow progession even to get to the auditions. You start when you're a child, the way Mom started me. Singing classes, coaches, parts in local plays and young artist programs where you get to sing with local opera groups. Later, auditions to join local opera groups as a performer, more voice coaching, more educating yourself in the operas themselves, learning foreign languages..."

"Foreign languages?" Stasia looked at her blankly.

"Well, yes. You sing operas in many languages, primarily Italian, French and German. You have to be able to pronounce the words correctly as you sing them."

"Good heavens, where is my mind?" Stasia asked, laughing. "Of course you do! But that's so much dedication, Odalie. When do you have time to go out on dates?"

Odalie grimaced. "Well, really, I don't," she confessed. "I've tried, but there was always a sudden change in schedules, or I had to stand in for a sick performer. Anyway, I'm dedicated to my craft. Just like you are," she added, smiling at Stasia.

"I hope I can continue being dedicated to mine," Stasia said hopefully. "I've finished my one big, expensive project, but I'm not likely to be getting commissions out here in the boondocks."

"Maybe your benefactor knows other people who want to be immortalized," Odalie said helpfully. "You never know!"

"I suppose not." She put a hand to her head. "I've been in the sun too long. My head's throbbing again."

Odalie got up. "Lie down for a while and take your meds. I have to phone my voice teacher in Italy and tell him I'm not coming back for two weeks. There's an opening in the local opera company in San Antonio. I'm going to try for it!"

"That's so exciting," Stasia said.

Odalie laughed. "It doesn't mean I'll get it. There's so much competition. How about lunch tomorrow?" she added. "We can drive up to San Antonio and have lunch and shop at El Mercado."

"That sounds lovely. I haven't been out to eat or anything since…" She stopped, not liking to say the words.

Odalie knew what she meant. "It's all right. You just need time. It will pass."

Stasia looked into her soft, pale blue eyes. "I hope you're right."

"You'll see. I'll come to get you about nine tomorrow. That okay?"

"That's fine. I'll look forward to it."

"So will I. See you!"

Stasia put on a simple yellow patterned sundress and sandals and left her hair long for her trip to San Antonio with Odalie.

"You should pose for yourself," Odalie teased as they drove into the small town of Branntville, a bigger town than Big Spur, which had grown up around Cole's ranch. Branntville even had an airport that would take baby jets. It was named for the Brannt family, King and Shelby, who were close to the Everetts. They arrived in Odalie's convertible BMW and parked in front of several shops on the square. One was an exclusive dress shop, the sort Stasia had gone to for her prom dress. John had taken her to the senior prom. It wasn't that Stasia didn't have friends, but she was standoffish about boys because she'd been in love with Tanner for so long that she didn't see other men. Besides, she told her father, it was stupid to go to a dance with a boy you didn't even like, just because it was the thing to do.

Soon after that, John had volunteered to take her. She'd accepted. It was in those heady days when she hadn't realized how John felt about her. When she knew, she refused any dates with him at all. It would have been cruel to encourage him, when Tanner was the only man she wanted.

"Deep in thought?" Odalie teased as they got out of the car.

"I was just remembering that I came here to buy a prom dress. John took me to the senior prom. I had no idea how he felt. It must have been so disappointing to him."

"Not at all," Odalie said gently. "He lived on that night for a long time. He's still got the flower he wore on his lapel. He pressed it."

"My goodness," Stasia said. "I'm so sorry!"

"Don't pity him," Odalie replied. "He knows the score now. But it doesn't diminish the way he feels. He can't help it. Any more than you can help what you feel for Tanner." She sighed. "Isn't life a steaming mess?" she added with a grimace.

Stasia laughed. Odalie, looking over her shoulder, seemed uneasy.

Before she could turn around, Stasia heard Georgette Purlow's silken drawl. "Well, there you are, all alone, and you just married," the grating voice said in mock regret. "We saw your husband on the front page of that new tabloid paper. He's very good-looking."

Stasia turned, her dark eyes faintly glittering. "Yes, George, he's quite handsome."

"Don't call me George," the other girl said flatly.

"Then don't purr and gloat over the fact that my husband walked out on me with his mistress," Stasia said. "If I cared, it would probably be devastating. And isn't your mother having a flaming affair with our mayor? Wouldn't that look juicy in the tabloid if somebody told them?"

Georgette clenched her hands at her sides and glared at Stasia.

"Oh look, George, isn't that boy about to key your car…?" Odalie said.

"My car?!" Georgette had turned and was running like a madwoman in the general direction of the parking lot.

Stasia stared after her. "I don't see a boy."

"Why, I must be going blind," Odalie purred.

"You devil, you," Stasia said.

"You handled that very well, I thought," Odalie said. "Now come in with me while I find something stunning to wear to my audition in San Antonio next week!"

"That will be a pleasure," Stasia said.

Besides the pitying glances of the two elderly women who ran the shop, it was exhilarating to watch Odalie go through dress after dress trying to find the one that suited her most.

"It's the red one," Stasia said finally. "It's striking, it suits you and it's one of a kind. You won't meet someone wearing the same dress."

"The red one?" Odalie asked blankly, still twirling in front of the mirror in a black satin dress that did nothing for her.

"Yes," Stasia replied.

"I suppose I could try it on again. I thought it was too, well, too flashy," she confessed.

"Flashy is you," Stasia pointed out. "If you camouflage

your natural tendence to be flamboyant, you'll be hiding an essential part of your makeup. Red. Definitely red."

"Well, all right," she said slowly, but she did put the dress back on.

She walked into the showroom and struck a pose. Stasia and the saleslady were both beaming. Odalie looked in the mirror. "You're right," she said after a minute. "It does suit me. Okay, I'll take it!"

A relieved saleswoman plowed ahead to the checkout counter.

"That wasn't too painful, was it?" Stasia teased.

"I suppose not," she replied. She stopped outside the door. "Shoes! I simply must have shoes!"

"Onward, then, to Fricks," Stasia said. "Nobody has better shoes in all of south Texas!"

"Or north Texas either," Odalie agreed. She grinned.

Back at home after a hectic afternoon of shops and more shops, Stasia almost fell onto the sofa when they got back to the ranch.

"Are you all right?" Odalie asked worriedly.

Stasia laughed. "I'm just dizzy. I have these spells lately. I think it's the heat."

"It may be, but I'm very glad that you're going to see a doctor," Odalie replied. "I don't have so many friends that I can afford to lose one!"

"You won't lose me," Stasia promised. "I'm like a weed." She yawned. "Gosh, I'm so sleepy. I get tired at the most awkward times."

"Summer heat," Odalie replied. "We have a cowboy who does the same thing. It's a good thing that my dad likes him so much. We found him asleep in the barn one day, leaning on the rake. He's notorious."

"We have a guy like that, but he just falls asleep watching TV. Dad always said…" She stopped. It was painful to realize that her father was gone.

"Your father was a terrific dad," Odalie interrupted. "I know you miss him. But he'd like to see you perk back up and get more of those fabulous commissions. He'd be so proud of you."

Stasia swallowed, hard, fighting tears. "He was proud of me when I didn't do fabulous things," she said. "He was sure that I could make it as an artist. We used to talk about it all the time."

"They're not gone," Odalie said solemnly. "Not as long as we remember them."

Stasia smiled. "Thanks."

"Go lie down. I'll take my outrageous red dress home and model it for Mom. She'll love it!"

"I'll bet she will. Thanks for getting me out of the house. I needed it more than you know. And," Stasia added, "thanks for the super defense when Georgette started on me. Imagine, running into her in Branntville. It's not that small."

"Yes, but Fricks is the best dress shop. I'll bet she'd just come from there."

Stasia grinned. "She may still be looking for the boy who was about to key her car."

"Funny coincidence," Odalie said, "because I wasn't lying. There really was one. He had keys in his hand, but he might have considered using them on her car. I had no way of knowing."

"Well, it was excellent timing, just the same."

"Especially when I saw your hand making a fist. I've never forgotten what you did to Cherry in our homeroom when she made a nasty remark about my getting arrested when that internet nightmare erupted." She shook her head. "Looking back, I can't understand myself. I was so mean to Maddie Lane—the lie I told to that boy almost got her thrown out a second-story window…!"

"But it didn't," Stasia said gently. "And now she's your friend. You and John were so kind to her after the accident."

"I caused the accident." Odalie shook her head. "When I knew what I'd done, I was eaten alive with guilt. I did things for Maddie because I felt sorry for her, but very soon I learned why Cort Brannt was so fond of her. She has a heart as big as a city. I'm just glad that she recovered. She sculpted a little fairy that looks just like me. I was overwhelmed. She makes them for sale now, and gets a king's ransom for every one she sells. A true success story. And a moral tale," she added with a smile. "I had to take a long look at myself, and it was painful."

"But from pain, we grow," Stasia said.

"True words." She glanced at her watch. "I have to get home. We need to do this more often."

"I'm game whenever you are," Stasia said, and hugged her. "It was a great day. Thanks."

"I enjoyed it, too." She frowned. "You really do look pale. You need to lie down and rest."

"I will."

"Indeed you will," Minnie said from the doorway. "And right now. I'll bring you something to eat and some coffee. Would you like some, too, Miss Everett?" she added with a smile.

"No, thanks, Minnie, I have to get home. Keep an eye on her, will you?"

Minnie laughed. "You can bet I will."

After Odalie left, Stasia dropped down on her bed and fell asleep at once. Minnie took off her shoes and pulled an afghan over her and turned out the light.

When she woke, hours later, Minnie had pinned a note to the bathroom door. *Sandwiches in fridge, coffee ready to make, call if you need me.*

She chuckled. Minnie was like a mother hen. She was growing fonder of the woman every day. She started toward the bathroom and had to hurry. She lost all the food in her stomach. She was getting really worried. There had to be something major wrong with her. She dreaded being sent to specialists with all their tests. But that's what her doctor would do. It was what any doctor would do. She put it out of her mind while she ate a ham sandwich and drank coffee.

She couldn't forget Georgette's gleeful, sarcastic comments. It was humiliating to have people know how her new husband treated her. She'd wanted to keep it to herself, to bear her shame in private. After her mother's suicide over her affair with a married man, all those years ago, the gossip was equally painful. It seemed that her family had given Branntville and Big Spur more than enough to gossip about.

She knew Tanner wasn't going to keep the vows he made. He didn't live by any conservative morality. He was a free spirit. What did it matter to him if his unwanted wife was gossiped about? He and Julienne were having a whale of a time overseas. They weren't around to be bothered about it.

She was going to have to find some way to protect herself from people like Georgette, who thrived on other people's woes. If there was one.

It was late in the day, and the Bahamas in early summer were lovely. Tanner and Julienne had just returned to their hotel suite after dinner in the restaurant downstairs.

"Isn't this hilarious? Imagine a little private wedding like yours ending up in a national gossip magazine?" Julienne was laughing as she read a piece in the tabloid.

"My wedding?" Tanner asked, looking up from his coffee.

She turned the paper so that he could see the headline. An outburst of range language ensued, with the tabloid being dragged out of her hands.

He read the story, still fuming. Did this tabloid circulate in as small a town as Branntville? He groaned inwardly. Of course it did. The damned magazine circulated all over the country. Stasia would be shamed and embarrassed in places she'd never even seen. Because of him. Because he'd mocked the ceremony and all connected with it.

If he hadn't been so notorious, something that Julienne helped bear the guilt for, this story would have had no wheels. But his name was known, not only for his antics abroad, but because his mother was who she was. Heather Everett had written two Grammy-winning songs, and that was in the story as well.

He'd not only shamed his wife, he'd dragged his poor mother through the mud as well.

He groaned aloud.

Julienne just stared at him. "Well, who cares?" she asked. "It's just a story. They'll find somebody else to pick on in a week or two, and they'll drop this story like a hot rock," she said carelessly.

He turned and looked at her. "I wonder," he said curtly, "if you'd feel the same if it was a member of your family on the front page of this rag? Your sister, perhaps…?"

She tautened. Her sister had been involved in a bank robbery. The robbers had put a gun in the poor child's hands and told the police she was responsible for the heist the minute they showed up. Promising to be available for questions, the real robbers took off with pockets full of diamonds, and poor Clare was put in jail. Tanner had helped get her out, found a good attorney to represent her. But the gossip columns had gone crazy. Julienne's father was a TV personality, so the gossip was hard on the family.

"I see that you get my meaning," Tanner purred. "It's not so funny when the shoe's on the other foot, is it?"

She stood up and glared at him. "You're turning into your brother."

"John?" His eyebrows rose. "I'd have to grow two more inches and weigh thirty pounds more."

"Oh, you know what I mean," she grumbled. "I never thought I'd see the day that you'd turn conventional!"

He shrugged. "I'm not. But Stasia has had more than enough gossip already."

"Yes, her mother killed herself over an affair, didn't she?" she asked absently, twirling a finger around a stray curl in her hair in the mirror. "And her husband actually mourned her!"

"He loved her."

"Oh, love." She waved it away, still eyeing her face in the vanity mirror. "I'll take money, any day."

He cocked his head and stared at her. He'd been here for what seemed ages, and Julienne had done her best to make the holiday a trip to hell. The worst of it was that he no longer wanted her in bed. He didn't understand why. It was making the woman snappy.

"I've got a lacy blue negligee," she began in a beguiling tone.

"And I told you, I'm fighting an infection," he shot back, lying convincingly.

She glared at him. "If you'd go to a doctor…!"

"I've got meds for it. It's an old problem."

She stood very still. "Old problem. An STD?" she asked, all eyes now.

"Something I picked up overseas," he added.

She made a face. "So much for having a good time here,"

she said, her eyes shooting daggers at him. "I might as well have come alone."

"Certainly. And you would have afforded this trip, how…?" he asked with a smug smile.

She averted her eyes. "I guess it's worth my time to wait out your problem," she said. "I'm bored stiff. How about the casino?"

He looked at his watch. "Sure. I need to make a phone call first."

"I'll wear something trendy," she said, talking to herself as she went toward the smaller of the two bedrooms in the suite. Tanner had insisted on privacy at night, all through their relationship. Julienne was fascinating in bed, but he got little enough sleep as it was. When he finished with her, all he wanted to do was sleep, not hear the results of the latest audience-picked talent in some television show, or the on-going plot of a series. Julienne was educated, but it hardly showed. She'd been going with a French millionaire at the time, and he'd been kind enough to hire people to help her with homework and even take tests for her. She had a degree that she'd never earned, never used and likely never would need. It was, like her fancy wardrobe, stage dressing.

He went into his own bedroom and closed the door, pulling out his cell phone.

The phone rang and rang. Just as he was about to hang up, a soft, pleasant voice picked up on the other end.

"Mom?" he asked.

She paused. "Tanner?"

"Yes."

There was another pause. "Yes, I'll be there in a minute, sweetie," she called. There were footsteps and a door closing. "Odalie's here, trying on a dress she bought. You are in the red in her ledger right now."

"I don't know why the Lombards printed that story," he said curtly. "It was mean-spirited. Stasia has never hurt another human being."

"Stasia isn't the one living it up in Greece with his mistress," Heather said flatly.

He drew in a breath. His sweet mother's voice was dripping with venom.

"Hasn't Stasia had enough gossip around her already, Tanner?" Heather asked. "People are still talking about her mother's affair, and the suicide, all these years later. Small towns are…well, people gossip."

"That's why I hate small towns," he said flatly. "It's why I won't live in Big Spur and raise cattle."

"It breaks Cole's heart that you wanted no part of the Big Spur."

"John will grow it," Tanner said. "He's a born cattleman. He was the better choice. I love my freedom."

"Yes, we all noticed that when you walked out on Stasia the morning after the wedding without even saying goodbye!"

"How do you know that?"

"Minnie loves her. She's staying at your place, but she says it's temporary. That man who offered her money for a painting knows someone in law who says there is a way to break the will, a loophole none of us considered."

"A loophole?" Hope raised its head. "What is it?"

"I don't know. He said he'd talk to the attorney and have him call us. Mr. Dill called over here to see if he could get permission to give our number to the attorney. Cole agreed at once."

"Then there's light at the end of the tunnel," Tanner said.

"Always."

"Tanner, are you off the phone yet? I want to go, now!"

He groaned silently.

"My, my, I heard a woman at the vet's talk to her dog that way," Heather said sweetly.

Tanner ground his teeth together. "Stasia will do fine without me," he said at once.

"Yes, she will. We're all going to pitch in and do our best to make her fall in love with John after the divorce!"

He felt a sudden emptiness and wondered why. He forced it down. "Go for it," he said with convincing apathy. "I'd better get dressed. We're going to the casino. In the Bahamas."

"How nice. You can come home naked on a budget airliner..."

"I don't lose," he chuckled. "I've been barred from a couple of clubs here and there. And I never cheat."

"Yes, you do," Heather replied. "What would you call going to Greece with your...friend?"

"Night, Mom," he said, biting his tongue. "Love you."

"I love you, too, even if you are making one colossal mistake..."

"I'll call again soon. Night." He hung up while she was still mid-tirade.

An irritated Julienne stuck her head in the door. "Will you get dressed? For God's sake, I don't want to get there next year...!"

"One more damned word in that tone of voice and I'll pack my bags and go home," he interrupted, throwing her an icy glance. "Alone," he emphasized.

Her eyes were the size of saucers, but she swallowed the hot words on her tongue. If he left, she had no way of getting home. She didn't have a dime of her own, and he held the tickets. "Okay," she bit off. She closed the door.

He stared after her for a minute. She really was a pain to be around. Now that he felt less than attracted to her physically, he was seeing things he hated. She did talk to him with a noticeable lack of respect. He'd let her get away with it because he thought it didn't matter. He could snap back. But when his mother mentioned it, Julienne's attitude hit him in the face. He didn't like her. In fact, he was beginning to curse the day she'd walked into his life.

On the other hand, he didn't want to get mixed up with Stasia. Well, no more mixed up than he already was. He almost groaned, remembering that night with her. He'd never had so much pleasure from a woman, not even Julienne, and Stasia had been a virgin. He recalled soft cries of delight, moans of anguished ecstasy, and he felt himself go rigid just from the memory.

Irritated, he turned and went to his closet. A change of scene and the casino would take his mind off his female issues. And he had a man to see when he got there. Someone unknown to his family, even to Julienne. He'd just made a decision that was going to affect his life far more drastically than he even imagined.

SIX

Odalie came out of the living room, beautiful in her red gown. She twirled around. "Will I do?" she asked.

"You look beautiful," Heather said softly, but she was preoccupied, and it showed.

"You aren't paying attention. Who were you talking to?" her daughter asked.

Heather sighed.

"Tanner," Odalie muttered. "That man! How could you!"

"He's my son, whatever else he is," Heather replied. "When you have children of your own, you'll understand."

"Don't hold your breath," came the reply. "Right now, opera is my whole life."

"If you meet somebody who takes your breath away, opera will go out the front door," she replied.

Odalie put her arms around her mother. "Like you and Dad. You gave up so much for him."

"I gave up loneliness," she said gently. "I loved Cole from the time I was barely in my teens. He was my whole world. He still is. He always will be."

"I can't imagine loving like that," Odalie said.

"I know. It's all right. Where are you going, and with whom?"

"Just to the local cattlemen's ball. John's taking me."

"You're going with your brother?!"

"Well, I don't want to encourage the three men who asked me out. I don't want a relationship right now. I don't have the time."

Heather just smiled. She hugged Odalie and then let her go. "I remember feeling that way, when I thought I'd lost Cole. I wanted nothing to do with other men."

"Dad was lucky."

"So was I. Well, go be the belle of the ball."

"I'll do my best."

"Are you ready?" John called from the living room. "If you don't hurry up, all the best beer will be gone!"

He came into view, resplendent in a white suit with a blue striped tie. His blond hair was like spun gold in the light of the hall.

"But, John, you don't drink beer," Odalie pointed out.

He grinned at her. "All the more reason to get there early," he said.

"Brothers!" Odalie muttered.

"Sisters!" John echoed.

"Now, now," Heather began.

"Mothers!" her children chorused.

And they all laughed.

But neither one was smiling on the way to the civic center, where the ball was taking place.

"He's breaking Stasia's heart," John grumbled. "He knows it, and he doesn't give a damn."

"We can't interfere, as much as I'd like to," Odalie said. "Mom was just talking to him."

"He called her?"

"Yes. She told him what Stasia's benefactor said, about finding a loophole in the will."

John brightened. "That sounds hopeful."

She bit her lower lip. "John," she began.

"I know. She doesn't love me. But I'm here, and Tanner won't be," he added. "Water drips on stone and eventually dissolves it."

"That would take one powerful drip."

"So, hope springs eternal?"

She laughed. "You are truly hopeless."

"I always seem to get hung up on the wrong girls," he sighed.

"You get hung up on the very best girls," she replied. She smiled at him. "And one day, she'll be the right one. You wait and see."

"I'm growing older by the day. I'll lose all my teeth and my hair will fall out. I'll have to wear dentures and a wig just to get women to look at me," he wailed.

"Oh, put a sock in it," she murmured dryly. "You're gorgeous. Women mob you, everywhere we go."

"Maybe someday that will matter," he said. "But I doubt it. There's only one woman I want."

She started to argue, but it was useless. Let him dream of Stasia. It didn't hurt anyone. Well, anyone except poor John.

The casino on Paradise Island in the Bahamas was full. People were dressed in all sorts of ways, from evening gowns and suits to jeans and sweatshirts. The glitter was off the charts.

It was a famous casino, too, the Bow Tie, where a movie had once been filmed. There was a plaque with the details.

"Look!" Julienne exclaimed, nodding toward a handsome man speaking to one of the workers. "Isn't that the star of *Reckless*, that new TV series?!"

Tanner glanced at him. "I wouldn't know. I don't watch television."

She made a face at him. "Oh, I wish we could just walk up and introduce ourselves," she wailed. "He's my favorite TV star!"

"I'm sure it's his loss."

She frowned up at him, but he wasn't listening. His eyes were on a burly man with thick black hair and dark eyes, dressed in a suit, standing idly by the roulette table.

"Why don't you go over and tell him you're a fan?" Tanner suggested. "I see an old military buddy. I'm going over to talk to him."

She started to protest, but he was already walking away.

Stasia worried about the throwing-up episode. She must have some sort of stomach virus. But the other symptoms, the ones that wouldn't go away. She was only nineteen. Surely it couldn't be cancer!

She grimaced. Why couldn't it? Even little children got it. She was going down the roster of people in her family who'd had it when Minnie came into the kitchen where Stasia was pouring herself a cup of black coffee.

"Sweetheart, you're so pale," the older woman exclaimed. "Are you okay?"

"I'm fine, Minnie, just a little uncomfortable. I've got an appointment to see my doctor day after tomorrow. I'm just worried. I think there's something wrong in my stomach," she added worriedly.

"You've been under a lot of stress," the other woman reminded her. "It has an effect. And you don't sleep well or eat right."

She grimaced. "I know. I'm sorry." She smiled. "You're such a good cook, Minnie, and it's just wasted on me!"

Minnie hugged her gently. "It's not. When you get hungry, you'll eat. You just tell me. I'll fix you anything you want."

Stasia hugged her. "Thanks."

She went off to the bedroom, too sleepy to even sit up.

Behind her, Minnie's face no longer concealed her concern. If she was right, Tanner was about to find himself in really hot water, and likely with no way out. No way at all!

Later that day, on a truly incomprehensible impulse, Stasia phoned Tanner. Yes, it was overseas and would probably cost a packet, but she had a commission that would easily settle the debt. Besides, she wanted to tell her reluctant husband about her windfall—and pick his brain about the loophole in her dad's will.

Just for a few seconds, she toyed with the idea of hanging up. What if she caught Tanner at some awkward moment with Julienne? On the other hand, his phone had a Silent switch, so he could turn it off when he wanted to.

And as her apprehension grew, suddenly Tanner's deep voice came on the line.

"Isn't this a rather unusual call for you to make?" he asked, obviously having checked the ID of his caller.

"Couldn't help it," she said. "I'm excited!"

He felt a skirl of apprehension. "About what?" he asked suspiciously.

"This guy who came through town and raved over one of my paintings sent me a commission through Mr. Dill. He paid me ten thousand dollars to do a portrait of a friend of his!"

"Ten grand?" Tanner asked blankly.

"Yes! And there's something else, he told Mr. Dill that if I was interested in art restoration, he knew a good school in New York and he had contacts that could get me in. He says it's a highly paid profession!"

"It is," Tanner said, surprised. "I read an article about it just recently." He paused. "How trustworthy is this guy?" he added, worried about having some strange man take advantage of her. She was naïve to a fault. Or she had been. He flushed with remembered pleasure and forced it out of his mind.

"So is that what you want to do?" he asked. "Art restoration?"

"Well, obviously I want to keep painting as well," she said. "But a profession isn't a bad idea, for in between those huge fees for original work."

"At least you have an eye to the future," he remarked, and felt suddenly rootless. Stasia, at her age, knew what she wanted to do—thank God, it wasn't stay at home and fawn on her husband! But Tanner, with his advantage in age, had no advantage in future plans. He owned a ranch. Big whoop. He hated dust and cattle. It brought him a sizeable annual return; he could buy most anything he wanted. But he had no real purpose in life.

Well, that wasn't exactly the truth. He was going back to work again with a covert secret agency. He wasn't even sure why. Certainly, he hadn't told his family. Or Julienne.

"Oh, did you think I wanted to sit in a rocking chair and knit and send smoldering glances your way?" she asked, only half teasing.

He laughed, but without any real humor. "Not really," he said.

"Good, because the same guy who's busy planning my professional future said he thinks his lawyer may know how to get the will overturned. He says it wouldn't be the first time he'd done it."

"You don't want to do anything illegal," he said abruptly, because the description sounded like one he'd heard several times during his stint in special operations. He'd dealt with the underworld.

"It won't be. He isn't going to take the case, he's going to talk to Dad's lawyer. If it's something shady, you know Dad's attorneys won't go for it."

He relaxed a little. "Probably not," he conceded. He drew in a breath. "Well, so that takes care of you when we go our separate ways. Do you really want to live in New York, though?" He hesitated, feeling an odd sort of possession that made no sense. "John will be devastated," he added sarcastically.

She heard that mocking note and accepted that he was never going to fall head over heels in love with a little backcountry Texas girl. But it wasn't something she hadn't faced before.

That one sweet night in his bed would have to be a memory to last all her life. He sure wasn't lining up to be her Mr. Right.

"I know you think I'll eventually give in and marry John," she said easily. "But I'm not that cruel."

And she wasn't. He ground his teeth together. He knew her right down to her bones. She was Julienne's exact opposite: a kind, sweet girl with no malice, no greed, no meanness in her.

"You're going to need to grow a thick skin before you try to live in New York City," he said abruptly.

"Oh, I already have," she returned on a sigh. "You'd be amazed how many times a day I have to explain to people why my husband is spending his honeymoon with his mistress overseas."

His whole body tautened. She wasn't accusing him. She

wasn't even being sarcastic. But he didn't have a comeback. He was publicly shaming her. It hadn't bothered him before. Why was it so disturbing now?

"Sorry," she said pertly. "Forget I mentioned it. I just wanted you to know that I won't be dependent on you for my living, even if we can't get out of the marriage right away. I have prospects."

He didn't tell her, but he was going to check out her "prospects." After all, she was legally his wife. He didn't want strangers hitting on her; especially strangers who might have mob ties and wish her harm. She was a pretty girl, but very naïve.

"I'm happy to hear it," he said slowly. He hesitated. "Stasia," he began, his voice deep and quiet.

The door opened suddenly. "What are you doing in here? We'll be late for the floor show! Will you get a move on, please?" Julienne said rudely. "Who are you talking to, anyway?"

He held up a hand and glared at her until she went out, slamming the door behind her.

"Wow," Stasia murmured. "Sorry if I got you in trouble."

He drew in a breath. "I'm not. Listen, don't agree to anything unless you let my attorneys, or my dad's, look over any papers you're asked to sign. Okay?"

"Okay." There was a wistful smile in her voice. "Take care."

"You, too." He paused. "I'll be back in a week or so. I need more clothes," he added, so that she wouldn't get her hopes up.

"No problem. I'm having Odalie over a couple of times a week so I can teach her to swim. That all right?"

"My sister can move in with you for all I care," he chuckled. "How did you ever get her to agree to go in the water?"

"I took her to an exclusive shop and let her try on bathing

suits," she said. "She bought eight. Now she has a place to wear them. Half the cowboys find bushes to trim and grass to cut around the pool when she shows up."

He burst out laughing. "That's my sis."

"She is very beautiful," Stasia replied. "And very sweet."

"Only because she likes you," he said.

"Well, true enough. I have to go. Have a safe trip."

She hung up before he could answer her. He hung up. He didn't like the idea of her strange benefactor. And he was going to do some checking before she got herself into hot water.

"Who were you talking to?" Julienne asked irritably. "We're going to be late," she grumbled as they headed across to Paradise Island in a cab.

"None of your business," he said pleasantly.

She glared at him, but he paid her no attention. She drew in a suffering breath. "Well, just ignore me, and I've just bought this adorable dress…!"

He glanced at it. Mostly black lace and almost see-through in places. No doubt she'd be fishing for tabloid photographers, and there were plenty around Marcus Carrera's Bow Tie Casino. Marcus didn't discourage them. As he said, a guy, or a girl, had to make a living somehow. Not an easy thing in the modern world.

"Advertising?" he asked.

She gave him a hateful look. "I might as well," she muttered, and the glare became heat-seeking. "I don't seem to do anything for you these days."

"I told you, I've been under a lot of stress," he lied. The fact of the matter was that he found Julienne far less appetizing than the wife he'd left back in Texas. He hadn't been able to work up enough interest to touch Julienne since he'd joined her in Greece. Stasia had left a decided addiction in her wake. He was so confused that he could barely function. He didn't understand himself lately.

"Stress. Sure." She glanced at him. "I hope you don't mind if I advertise?" she added in a sarcastic purr. "After all, a girl never knows when she may need a safe harbor."

"Suit yourself," he said casually.

She made an irritated sound. It infuriated her that she could never make him really mad. He had perfect control over his temper—and he needed to have it, because his temper was all too terrible. She'd only seen him lose it once, when a young girl on one of their foreign trips had been accosted by two toughs. One of them had pulled a gun on Tanner.

Until then, Julienne had been a stranger to real physical violence. Tanner had opened her eyes to its dangers. Tanner had taken on the two toughs with no appearance of menace, until he dropped them both in less than ten seconds. The police were called, the men arrested, the girl returned safely to her family. There was a lengthy stop at the local emergency room for the two predators. Julienne had needed a whisky highball to get her past what she'd witnessed. After that, she was careful about how far she pushed Tanner. He wasn't a woman-beater. But he was scary in a temper, even when it wasn't directed at herself.

Stasia heard from Mr. Dill at the art store the next morning. He was jubilant.

"You have to come by here," he told Stasia excitedly. "I have several brochures for you, about exclusive art schools in New York City!"

"I hope my fee will cover the cost of admission," she began worriedly.

"That's the thing, you don't have to! This gentleman is

willing to finance your college! He says he's widowed and has no kids and he'd love having somebody around who could share his fascination with art."

"Is he on the up-and-up?" she asked suspiciously.

"I anticipated that. I called Mr. Bellamy, your dad's attorney. He said that he checked out the gentleman. He does have some, well, some interesting acquaintances and a background that's, uh." His voice trailed off. "But he's a legitimate businessman and he does have the money to back up his offer. He's very wealthy."

"Goodness!" She hesitated. "Do you think it's going to be all right? I mean, no strings, or anything…?"

"No. I had your dad's attorney check that out, too. That's why I haven't been in touch sooner. I wanted to make sure that it was a legitimate offer."

"Wow," she sighed, and sat down. "It's like a dream come true." Well, almost. A true dream fulfilled would be Tanner Everett coming home, sweeping her into his arms and wanting to love her forever.

She started laughing hysterically.

"Stasia?" he asked hesitantly.

"Oh. Sorry. Sorry!" She wiped away tears of mirth. "Sorry, I was just thinking of something else. No, I'd love to see the brochures. I'll drive over after lunch and get them, that okay?"

"It is. Also, Mr. Bellamy says he's expecting a phone call from your benefactor's attorney. It's going to get interesting."

"I know it is. I can't wait!" she lied.

"Well, I'll look for you later today then."

"Yes, sir. I'll be there. Thanks again!"

She hung up. Minnie came in with a glass of milk.

Stasia took it and made a face at her.

"Milk makes little bird bones strong," she teased. "Come on. Drink it."

"I don't have any appetite," she complained.

"Hence, the milk. Drink it. What did Tanner say yesterday when you talked to him?"

"You were eavesdropping," Stasia accused with a grin as she drank the milk.

"Of course I was!" Minnie replied. "Honestly, my life is so dull that nobody would pay to watch me for five minutes! Your life is much more interesting!"

Stasia sighed and handed her the empty milk glass. "I guess it is temporarily. But if my benefactor's attorney knows a loophole to break the will, I'll be free. So will Tanner. We'll have no more ties."

Minnie didn't say a word. She murmured something and smiled and went back into the kitchen, where the fake smile was dispensed with. Unless she was far wrong, Stasia was pregnant. How was that going to play into the mysterious wealthy man's offer, and Tanner's freedom? A baby was a tie that neither one of those fiery people could break. And Tanner would go nuts when he was told. Absolutely nuts.

Stasia, blissfully unaware, had a call from her doctor's office, changing her appointment to one ten days later because the doctor had a family emergency. She was secretly relieved. If she did have something terminal, better to put off the reality of it as long as she could!

Another slow week passed. Tanner was bored to death. All Julienne wanted to do was shop, gamble, lounge on the beach or mingle with other couples in the bar nightly. The Bahamas were far more lively than the place in Greece where they'd been vacationing. Julienne was addicted to bright lights and loud music. Tanner preferred the lonely, haunting nightly landscape of the Greek isle their hotel had been on. Julienne had complained nonstop about the lack of a casino.

Her pleading hadn't bothered him. He was tired of Greece as well, so they'd moved down to the Bahamas.

It was certainly livelier. Marcus spotted him at once and came over to where Julienne was leaning seductively against a roulette table, flirting with the gamester.

"Still with her, I see," Marcus muttered, shaking hands. He was about the same height as Tanner, but husky and muscular. He'd married a Texas girl some years before and they had two small sons. Marcus was an absolute fool about his wife and kids.

"Still. How's it going?" he asked the older man.

"Business is picking up again," he replied. "About damned time, too."

"Where's Smith?" Tanner asked, scanning the rooms for a tall, bald man with a five-foot iguana curled around his shoulder and upper arm.

"Mr. Smith is at the villa, helping my wife with the orchids," he replied, smiling. "She can't get through them as fast as she usually can, and it's fertilizing day."

"What's different?" Tanner asked.

"We're pregnant again," he confided, his black eyes twinkling. "This time, it's got to be a girl! Listen, I've invoked a local witch doctor! He made herbal bundles and charms and all sorts of stuff!"

"Hoodoo," Tanner chuckled after congratulating him.

"No, just legitimate pleas for a daughter who'll look like my sweetheart," he said, absolutely besotted and not hiding it.

"You and your kids," Tanner said, shaking his head. "I'd never have pegged you for a family man."

"It comes to us all eventually," Marcus replied. "The older generation having kids to take over, when they move on. Old plants going to seed, returning from the earth. The unbreakable cycle."

"Not for me," Tanner said with a mock shudder. "I have no desire whatsoever to become a father!"

Marcus lifted an eyebrow. "I have contacts in San Antonio who have contacts near Big Spur and Branntville," he remarked. "Didn't somebody tell me that you got married?"

"Business stuff," Tanner scoffed. "We had to go through a ceremony to save my…wife's ranch from being bought by a man with an entertainment complex in mind. My livestock and my dad's would have been history. Impossible to tear down a six-million-dollar animal breeding complex and put it up again somewhere else."

"So your livelihood was tied to it."

"Exactly." He looked around to where Julienne was draping her low-cut bosom over the croupier. "I have an inheritance that Mom gave me from her mother, but frankly it wouldn't finance three of Julienne's couture gowns." He laughed. "I really would have to get a job."

Marcus gave him a long look. "Eb Scott's recruiting, down in Jacobsville," he remarked. "Delia still has cousins there," he said. "We visit Jacobsville from time to time. I know Eb from way back."

"So do I," Tanner said without elaborating. He sighed. "I do have a prospect. I'm bored to death and sick of my…companion," he added grimly. "I wouldn't have to work, anyway. But now Stasia and I are looking at a loophole that will let us out of the marriage. Then she's got a career in art lined up, starting with a school in New York City and a benefactor who's willing to fund it."

"Not somebody taking advantage of her? Is she pretty?"

Tanner hesitated. "Yes," he said, surprised at the image he had of Stasia in his mind, all golden and laughing up at him. "She is pretty."

"Pretty and young. I'd check out the benefactor. Know

who he is? I have contacts in New York. Lots of them," he added with a dark smile.

"I'll find out," Tanner said. "I don't want her taken advantage of. Our families have been close for a long time."

"Not a bad idea, to make sure what she's getting herself into."

"Just what I was thinking," Tanner mused.

Stasia, unaware of the multiple plans for her future, was just getting into her car after a fraught hour in the doctor's office.

She just sat there in the car, without turning on the ignition, staring into space. She should have said something to Tanner, told him she was unprotected. She was pregnant, very pregnant, and she could only imagine what Tanner's reaction would be.

She placed her hands protectively over her flat stomach. Amazing how all at once she felt protective of the tiny life inside her. The doctor was outlining tests they needed to do, going over vitamins and talking about morning sickness. It all went over her head. She was pregnant. She was going to have Tanner's child.

It was glorious. Just that first, profound thought, that she was carrying the child of a man she loved more than life, was exhilarating. But seconds later, she faced reality. Tanner was not going to want this child. If anything, he'd be looking toward clinics.

She could go away and have it, she thought for one blind instant. Oh, sure, and his family would certainly keep the secret. They'd never know that Stasia had a child who looked just like Tanner. He'd never find out, either. She could live with some pretty white unicorns in a magical forest and eat flowers...

She started laughing hysterically. *Well, this is just lovely*, she thought to herself as she sat in the hot car, both hands on the steering wheel, staring straight ahead. *This is just lovely. Tanner is going to go through the roof. And how do I tell him?*

It was late when she got back to the ranch. Minnie had already gone home. Stasia had phoned when she stopped by the art store, to tell Minnie to go ahead and take her time off. She'd come home when she finished talking to Mr. Dill.

She tossed her car keys onto the counter and leaned against it for a minute. She had periods of dizziness, and rounds of nausea that kept her unsettled. Having to hide them was difficult. At least she wasn't having to hide them right now. Nobody was here.

She dropped down onto the sofa and unfastened her jeans. They were already too tight.

She lay back on the sofa and fanned herself with a magazine. The nausea was rising again, hot and thick in her throat.

It bubbled up. She rolled off the sofa and ran, staggering, to the downstairs bathroom, almost colliding with a dripping wet Odalie wrapped in a towel on the way.

"Sorry," Stasia choked, and ran into the bathroom.

Odalie stood there, stunned for just a minute before she poured herself a strong snifter of brandy. She carried it out to the patio and dropped into a lounger overlooking the pool.

Minutes later, a toilet flushed. Soon, a subdued Stasia appeared, dropping down into the lounger beside Odalie's.

"Hand me that," Stasia said, holding out her hand.

"You shouldn't drink," Odalie groaned.

"It beats rolling the truck over a cliff. Not that we have cliffs in this part of Texas. Give it," she repeated.

Odalie handed her the snifter.

Stasia took a sip, made a face and handed it back. "How can you drink that?" she groaned.

"The more you drink, the better it tastes," Odalie teased. Then she sobered. "What are you going to do?"

"Find a nice hidden valley with unicorns and a full-time full service restaurant and hotel, and move in for the duration. Then I'll hide the baby in my art bag while attending classes in New York." She glanced amusedly at Odalie's wide-eyed expression. "And of course, none of you will ever tell Tanner about the baby."

"Stasia…"

Stasia sighed. "I don't know what to do," she confessed. "Tanner will want a termination. I've heard him say that he wasn't ready to settle down before he hit forty, and he meant it. He won't want the child. On the other hand, I can't step on an ant deliberately, and I want the baby more than anything in the world."

"Irresistible force, meet immoveable object," Odalie sighed.

"Exactly."

"Tanner might…" Odalie began.

"Don't," Stasia interrupted. "I have no illusions about his reaction. You know him even better than I do." She lay back with a long sigh. "Dad always said, just sit tight for a bit, and most problems will resolve themselves." She turned her head toward a worried Odalie. "Not this one."

"No," Odalie said with a sad sigh. "Not this one."

Another week passed with Julienne trying to seduce Tanner and becoming enraged because he was impervious.

"What is wrong with you?" she raged, throwing things around the bedroom when her latest attempt had failed.

"I told you. Fatigue." He got up and dressed. "I need to go home and get a change of clothes."

"You could just buy clothes here," she protested.

"I want my own stuff." He glanced at her. "Don't worry.

You can come along. We'll head to Fiji next. I'm bored with the Atlantic and the Med."

She brightened. "Oh, I love Fiji! I can buy new clothes…!" She went off into the other room, happily musing about future purchases.

Tanner was uneasy. Something was wrong, and he didn't know what. He was worried about his family. From time to time he had premonitions about the future; not spelled-out, concrete ones, but just feelings of doom. He had one now.

Perhaps he should leave Julienne in the Bahamas for now and pick her back up after he'd spoken to Stasia and they'd discussed that loophole in the will. On the other hand, he was vulnerable right now, and he didn't want to end up making Stasia promises he couldn't keep. He didn't want to continue what was, after all, a forced marriage. Certainly not.

It would be wiser to take Julienne along. After all, he wasn't likely to soften toward Stasia with Julienne around. Not one bit.

SEVEN

Odalie was becoming a fixture by Tanner's indoor pond, as Minnie called it. They did have a heated indoor pool at home, but Tanner's was more open to the sun, and newer. Besides, Odalie was becoming very fond of Stasia and enjoyed her company.

They went to Big Spur for supper one evening and sadly for Stasia, the morning sickness that came at all sorts of inconvenient times hit her just before dessert was served. She spent time in the downstairs bathroom and was then carried by a distraught John into the living room and placed like priceless porcelain on the sofa.

"What can I do?" he asked, all concern.

"I'll be okay in a minute," Stasia said, fighting down more nausea.

"Should we get the doctor?" he asked his sister as Odalie joined them, just after closing the sliding door panels.

"It's a baby, not a medical condition," Odalie muttered as

she handed Stasia a cold, wet washcloth. "That might help a little. Want something cold to drink?"

"Not just yet. Thanks!" she said huskily from under the cold cloth.

John was almost vibrating with anger. His big fists were clenched at his side, something Odalie noticed but Stasia didn't.

She caught her brother's eye and jerked her head from side to side in warning. "If you need anything, call me, okay?" Odalie told her. "We'll be close by."

Stasia just nodded.

Odalie pulled John onto the moonlit patio and closed the door. "Don't make it harder for her," she cautioned.

"Does he know?" he asked angrily.

"I'd bet real money that he doesn't." She sighed, wrapping her arms around herself. "And I think you'll already have guessed what his solution will be."

"She'll never agree to it," he replied, jerking his head toward the woman on the sofa inside.

"I know." She faced the pasture. "What are we going to do? Mom and Dad will be furious." She glanced at him. "Dad even told him not to make any mistakes he couldn't fix."

"He should have had the common decency to walk by her," he said, furious. "He knows she's in love with him, why rub her nose in it?"

"Tanner doesn't know what he wants, John," she said, not looking at him. "In many ways, he's the most unsettled of all of us." She turned. "You want to be a rancher, I want to sing opera. What's Tanner want?"

He blinked. "To bum around the world with his would-be ingenue, I guess."

"Is that a purpose?"

He frowned.

"A purpose," she repeated. "He doesn't have one. He lives day to day. He only cares about his own needs, his own pleasure. He has nothing that denotes him as a person, that gives usefulness to his life."

John was quiet for a minute. "I hadn't thought about it."

"Mama spoiled him," she replied. "Dad says it's the only real regret he has about the years of happiness they've had, letting her have her way when Tanner was small. She had problems while she was carrying him, almost lost him. So she was much more possessive about him than she was about us, when we came along."

"Tanner's not that spoiled," he commented.

"Yes, but he's an anchorless, rudderless person. Someday he'll be too old to vagabond around the world with slinky women. Then what?"

He sighed. "No idea."

"He just leaves all the ranch work to Minnie's husband and Dad and the cowboys. He contributes nothing." She turned to John. "Nothing he does matters, don't you see?"

"I may. He doesn't."

She sighed. "I guess I'd do better to worry about the baby," she said. "And how are we going to keep Mom and Dad from finding out?" she added.

As she spoke, inside the door was opening and Heather and Cole were around Stasia, all smiles and beaming looks.

"Oh, no," she murmured, glancing at John.

He ground his teeth together. "Minnie," he said. "Minnie told them!"

"Of course I told them," Minnie justified herself to Odalie and Stasia the next morning as they sat around the pool.

Stasia felt better than she had since the pregnancy started. She was barefoot, her long, pale blond hair rippling around her bare, tanned round arms in the yellow floral sundress with its twin ties on her shoulders. She had a sunflower in her hair, above one ear. She looked young and radiant. Beautiful. Odalie was glad that John wasn't with them. It wouldn't do for him to see Stasia looking so pretty. He was far too susceptible.

"You look radiant," Minnie said with a warm smile. "It suits you, darlin'."

"It won't suit him," Stasia groaned. "What am I going to do? What am I going to say?"

"You run toward him like he's the sun itself and tell him he's going to be a dad," Odalie offered.

"He'll duck and throw Julienne at me," Stasia sighed.

"Men don't want babies until they know they're having one," Minnie said with a grin. "You'll see. It's all going to work out."

"You think?" Stasia wanted to be optimistic, but she knew Tanner too well. So did the other two.

A car door slammed. Odalie glanced at Stasia, who was already on her feet and heading for the doorway.

"Are you expecting anybody?" Odalie asked.

"Just John," she replied with a grin. "I thought he might have to rescue you if you fold up. I'm not messing up my dress...oh, my gosh!"

She took off running, her face full of unbounded joy, her eyes alight, laughing. "Tanner!" she cried.

He stopped dead. She was beautiful. He'd never seen a woman so radiant, so utterly incandescent. He just gaped at her. Barefoot, a flower in her hair, the sundress exposing her lovely figure, leaving bare her shoulders, just the swell of her small, pert breasts. She took his breath away.

Julienne appeared beside him suddenly, and Stasia stopped in place.

"Oh, good Lord, would you look?" She burst out laughing.

"She's barefoot, for God's sake, and that stupid flower…you look like some backcountry drooling idiot!" she told Stasia.

Stasia just stood there, stunned. She'd thought Tanner was going to open his arms for her. He'd looked like that. Now he stood scowling at her.

"How backward and unsophisticated can you get?" Julienne gasped.

Stasia looked at Tanner with eyes that grew darker and sadder by the second.

"And who pulled your chain?" Odalie demanded as she joined them. She glanced at Julienne. "Oh, hello, Jules, still vying for Playmate of the Year, are you?" she added, her eyes all too eloquent on Julienne's very brief shorts and tie-halter that left far too much skin bare.

"How dare you!" Julienne spat.

Minnie joined the group. "No, how dare you bring your mistress into the house with your pregnant wife?" she burst out, instantly regretting the hasty words but unable to call them back.

"Pregnant?" Tanner's face went from astonished color to pasty white in seconds. "Pregnant?" he said again, his face furious as his pale blue eyes stabbed into Stasia's dark ones.

"I'm sorry," she choked.

"How convenient!" Julienne said with a sarcastic smile. "Do you really think Tanner will fall for such an obvious lie? And why would he want to be tied to a stupid little country dumkin like you?" she concluded, her eyes disparaging the dress and bare feet all over again.

Stasia had always been a fighter, but this was just too much. She couldn't take on Julienne and Tanner all at once, and she was sick with disappointment. She'd thought, she'd prayed, she'd hoped…!

All for nothing. Tanner didn't want her or the baby and

he was throwing off actual sparks in his surprised fury. That wasn't a man who wanted to be a father. That was a man who looked capable of homicide.

Stasia turned and ran, her voice breaking on a sob.

"Well, you certainly handled that beautifully," Odalie told her brother. "What do you do for an encore, slap babies?"

"Did you hear what she said to me?" Julienne was still protesting Odalie's earlier comment and pointing to her.

"Oh, hell!" Tanner took Julienne by the arm. "Let's get out of here until everyone cools down."

He dragged her out the front door and put her into the convertible he'd rented at the airport. "Did you have to start a cat fight?" he demanded as they roared away.

"You didn't even defend me!" she raged.

He just drove, ignoring the complaints. He'd already decided that, whatever happened, he'd definitely had enough of Julienne. About the baby, he wouldn't think, not now. He felt trapped and sick and furious. He needed time to sort those emotions out so that he could reason again. It would take a little time.

There was a sharp cry as Odalie walked out onto the patio. She screamed.

Minnie ran to the pool and got there just in time to see Odalie diving in. Stasia was floating just a few feet away.

"Ambulance!" Odalie called, making a valiant effort to remember how to keep her head above water. "She fell. There's blood on her head!"

"Is she conscious?" Minnie yelled as she pulled out her phone.

"No!" Odalie wailed. "Call 911 and call one of the men to come help me! I can't get her out of the pool!"

"I'll get help." She phoned 911 and while she was giving

the information to the dispatcher, she was motioning two men in the corral to come to the ranch house.

The house was dark and quiet when Tanner and Julienne pulled back up in front of the ranch house.

"Minnie should be in the kitchen," Tanner murmured. "It's barely suppertime."

"Maybe they're all sitting around talking about us," Julienne laughed.

He didn't reply. He walked into the dining room with Julienne right behind when suddenly the lights came on, revealing a cold-eyed, furious Cole Everett and an equally taciturn John standing by the counter.

Tanner let out a breath. "Okay. You obviously know what's going on," he said. "So where do we go from here?" He smiled coldly. "Just don't assume that I won't fight letting her have the child…"

"There isn't going to be a child," John choked. "Not anymore."

Tanner blinked. Things were moving too fast. Beside him, Julienne seemed to shrink under Cole's icy gaze.

"No child…" Tanner just stared at his brother.

"Stasia fell," Cole bit off. "She hit her head and her stomach when she slipped on the wet tiles. She lost the baby."

Tanner's lips split on a shocked breath. "Is she all right?"

"She was unconscious for an hour," Cole said. "Concussion."

Tanner was recalling too many cases of concussion that had ended in death overseas in the military. "They're keeping her overnight?" he asked.

"Of course," John said. "She's conscious now, but they had to sedate her. She was hysterical when they told her…about the baby." He closed his mouth tight. It was emotional, remembering.

Tanner drew in a long breath.

"Shouldn't we go?" Julienne was asking Tanner almost plaintively.

Cole smiled icily. "Yes, you should. I'd advise packing. Quickly." He stared at her until she excused herself, flushing with nervousness, and ran up the steps.

Tanner shoved his hands into his pockets and raised his chin. "Okay. Why the smile?" he added, because he knew that smile. It usually preceded some idiot cowpuncher getting knocked down when he tried Cole's temper.

Cole cocked his head. "You've made a mockery of marriage. Held Stasia up to ridicule and gossip. You've played at life with no purpose whatsoever, and I've let you get away with it. Your mother spoiled you too much. You need to learn responsibility."

"I have a ranch," Tanner pointed out.

"You had a ranch," Cole returned. He moved closer, and his eyes were glittering like silver fire. "I've exercised my option to do an outright purchase. You have your grandmother's legacy. It won't keep you and your paramour in the splendor you're used to, but you can afford food and lodging with it, until you find a job of your own."

"You're taking the ranch?" Tanner asked indignantly.

"Yes. The ranch, the livestock, the fancy cars, the overstuffed house…" He looked around distastefully at the so-called decorating that Tanner had let Julienne do. It wasn't his taste at all, too modern, but he hadn't cared overmuch about how the house looked. He spent little enough time in it.

Tanner was feeling more unsettled by the minute. "You're overreacting…"

"Really?" He moved even closer, taller than his son and

far meaner. "You've disgraced us all. And I've let you. But no more. Until further notice, you're banned. You will have no contact with us or your siblings from now on. And that goes double for Stasia."

"Stasia cheated," Tanner said icily. "She told me she'd been to see the doctor!"

"She did," John said. "And Odalie said you never asked when she was supposed to start the stuff the doctor gave her!"

Tanner's eyes closed. Nor had he. His eyes opened and he looked straight into his father's. "So I'm a leper now?" he asked, not losing his cool. He had to appear less ruffled than he really was. You never showed weakness to Cole Everett. It was invariably fatal.

"You were my eldest," Cole replied. "I thought some of your heritage might one day appeal to you, that you'd see the history here and be proud to be part of it. I thought you'd settle down. But you haven't. You never will, as long as you're allowed carte blanche at the expense of the ranch."

"So where do I go?" he asked with faint sarcasm.

"Somewhere I can't get to you," John said icily. "Damn you for what you did to Stasia!"

"That's enough," Cole said, pushing John back. "Go bring the car around. Go on."

John gave his brother one last vicious glance and went out the door.

Cole turned his attention back to Tanner. "It might surprise you that your mother and I were looking forward to our first grandchild. We'd all been sitting around, making plans, thinking about the future. We thought, hoped, you might want the baby." He glanced toward the stairs, where a dressed Julienne was hovering. "Of course, that was a fool's dream," he added.

"I'm not cut out to be a rancher," Tanner said curtly. "I never was."

"I know that. Years too late." He moved away.

"I hope I can still wish my mother a happy birthday," Tanner remarked.

Cole turned at the front door. "You can do it from a safe distance. I'd better not catch you on Big Spur land. Not ever."

Tanner drew in a breath. "Sure. No problem."

Cole went out the door without a backward glance. He didn't even slam the door.

"Well, are we going to Fiji now?" Julienne asked, peering around corners to make sure neither of the other Everetts were nearby.

"No, we're not going to Fiji," he said angrily. "My father just bought the ranch out from under me and kicked me off the property."

"Excuse me…he what?"

"You heard me. Are your cases packed? I'll drop you off at the airport on my way out of town. And I'll buy you a ticket. Assuming Dad hasn't canceled my credit cards yet."

Julienne was just beginning to get the picture. "You mean, you aren't rich anymore?" she wailed.

He sighed. "Not rich at all," he agreed heavily. "I'll pack and we'll leave."

All the way to the airport, he was reliving the fraught moments with Stasia when he'd just arrived at the house. She'd looked so beautiful, so radiant, and he hadn't remotely decided why. Then Minnie had spilled the beans.

Poor Stasia, who loved him, being ridiculed by his mistress in her own home, while she was carrying his child.

For the first time he thought about a child, about how it would have looked, if it would have favored him or Stasia. It was ridiculous. He didn't want a child! Would its eyes have been blue like his or brown like hers? Would it have been a happy baby, like one he'd seen gurgling in its parents' arms in one of the venues he'd taken Julienne to in the Bahamas?

Poor Stasia! And she was in the hospital, grieving for her child, probably hating him, and he couldn't even call and ask how she was. Once he'd have asked John, but he wasn't willing to open that wound right now. John was murderous. Well, his brother loved Stasia and probably felt he'd been betrayed horribly when he knew she was pregnant with Tanner's child.

Stasia didn't belong to John, of course, and she never would, because she was Tanner's. His wife.

Not for much longer, though. He wondered how they'd manage the…annulment? No annulment, the baby was proof that it would have to be a divorce. Should he go ahead and start proceedings himself, or let Stasia do it?

She wouldn't have money. Not yet. Not unless she'd been working on that portrait for her mysterious benefactor. He wondered who that was and worried that she might be taken advantage of. He needed to find out who the man was. Marcus could tell him if he was trustworthy. Marcus could find out anything he wanted to know. Meanwhile, there was nobody he could ask for progress reports on her.

On second thought, there was. He and her father's lawyer, Bellamy, had done business together. They weren't friends, but on the other hand, they were more than acquaintances. He could ask Bellamy to find out for him. Not only that, he was going to need someone to handle the paperwork for him, whoever filed for divorce. His father would likely have Stasia use his own attorney, so Tanner would definitely need one of his own.

He dropped Julienne off at the airport.

"You could come with me," she pointed out. "I've got relatives in LA. Surely somebody in Fiji can invite us to stay for a month. I can ask…"

"I have a life to make," he pointed out.

She made a face. "Well, it was fun while it lasted."

He nodded.

She reached up and kissed him passionately, noting that the kiss wasn't returned, even lukewarmly. "Well, don't let yourself be put out to pasture here with a woman who doesn't even know how to dress," she drawled.

He let the insult pass without registering how much it irritated him. "Bon voyage."

She shrugged. "So long, cowboy," she said, and walked away.

"Cowboy." He made a harrumphing sound and went to get his ticket.

Eb Scott just stared at him. "I thought you were in Europe."

Tanner shrugged. "Too boring. I need something to get my senses honed. I think I may go freelance."

"Well," Eb exclaimed, "I think I have something that's right up your alley. With an old friend," he added. "Come on in! Of all the coincidences. I was just telling my guest about your wedding. I don't go to many these days."

"I know that. I was grateful that you came."

Eb glanced at him. "Not the happiest day of your life, I noted, and you didn't even introduce me to your bride."

"I didn't expect to stay married."

"Still feel that way?" Eb asked suspiciously.

"Nope. Getting divorced very soon," he replied. It was the truth. He'd been on the phone with the attorney, Bellamy, already.

"I'm sorry for you. I've been married, happily married, forever and a day."

"It works for some people," Tanner said quietly, not revealing the turmoil that still raged inside him.

"So they say. Come on in. Hey, Bruce, here's the guy I was talking to you about," he added.

"I don't believe it," the other man chuckled. "Tanner Everett! It's a small fricking planet!"

"It is, indeed. How's tricks, Bruce?" he added.

Bruce Willoughby, a senior agent for a largely mythical government agency, grinned. Tanner was forcibly reminded about the Shakespeare line, the man smiled too much. "It's good to see you! I was just asking Eb if he had any prospects that I might want to recruit. And here you walk in the door!" He turned to Eb. "This guy worked under me briefly when he was in the service. He really has mad skills."

"Thanks, but they're mostly honed instinct," Tanner said. He tossed a thumb toward Eb. "He did most of the honing."

"Worst recruit I ever trained," Eb said, glaring at Tanner. "These ex-military types are the devil to get in line."

"Exactly why I covet them," Bruce said. "I've got an operation going. If you're interested, I'll interview you for the position right here." He glanced at Eb. "I don't need to ask for privacy, do I?"

"No problem." Eb went to the door. "I won't mention that my security clearance trumps yours," he pointed out.

"In most areas. Not in this one, I'm afraid. It's a compartmentalized operation. Top secret."

"Then don't mind me," Eb chuckled. "I'll go flog the trainees."

"I'll be along in a few minutes," Bruce called after him. Eb threw up a hand and closed the door.

Bruce turned back to Tanner, deadly serious. "I've got a mole in my department," he told the other man. "I don't know who it is, and it's going to take some international travel to track him down. This is a short operation, but it pays well. And who knows, somewhere down the road, you may need a job and I may have one available!"

Tanner smiled. "Okay. I'm in." After all, he was rootless, with no family. That hurt. He didn't like to remember that he'd brought it on himself. He never should have married Stasia knowing how she felt about him. He should never have touched her, either.

He groaned inwardly, remembering his last sight of her. Radiant Stasia, running toward him, jubilant, joyful, with the sun in her eyes and her smile. Stasia, pregnant with his child. And he'd let Julienne savage her...!

"Hey, are you okay?" Bruce asked at once when he saw the tortured expression.

"What? Oh." Tanner managed a smile. "Sorry. I was thinking about another job I just finished. Go ahead. I'm listening."

Bruce nodded and laid out the assignment. Tanner did pay attention. He knew that Stasia was going to be okay. They had her sedated, and she'd be watched by his whole family to make sure she didn't do anything crazy. He recalled all too vividly her mother's suicide. He and Cole had taken down the body, and Tanner had consoled a very young Stasia. So many of her traumas had been soothed by his arms. He'd forgotten that.

But now he had to put her out of his mind and concentrate on how he was going to support himself. All these years he'd coasted, letting his father handle the money, the ranch property, all the investments. He'd never offered to help. He'd been too busy jet-setting, and not just with Julienne. He'd been doing it with several women over the years, in between college classes and work with the military and the intelligence community. In fact, they could paste a picture of himself in the dictionary under "irresponsible." He looked the very definition of the word.

Well, he'd have a job now at least. Maybe he could make it up to Stasia one day, somehow. He had no idea how. He couldn't think about it at the moment, it was too traumatic.

His dad and mom, his whole family, would take care of Stasia. Mr. Bellamy was going to find out the name of Stasia's patron and give it to him. He'd check with Marcus to make sure she wasn't being railroaded or trafficked. Cole didn't have underworld ties, but Tanner did. He was going to look after Stasia regardless of their circumstances. He owed her that much.

Stasia came in and out of consciousness at first. When she stabilized, her hand went to her sore and very bruised stomach and she looked suddenly up at Heather with wild eyes.

"My baby…?" she asked, her lower lip quivering, the bruise on her forehead purple and violet.

Heather's face gave it away.

Stasia collapsed in tears. They sedated her, and Heather and Odalie shared the time keeping her company. John wanted to, but Cole kept him occupied. It wasn't wise to let Stasia start depending on John, not when she was this distraught. She could make a wrong decision. Especially right now.

She did bounce back quickly. She was young and healthy and the world hadn't completely ended.

While she was recuperating, Mr. Bellamy, her father's attorney, called and gave her the information he'd gotten from her would-be benefactor's attorney.

"There is a loophole," he told her over the phone, sounding unusually jubilant. "It's a tiny one, but we can use it. I've already started divorce proceedings in your name."

She hesitated. "You'll have to get in touch with Tanner's attorney…"

"I am his attorney," he answered. "It's okay, you're using

Cole's firm, so there's no conflict of interest. You'll be free in a matter of weeks."

"Oh." She felt raw inside, still. "I don't want anything from him," she added.

"You'd be lucky to get anything," he said amusedly. "Cole disinherited him, I hear."

"What?" She caught her breath. "But how will he live?" she asked sadly.

"He already has it figured out, from what I understand." He didn't add that he'd just spoken to Tanner. "And one more thing, I've had your benefactor checked out. He's rich beyond the dreams of avarice—has his own baby jet, a mansion in New Jersey and a townhouse apartment in New York City. He's the real deal. And he is a connoisseur of art. He's got a portfolio that even I envy, and he collects rare art as well as sits on the board of directors of two art museums. Plus he owns one."

"Wow," she said. "And he really wants to help me?"

"He does. He's crazy about artists. He was trying to encourage one down in Jacobsville to go professional, but she married a Wyoming rancher and has no interest in it. He's been sort of looking for someone to nurture. You're it."

She laughed. "What a strange coincidence."

"There are no coincidences," the attorney said drolly. "Not in my experience. Now let me explain how this is going to work. About the will, I mean."

"I'm all ears," she agreed.

In the end, they did manage to get the will set aside on a minor bout of language that could be interpreted either way.

"I should be flogged for the way I framed that paragraph, by the way," Bellamy explained. "Your father didn't catch it, and neither did I. It does at least work to yours and Tanner's advantage at the moment."

"It does. We can assume that marrying and living together for a day fulfills the condition of the will. So the divorce will go through without challenge."

"Tanner agreed to that?" she asked, averting her eyes.

"He won't challenge. He said if you wanted him to settle any sum on you, he was willing."

"He can save it for Julienne," she said bitterly.

"Not really," he replied. "She just went extinct."

"How lovely," she muttered. "I guess the money was the main attraction after all."

He cleared his throat. "I understand that she offered to find somebody in Fiji to have them as houseguests for a month or two."

"I can see Tanner agreeing to that," she laughed.

"Yes. So can I. But she's history."

"He'll find somebody else," she said quietly. "He always does."

"Well, the next one he finds had better have simple tastes," he said. "Because there won't be any more jet-setting. And he's got a job."

"Already? What doing?" she asked, almost stammering.

He hesitated. "Sorry. I'm not allowed to say."

"Nothing illegal?" she asked abruptly, worrying.

He felt the concern even over the phone and ground his teeth together. Tanner could throw away a woman like that! Idiot.

"Nothing illegal," he assured her. He hoped it was the truth.

Tanner faded into the shadows. Stasia finally met her bene-factor face-to-face. He came to supper and outlined his plans for her, to the delight and amusement of the Everett clan, who all gathered around to be introduced.

Tony Garza was amused that Stasia had so much support. He was amazed at her talent and happy to be the one to discover her. She had great potential, and not only as an artist. He was convinced that, with the right training, she'd be a wonder as a restoration worker, and he had stock in a big gallery in New York City that could benefit from her expertise even in her spare time.

He was big and bluff and intimidating in his way. He had a husky build, like a wrestler, and hands like hams. He had big feet and a chiseled face. Wavy black hair with just a hint of silver, and big dark brown eyes that glittered with feeling. He had a light olive complexion that went well with white shirts. He was a handsome man. A widower, he told them, but with no plans ever to remarry.

He glared at Odalie as he said it. Nobody understood why, but he'd been antagonistic toward Odalie ever since he walked in the door.

"Oh, I hope you weren't saying that to ward me off, Mr. Garza," Odalie purred. "I mean, I'm just nineteen, you know…"

"I don't rob cradles, little girl," he drawled in a grown-up way.

"Mind I don't knock out your crutches, old man," she shot back with glittering pale blue eyes.

"This is a happy occasion," Heather broke in, deliberately bright.

Tony glanced at her and grimaced. "Sorry," he muttered, avoiding Odalie's bright eyes. "I meant to say that I'm still devoted to my late wife."

Cole's arm pulled Heather close. "I'm sorry for you," he said quietly.

"Life isn't always kind," Tony replied.

"But sometimes it is, abundantly," Stasia said. "I don't even know how to thank you, Mr. Garza!"

"That will work itself out, when you graduate from art school and you're qualified to restore paintings for my own collection," he chuckled. "As you see, I have ulterior motives. But only a few."

"I don't mind," Stasia said. "So. When do we start?" she added, smiling.

EIGHT

Five years later...

It had been a long day at the art gallery. Stasia shook off her slingbacks, tossed her purse onto a vacant armchair in her modest apartment in New York City, and threw herself down onto the sofa.

She no sooner relaxed than her phone burst out with the theme from a box office summer motion picture. She answered it, glancing at the caller ID as she did. "Hi, Odalie!"

"Oh, what a long, long, long day!" came the reply. "I'd love to invite you to supper. But, one, I'm in Texas and you're in New York and, two, I've just eaten. How's it going?"

"I love my job," she said on a long sigh, and with a smile.

"Besides your job," her friend interjected. "What about the assistant gallery manager...?"

"Oh, the one with a wife and two kids who isn't understood at home and longs to be free? That assistant manager?"

"Well, darn!"

Stasia laughed. "He's nice, but we had a long talk and then I introduced him to Tony."

Odalie didn't say anything for a moment. "That wouldn't have gone over well. Tony has designs on you."

"Actually, he doesn't," she replied easily. "He's got women of his own. One is really glossy, she was a fashion model. He brought her by the gallery on the way to the opera."

"Hmmmph. I hope he won't show up at the Met one day when I get accepted there, and make nasty remarks about my career choice."

"He's never heard you sing, sweetheart," Stasia reminded her.

"Never will, if I have my way!"

"He loves opera," Stasia teased.

"He can love opera with some other woman. Never me! I know he's been kind to you, but I can't stand him!"

Stasia, who'd seen the two of them together infrequently, disagreed with that impassioned statement. She'd seen the way poor Odalie looked at Tony, who was deliberately offhand with her and never even smiled in her direction.

"He still hates my guts I guess?" Odalie asked with some venom.

"He hasn't mentioned you," came the reluctant reply.

"Doesn't bother me."

Sure it doesn't, Stasia was thinking privately, but she didn't speak out loud. "When are you coming up for a weekend?" Stasia asked.

"I thought I might come late next week," Odalie said. "I start singing lessons in New York. I'm tired of singing in local operas. I want someone who actually has ties to the Met."

"Your voice is awesome. All they'll have to do is hear you at an audition…"

"Don't say audition," Odalie pleaded and sounded sick.

"I'm so scared, I can't even force myself to ask for one. What if they said no? I'd never get over it!"

"What if they said yes, and you were too afraid to ask?"

"Don't clutter up my misery with a bunch of irrelevant facts," Odalie sighed.

"It's still the truth. Come on up. We'll go out on the town. If I need to go places, Tony lends me Big Ben. He's not only a great chauffeur, he's so big that he intimidates anybody I don't want around."

"Tony spoils you," came the soft accusation.

"I'm an adoptive child," Stasia teased. "He doesn't have kids, so I've become his."

"You're gorgeous!"

"Not to Tony," she laughed. "I'm a big kid with skinned knees. That's all." Her laughter trailed away. She sighed. "I don't get over things," she added softly. "I'll never get over Tanner. God knows, I've spent the last five years trying."

"He hasn't been in touch?" Odalie asked.

There was a long pause. "No." She hesitated. "Have you…?"

"Heard from him? No. I think he corresponds with John, but I've always been afraid to ask. John keeps his cards close to his chest and he knows I can't keep a secret. He and Tanner were always close. And John doesn't really know how to hold a grudge," she added softly. "But Dad's still volatile. He found out that Mom met Tanner in Dallas to treat her to a birthday lunch and he hit the ceiling. Mom calmed him down, but he was furious. He doesn't want any of us around Tanner."

"Why?"

"Because of the way he treated you, of course. My family thinks you're one of us. Sisters-in-law don't lose the title with the divorce, you know. You're still family."

"That's sweet," Stasia said. "I feel just the same way. But it's been five years, you know."

"My father is still holding a grudge against the woman who told him my mom was his half sister. He won't hear her name mentioned, even though she's happily married and lives in another state! Do you know how many years ago that was?"

"Good grief!" Stasia exclaimed.

"That's what I'm talking about. Dad doesn't forgive. Well, he forgives Mom. But not Tanner. Not ever."

"That's so sad. I hope it's not over me. I don't have a family anymore, so I can appreciate how important they are. Anything could happen to Tanner, and how would your dad feel then?"

"Awful," Odalie confessed. "But you'd never hear him admit it."

"Probably not."

"You should get some rest. I'll see you next week."

"Text me when you're getting on the plane with your flight number. Big Ben and I will meet you."

Odalie laughed. "That will raise eyebrows."

"In New York? Bite your tongue! See you then!"

She hung up and changed into yoga pants and a T-shirt, letting her long blond hair down from its neat knot behind her nape. She was twenty-four now, mature and competent in her profession. She'd graduated art school with honors and immediately taken a position with the gallery Tony had an interest in. She'd worked her way up steadily, and now she was gaining a little reputation as a restorer.

She loved the job. It was just that Tony was so overprotective. She felt like a beloved child. Tony was big on spoiling her. She'd long since learned that if she admired anything, no matter how expensive, it would turn up as a Christmas or a birthday present.

It was nice, to be pampered. Stasia still missed Tanner, but the years had been kind. The pain had receded, a bit. She had no interest in men, though. The loss of her baby had taken a lot of time to process, and the memory hurt. Julienne's unkind laughter and ridicule had only added to the pain. Stasia knew she was a country bumpkin. Or, at least, she had been. Not so much anymore.

She had traces of her Texas accent left, but only traces. She'd learned sophistication and she'd become accustomed to five-star hotels and restaurants. Her father had lived from pillar to post just at the last; there had been no big money at home. She just wished she'd known that her father was facing bankruptcy. That was the only reason he'd put that insane clause in his will, the one that had forced Stasia and Tanner to get married in the first place. He'd expected that Tanner would take care of Stasia, who was pretty and naïve.

Stasia often wondered what her father would have thought if he could have seen the results of his scheming. It had brought untold tragedies to two families.

She put Respighi's *Pines of Rome* on the stereo and stretched out on the sofa. It seemed like a bad dream sometimes, those days when she'd lived in Tanner's house and hoped against hope that he might want her. She should have known better.

The hardest part of her life had been keeping John out of it. She knew he had feelings for her, but she didn't dare indulge him. Love on one side was never enough; her feelings for Tanner had taught her that. It would have been destructive, to let John hope for any return of the emotion he felt for her.

She knew that Tanner kept in touch with John, so the younger brother had apparently forgiven his sibling somewhat for the pain he'd caused Stasia. She didn't blame John for it. Families stuck together. Well, Cole hadn't relented, and it seemed as if he never would.

Heather told Stasia that Cole had gone all dreamy with the idea of a grandchild. It had been a blow to his hopes when Stasia miscarried. Heather had wanted a grandchild, too. It was sad that Tanner hadn't had the foresight to avoid Stasia's bed.

The marriage, the wedding night, all of it seemed oddly like a movie Stasia had watched a long time ago and half forgotten. She could forget about Tanner when she was working. He wasn't part of her new life, so there were no bad memories to get past.

Cole made sure that her father's house was kept in good repair so that Stasia would have a place to stay when she came home to Texas. The foreman and his wife lived in the big house, and took care of it when Stasia was in New York. Her bedroom was just as she'd left it, all those years ago. She could stand on her front porch and remember, oh, so well, the times she'd seen Tanner pull up in front of the steps.

But that was in the past. She had commissions now for paintings, as well as the restoration work she did for the gallery that Tony owned. She loved her work.

Supper was yogurt and a salad, then she went to work on her latest commission, a child's portrait for one of her coworkers at the art museum. It was of a little girl with dark eyes and hair and an olive complexion.

As Stasia worked on it, she thought about the baby she'd lost. She wondered who it would have favored, if it would have been a boy or a girl.

It hurt to look back. In a perfect world, she and Tanner would have been deeply in love with each other and looking forward to being parents. It wasn't a perfect world.

She wondered from time to time if Tanner ever thought of her. She figured not. He was doing private security, was the last tidbit she'd heard from Odalie. It didn't seem like the sort of job Tanner would take, but then, she didn't know him as an adult. She'd been a teenager living in dreams.

She got out her paints and uncovered the oil painting in progress on her easel. She was enjoying the commission. The little girl on the canvas was taking shape. She was going to be beautiful.

Odalie showed up a few days later. Tony had sent Big Ben along with the limo to pick up Stasia at the gallery and go on to the airport to meet the other woman.

"This is so nice of you," Odalie said, fanning herself as she plopped down in the back seat of the limo next to Stasia. "It's hot even for August!"

"Oh, tell me about it," Stasia laughed.

Odalie studied her with a curious smile, taking in the exquisitely braided hairdo that gave Stasia an elfin look with her platinum hair and big brown eyes. "You look gorgeous."

"Speak for yourself," Stasia said. "You always look gorgeous."

And she did. Odalie had long, pale blond hair that waved around her shoulders and pale eyes like her mother's. She was elegant.

"How's work?" Odalie asked.

"Fun," came the smiling reply. "I've never enjoyed anything so much. Tony was right. Restoration was the best choice of jobs for me."

"But I also like the original canvases you do," Odalie replied. "You're so talented."

"The best of both worlds. Want to stop and pick up something to eat on the way home?"

"Tony said how about coming over for supper?" Big Ben asked from the front seat. "He thought you might like something home-cooked."

"Is he cooking?" Stasia asked.

Big Ben grinned. "Yep. Spaghetti and homemade garlic bread."

"In that case, thank you, we'd love to!"

He reached for his cell phone. "I'll tell him." He powered the window back up between the front and rear seats.

"He might not mean me as well," Odalie said.

"Don't be silly. I told him you were coming."

Odalie made a face. "He'll have time to count out some poisonous toadstools to cook in my part of the spaghetti."

"I don't understand why the two of you can't get along." Stasia shook her head.

"Different generations," Odalie said nastily.

"Stop that. He's only twelve years older than us," Stasia pointed out.

"Thirteen," Odalie corrected harshly. She shifted on the seat and looked out the window. "I don't know why he doesn't like me," Odalie muttered. "But I don't like him because he's rude and obnoxious and antagonistic."

"Mmm-hmm," Stasia mused aloud, not believing a word of it.

"He starts it," Odalie said curtly. "I just defend myself."

"I think it's about fifty-fifty," Stasia said.

Odalie leaned back against the seat. The air-conditioning was heavenly. "I've been helping Mom clean out closets. It was such a relief to come and arrange lessons with my singing tutor. He won't be pushing me into closets."

"You hope," she answered. She stretched. "How's John?"

"Knee-deep in ranching politics," Odalie said. "It keeps his mind off you," she added.

"Poor guy," Stasia said. "I keep hoping he'll find somebody of his own."

"So do we. So far, no luck."

"You should send him on a vacation to somewhere exotic. John doesn't travel. He just works on the ranch."

"We've all tried. He's just not interested. He loves horses and cattle."

"Maybe find him a girl who loves horses and cattle, too."

"Hope springs eternal," Odalie said. "I hope this tutor and I can get along," she added worriedly. "The one I had in Italy was just so demanding and sarcastic. I began to think I should give up opera and get married."

"Any prospects?" Stasia asked.

"As if," she muttered. "Everybody I went to school with is married or divorced or trying to shack up with somebody."

"There's a man out there waiting for you," Stasia pointed out.

"Sure, he's at the bus station—that's where I'll be when my ship finally comes in."

Stasia burst out laughing. "Highly unlikely."

Odalie just shrugged.

Stasia looked out the window. "Have you heard anything from Tanner just lately?"

"John has. He's back into international intrigue, or so he told John."

"No more bodyguard stuff?"

"He wasn't needed. His client married and her new step-niece is under the protection of the underworld, so he went to another project. John said an old colleague of his had a hush-hush job overseas someplace. Tanner took it on."

Stasia kept her face averted. "He takes chances."

"He's the sort of man who can't live without them, I think," Odalie said after a minute. "He has a friend who runs a counterterrorism school in Jacobsville, the man who trained him all those years ago. Dad's best friend is King Brannt, and he loves mercs. He invites them to any big parties King and Shelby give on the ranch."

"Shelby is still beautiful, just like your mom," Stasia said. "They were my idols growing up. I couldn't decide if I wanted to be a famous model like Shelby or a songwriter like your mom."

"I think love is why they're both beautiful," Odalie said. "I keep hoping I'll find one of those happily-ever-after men like Mom did, but it never happens. I'm always the girl who has a shoulder for some poor, tormented man to lean on."

"That will change one day," Stasia said.

"Really? I'm ready to give up hope," the other woman sighed. "I think I'll go back to having crushes on TV stars. It was safer."

"If Heather wants grandkids, you and John are her best hope," she said, ignoring the faint pain of losing her own child.

"She'll have a very long wait in John's case. Maybe in mine, too. I only attract heartsick men hung up on other women."

"Baloney. You don't get involved because you want to sing at the Met."

"Yes, and my folks have spent a fortune having me correctly taught." She sighed. "Someday I'll have to justify that expense, one way or the other."

"You'll be great. You sing like an angel."

Odalie beamed. "Thus speaks a true friend."

"And don't you forget it!" Stasia laughed.

Tony wasn't dressed up. He was wearing a dark green designer shirt with dark slacks when he met them at the front door.

He glared at Odalie, but he smiled and hugged Stasia.

"I'm glad you could come," he told her.

"Thanks for inviting us," Stasia replied. "I was going to pick up some fast food on the way, but your spaghetti is worth waiting for."

"As long as you couldn't find any poisonous mushrooms…?" Odalie murmured.

He glared at her openly. "I don't poison guests. Even with provocation."

"Oh, I'll bet you'd make an exception for me," Odalie purred.

"I'm halfway finished with the little girl," Stasia interrupted at once. "You'll have to stop by and have a look at her."

"Maybe tomorrow," he said and smiled. "I've got a business meeting downtown. I'll pick you up at work and bring you home."

"Thanks," Stasia said.

"There's a cocktail party tomorrow night for our visiting artist, as well," Tony said, leading the way to the living room. "I'd love it if you could stop by. You can bring your…friend," he added, as if the word almost choked him.

"We'd love to," Stasia said, forestalling Odalie, whose blue eyes were spearing him like twin flames. "We don't go to a lot of parties."

"This one will be legendary," Tony told her with a grin. "It's a mixed bag of celebrities, outlaws, in-laws and sports stars."

"Not that sports star…?" Stasia asked worriedly.

"He's off the guest list permanently," he assured her.

Odalie was giving her a puzzled look.

"One of the better-known baseball stars got drunk and overbearing at a party last spring," Stasia explained. "I sort of helped him into a bowl of punch."

Tony burst out laughing. "He was wearing a white sports coat. It turned red."

"I felt bad about it."

"He felt worse," Tony assured her. "He's still trying to get his wife to come back."

"She seemed very nice," Stasia said. "I felt sorry for her."

"So did I," Tony said on a sigh. "He's been running around on her forever. I guess she finally had enough."

"Marriage works for some people. It doesn't work for others."

Odalie glanced at Stasia. "You'd still be married if my brother wasn't such an idiot."

"We both moved on long ago," Stasia said with a gentle smile. "Now we need to get you married."

Tony glared at Odalie at once.

She glared back. "She didn't mean to you," Odalie said with soft venom.

"Well, thank God, because I'm not in the market for a would-be singer."

"And I'm not in the market for the Godfather!"

"You listen here…!" Tony began.

Stasia got between them. "I love spaghetti," she said, wrapping her hand around Tony's arm. "And Big Ben said you even made garlic bread."

He hesitated, but just for a minute. "Yeah. I did. Helene," he called as they walked into the dining room, "make sure it's white wine. Yeah, I know, it doesn't go with beef, but I don't need a migraine tonight!"

Helene, middle-aged and rotund and gray-haired, smiled at them. "I know, I know, serve the white wine not the red."

"He won't let anybody nurse him through the headaches," Stasia explained to her friend.

"Red wine gives you headaches?" Odalie asked curiously.

"I'm allergic to the tannins in red wine," Tony explained. "Or aged cheese." He chuckled. "Just like her," he indicated Stasia with a fond smile. "In fact, one of my guys gets migraines. His wife was the only person he ever let nurse him through one. He lives in Jersey. She's from Texas."

"Texas?" Odalie asked.

"Jacobsville," Stasia explained as Tony seated her. Odalie

got into her chair so quickly that Tony didn't have the opportunity to seat her.

"Marcus Carrera's wife is from there, also," Tony said. "He's a gang boss. Or he was," he added with a cold glance toward Odalie. "Lives in the Bahamas with his wife and three kids—two boys and a girl." He made the last words sound poignant. It was no secret to his friends that Tony loved kids more than anything. His late wife hadn't been able to have children.

"That name sounds familiar," Odalie said, almost to herself. "Tanner mentioned him to John. He knows Carrera."

Tony sat down while Helene bustled around filling glasses and putting dishes of food on the table. "Tanner. Your brother, I gather?" he asked Odalie without looking at her.

"Yes."

He frowned. He studied Stasia. "You don't still have anything to do with him…?" he asked.

"As if," she laughed. "I haven't seen Tanner in five years."

He hesitated, as if he meant to say something. Then he shrugged and smiled. "Tell me about the painting," he said instead.

There was a painting of Tony over the mantel in the living room. Odalie stared at it as if mesmerized when they migrated into the cushy living room.

"Is that the painting you were telling me about?" Odalie asked Stasia.

"Yes. In fact, Tony's 'adopted' daughter did it," Stasia said. "Isn't it great? It looks just like him."

Odalie just nodded. She couldn't seem to take her eyes off it. "I've never seen anything quite like it, except the paintings Stasia does."

"That's why I coaxed her into going to art school here," Tony said. "She has one of the greatest natural talents I've ever seen. Merrie sees right inside people when she paints them, but she's married with kids and painting is just a hobby with her now."

"She was very talented," Odalie said.

"What time do you have to be at your tutor's tomorrow?" Stasia asked Odalie as they were getting ready for Big Ben to drive them back to Stasia's apartment.

"At eleven," Odalie said. "I'm a nervous wreck."

"Tutor? Tutor for what?" Tony asked.

"My voice coach," Odalie replied.

"Didn't she tell me," he indicated Stasia, "that you'd been coached for several years? Can't quite remember the lessons...?"

She hated that smug smile. "I remember them just fine, thanks," she gritted.

"Well, we'll be going. Thanks for supper, Tony, it was delicious!" Stasia said, half dragging Odalie out the door.

Odalie managed a jerk of her head to agree with Stasia's opinion of supper and then she was out the door.

"Do you have to bring her with you tomorrow night?" Tony groaned as he watched Odalie get into the limo, assisted by Big Ben.

"Yes, I do, and you have to be nice," Stasia teased. "She's not so bad."

He made a face. "I'll see you tomorrow night then, at the gallery."

"I'll be there," she promised, and waved as she went out to the car.

"He's just insufferable!" Odalie raged when they were back in Stasia's apartment.

"He's not. He just doesn't get along with most people."

"I noticed!"

"Let's watch a movie, unless you're sleepy?"

"No, I'm fine. What were you thinking about?"

"There's a new cartoon movie…"

Odalie rolled her eyes. "You and your cartoons!"

"You'll love this one. I promise!"

"That's what you said about the last one."

"Yes, and you loved it. Didn't you?"

Odalie just laughed. "Yes, I did."

"Wow," Stasia said, eyeing Odalie in the lacy black cocktail dress she'd donned for the drinks party the next night.

Odalie's hair was up in a complicated topknot, and all she wore with the dress were her Mikimoto pearls. She looked like a confection.

Stasia had a simple black dress of her own, with a cowl neckline and a bare back. Her pale blond hair was in a sleek chignon at the back of her head. She was wearing diamonds and emeralds, her favorite stones. In the art world, she commanded very high prices for her original canvases, which allowed her to afford such delights.

"You look glamorous," Odalie said with a sigh.

Stasia laughed. "You're the one who's glamorous, all lace and smiles," she teased.

"This old rag? I was using it to polish the piano just recently," Odalie said.

Stasia sighed. "Not hardly."

"You should learn to play," Odalie said.

"Your whole family plays, you don't need me to learn, too," she laughed.

"Dad doesn't play."

"One out of five," Stasia reminded her.

"Tanner played as beautifully as Mom did," Odalie replied. "Of course, she dragged him to lessons as soon as he could walk, from what she told us."

"I only heard him play once," Stasia said quietly. "It was

at a party at your house. He was all by himself in the living room, just sitting at the piano, when I walked in there. I guess I was fifteen or so."

"What did he play?"

"'Send in the Clowns.'" She sighed. "The Marks girl had just made fun of my big feet. She was the girl Tanner was dating at the time. He knew it was my favorite. He played the song to cheer me up." She smiled sadly. "I'd forgotten that. His girlfriends always seemed to have it in for me. Funny, because he couldn't see me for dust."

Odalie had always thought it was because they saw what Tanner refused to see, that he was as interested in Stasia as she was in him.

"John won't tell you, because it doesn't help his case. But Tanner still plays. And what he plays most these days is the theme song to that old Yul Brynner, Ingrid Bergman fifties movie, *Anastasia*."

Her heart jumped into her throat. It was so unexpected that she couldn't hide her reaction. Odalie grimaced.

"Sorry," she said.

Stasia drew in a breath. "Maybe it's guilt," she said. "He did have a conscience, and what Julienne said caused me to run away like an idiot. I should have poured water over her instead."

"You were younger then," Odalie said. "Wisdom comes through pain, with age."

"Don't I know it."

Still, it made her heart sing to think that Tanner played a song that was her name. Her mother had been fascinated with the song when Anastasia was born, so she named her baby for the heroine. If Tanner was playing it, maybe he remembered Stasia with something more than regret and blame.

"He probably still holds me responsible for what happened to him," Stasia said. "I ruined his life."

"He ruined yours first," Odalie said. "There was no reason to bring Julienne home with him."

Stasia shrugged. "He was probably afraid I was going to stalk him when he got home and try to keep him on a leash."

"Or something like that," Odalie said. "Maybe he wasn't certain he could resist you," she added, only slightly joking.

"If it had been more than that, he wouldn't have stayed away for five years," Stasia said with quiet confidence. "I'm sure he has all the women he needs. He always did have."

"He hasn't mentioned any to John."

She forced herself not to react. "He wasn't the pipe and slippers sort," Stasia said. "He'd never have settled on the ranch. He likes taking chances too much."

Odalie sighed. "Maybe so. But work seems to have become his life. He's making a living at least. John says he's piling it up in foreign banks."

"When he has enough, maybe he'll go get Julienne and head for Fiji," she laughed.

"I wouldn't bet money on that."

There was a knock on the door.

Stasia went to answer it. "Oh! Ben. I'm sorry, I lost track of time!" she apologized.

"No problem, but the boss said everybody's there almost."

"Let's go," she called to Odalie, who grabbed her purse and followed her out.

Tony always looked gorgeous in black tie, Stasia thought, admiring him discreetly. He was doing his best to ignore Odalie, who was giving him the same courtesy. Two people who had such obvious antagonism for each other might have gone looking for a reason, but not those two. They just went

right along, as if they were playing out some ancient griev-
ance against each other.

Stasia picked up a flute of champagne and turned, and
looked right into the eye of her ex-husband, Tanner Everett.

NINE

Tanner hadn't wanted to come to the cocktail party, but he'd been with a client when Tony phoned to invite them both. It would only take an hour or so, the client assured him, and then they'd be off to the assignment Tanner had been asked to do for an old friend.

It would be a boring evening. Tanner had resigned himself to it, though. He knew Tony, of course, because Tony knew Marcus Carrera. Marcus and Tanner had been friends for years. The client was an acquaintance who was having some issues with a double agent overseas. Tanner had been employed by this client, who also worked for the secret agency, to help him get the goods on the agent, who turned out to be a former partner of Tanner's. Sadly, the former partner, Phillip James, was now head of the secret agency Tanner had done black ops jobs for sporadically. And this client had revealed that he knew about a past incident that was under investigation. With Tanner's help on an overseas op, he might gather enough evidence to put James away.

At issue was the fact that James had done something unspeakable to a civilian village in the Middle East. The man had been high as a kite and fired on what he thought was insurgents while he and Tanner were on a covert mission the year before. Since then, with some under-the-table dealing, and blackmail, James had parlayed himself to head of the agency. He was literally untouchable without evidence Tanner could provide. He'd dared Tanner to ever speak of it, because he had great power in Washington, DC, and he promised him that he could have Tanner jailed for life if he even tried to speak of the incident. That was why Tanner had taken on a civilian job as a bodyguard, to distance himself from the agency. But it wore on Tanner's conscience like acid.

So when the client, an acquaintance of Tony's, had contacted him for help, he'd put on his tux and gone to the art gallery with his client, who was now off in a corner with a very seductive blonde. He'd found the drinks table, picked up a champagne flute and turned around right into his ex-wife.

Neither of them was able to pretend it was nothing to be concerned about. Stasia's face had turned pink. Tanner's one eye became slitted as he stared at her, trying to reconcile the woman he saw with the girl he'd married. She looked elegant and sophisticated and poised. Well, except for the pink cheeks.

She drew in a slow breath and held her champagne flute in both hands so that the faint tremor in her long-fingered hands wouldn't show so much. She hadn't been told that he'd lost an eye. He looked like a sexy pirate but she wasn't wading into that quicksand again.

"Didn't Tony tell you I was coming?" he drawled.

She raised an eyebrow and managed a stiff little smile. "He

might have mentioned it," she replied. She took a sip of the drink to steady her nerves. "Your sister's here."

"I know," he said, his voice deep and slow. "She's one of the reasons I agreed to come."

"She's taking up voice lessons here," Stasia replied.

He nodded, his black hair catching the light and glimmering. "I wish she'd have the guts to audition," he said.

"I'm working on that," she replied.

He turned back to her and studied her closely. "You've changed."

She shrugged, her eyes going to the other guests. "I grew up."

"I guess you did."

She took a breath. "What happened, to your eye?"

"I didn't duck fast enough," he said, his voice light and faintly amused. It wasn't quite the truth, but it would do.

She bit her lower lip. She knew what kind of work he did. It had always worried her. It still did, despite their estrangement. "I'm sorry."

"Fortunes of war," he replied. He cocked his head and studied her face. "How are you?"

She lifted her dark gaze to his. "Improving all the time," she replied. She managed a faint, sarcastic smile. "No more barefoot, bubbly teenage stuff."

He averted his eye. He could still hear Julienne laughing at her, making fun of the way she looked. His lips compressed.

Stasia took another sip of champagne. "Sorry," she said. "That just slipped out."

He took a long breath and sipped his own champagne. "I've had a long time to think about the man I used to be." He turned back and looked down at her with a closed expression. "I didn't like what I saw."

"We grow up and move on, Tanner," she said, her voice quiet and soft. She stared into her drink. "Life is a struggle, no matter what we choose to do. We were both caught up in my father's attempt to keep me safe after he was gone. I'm sorry."

"It wasn't your fault. I'm sorry that I blamed you for it."

She laughed hollowly. "I had a howling crush on you," she confessed, looking up at him. "Dad knew. Everybody knew. He thought it would make me happy." She took another swallow of champagne. "I wish he'd asked me first."

"And I overreacted," he said. He grimaced. "Dad was right, you know," he said. "I was a selfish spoiled brat."

Her eyes searched his hard face, seeing the faint scars, the new lines, the age. "I'm sorry that you were put in the position you were. It wasn't right," she added. "You lost everything because of me, because of what Dad did."

"I'm more guilty than you were," he said surprisingly. "I never should have touched you." He ground his teeth together and averted his gaze. "I didn't even tell you that I was sorry about the child..." He took a big sip of champagne. That memory was the most painful one of all. Over the years, he'd done a lot of thinking about the child. Certainly, it wouldn't fit in with his lifestyle. He'd blamed Stasia even for that. But it haunted him these days. Would it have been a little boy, perhaps, one who'd love the ranch and the country? Or would it have been a little girl, who'd look like Stasia? Odd, how much he missed the ranch these days, when he hadn't been able to get away from it fast enough five years before.

He stared into his drink. "Do you think about the baby, about what it might have been?" he asked in a curt tone.

"I try not to." She took a long breath. "It was a long time ago. We're not the same people we were."

"I guess not."

They stood awkwardly, both lost for words.

Odalie spotted her brother and came to join them. She went on tiptoe and hugged Tanner. "I had no idea that you'd be here!" She hugged harder. "Oh, Tanner, it's so good to see you!"

He held her close. "I missed you, too, sprout. How are the voice lessons going?"

"I only started today," she said, drawing back and smiling from ear to ear. "But I like the new coach. He sang opera in his younger days, at the Met, no less! We're going to get on fine."

"I'm glad. You really do have the talent."

"Thanks!"

"How's the family?"

She made a face. "John's trying to work himself to death. Dad just got into it with the head of the local cattlemen's association and punched him right in the middle of the spring meeting." She shook her head. "He's threatening legal action. Dad called his attorneys."

"Ouch," Tanner said. "Well, that sounds like Dad all right."

"I know. And Mom's just written another song for Desperado," she added, mentioning a hard rock group based in Wyoming. The family knew all the members of the band.

"That means a new video, I presume?" he teased.

"Oh, yes," Odalie said, pale eyes twinkling. "I'm so happy for her. She gave up a singing career to marry Dad. She said she never regretted it. But I don't think I could give up opera for anyone."

"If you ever meet the right man, that will change, sprout," Tanner teased.

"What about you?" Odalie asked. "Any entanglements?"

He laughed coolly. "In my line of work, that would be tricky."

"Why?" Odalie asked, frowning.

"Most women won't line up to be widows," Stasia said with a tight little smile.

"Exactly," Tanner said without looking at her. "I don't get involved anymore."

"You sound like Stasia…" Odalie broke off when she saw her friend's face. "I meant to tell you about the ranch you owned. It was featured on one of the networks; a documentary on the green tech that's gone into it. Dad made a lot of innovations."

"Not interested," Tanner lied easily. "I'm happy for him, but dust and cattle never appealed to me. He should let John manage it."

"Juan Martinez is still doing that, and very well, too. John's too busy managing Big Spur," Odalie replied. "He's never home. There's always a convention or a workshop or a sale…"

Tanner smiled. "That's my baby brother," he said affectionately. He sipped more champagne. "I suppose Dad's still on his high horse."

Odalie bit her lip.

"You don't have to look so guilty," he teased. "I know how Dad is. He doesn't forgive people."

Odalie took a breath. "I wish you two could just talk…!"

"Hold your breath, waiting for that to happen," Tanner replied.

Stasia's expression was pained. "That's my fault, all of it," she said miserably.

"It is not," Odalie said firmly. "Your dad was just trying to look out for you. He knew the ranch was almost bankrupt, and that he was in bad health."

"He ruined both our lives," Stasia said miserably.

"I wouldn't say that," Tanner replied seriously. "I landed a job that suits me very well, and you're not doing badly yourself," he added, his eye dropping to Stasia's flushed face. "If he hadn't altered his will, you'd still be living in Big Spur or

Branntville, trying to get rid of a bankrupt ranch and with no prospect of a life that wasn't one of deprivation."

She avoided meeting his eye. She thought of living on his ranch those weeks when she'd dreamed, prayed, that he'd come home and suddenly fall madly in love with her. Pipe dreams. Smoke.

"I might have been happy," she countered. "It sounds trite, but money really isn't everything."

He was studying her. She was wearing real emeralds and diamonds and a couture gown. "You've landed nicely," he murmured. "Expensive gear." He sipped champagne. "Tony must think a lot of you."

Stasia looked up at him with flashing brown eyes. "I do commissions on the side, and I make a lot of money doing art restoration. Tony doesn't keep me, in case it crossed your mind," she added with cold, icy fury. "I'm nobody's mistress."

Tanner's eyebrows rose.

She finished her champagne and put the glass down firmly. She glared at Tanner. "If you'll excuse me, I see someone I know." She turned on her heel and stalked off.

"Nice going," Odalie told her brother with a wicked smile.

He drew in a rough breath and finished his own champagne. "Does she know what sort of work her friend Tony does?" he asked.

"He does have mob ties," Odalie said reluctantly, "but she's really fond of him. She says he treats her like the daughter he never had. He spoils her."

"Is that all it is?" he asked, deliberately looking around at the crowd and trying to sound as if he didn't care.

"That's all it is," his sister said softly. "She doesn't even date."

He frowned and turned back to her. "What?"

"She said it's unfair to encourage men, and she gets offers, believe me. She said she never wants to get involved with anyone."

"She's only, what, twenty-two…?" he asked, stunned.

"She's twenty-four, Tanner," she replied. She grimaced. "She changed, after she lost the baby."

He swallowed hard and turned away. "So did I," he said gruffly.

Odalie bit her lower lip. "If only we could turn back the clock," she said softly, catching Tanner's big hand in hers, "and bring our family back together again. All of it."

He brought her hand to his lips and smiled down at her. "If only," he agreed. "Maybe someday Dad will speak to me again."

Odalie smiled. "He can't keep it up forever," she said.

"I don't think you know Dad," he said heavily. "Yes, he can."

"Then we'll have to hope for a catalyst. You know, something that will force him to change his mind."

"That would take a miracle," he chuckled.

"They do come around," she pointed out.

He made a face.

She reached up and kissed his chin, which was as far as she could reach.

Across the room, Tony, standing beside Stasia, was glaring toward Odalie and Tanner.

Stasia saw his expression and bit her lip, trying not to smile.

"Does she know what he does for a living?" he asked gruffly.

"Well, yes, of course she does," she replied, surprised.

"He's already lost an eye," he pointed out. "If he keeps going, he'll be missing half his damned body parts!"

She gaped at him. "Don't you know who he is?"

"Sure. He's your ex," he replied. He drew in a breath. "Beyond that, he's a mercenary with a bad attitude," he bit off. "We have mutual acquaintances. He's friends with Marcus Carrera, who said he could tell me stories about the man that would raise your hair!"

Stasia cleared her throat to keep from blurting out what relation he was to Odalie. This was interesting. Unless she missed her guess, Tony was jealous of Tanner. He didn't realize that Tanner was Odalie's brother! How very interesting...

"Do you know his name?" Stasia asked, trying to sound nonchalant.

"Tanner something," he muttered, glaring toward Tanner's back. "I wasn't that interested."

This was very curious. She'd never seen Tony like this. Apparently he had feelings for Odalie, perhaps in the beginning stages, but definitely there. He was jealous of Tanner and unable to hide it.

"You're laughing," Tony accused.

Stasia's eyebrows rose. "Who, me? Why would I be laughing?"

"That's what I'd like to know," he replied curtly.

"I just thought of something funny, that's all."

"Do tell? Share," he prodded.

"Not now," she replied. She grinned. "I'll tell you another time."

He rolled his eyes and turned away.

Odalie was reluctant to leave the party. She and Tanner had a long conversation about his work and his regrets. She hadn't seen him for such a long time, not since their mother's birthday when she and John and Heather sneaked into Dallas to have lunch with him.

"I wish you could talk to Dad," Odalie said sadly.

He grimaced. "Me, too, but that's not realistic." He shook his head. "God help me, he never lets go of a grudge."

"I'm sorry."

"Yeah, sprout. Me, too," he said gently. He bent and kissed her cheek. Around them, the party was winding down and guests were leaving. He noted Stasia coming toward them.

"I think your companion is ready to leave," he pointed out.

She glanced toward Stasia, who was motioning to her. Apparently, Odalie's best friend wasn't anxious to talk to her ex-husband again.

"I guess so," Odalie said. She hugged her brother. "You take care of yourself, okay?"

He smiled. "I'll do that. You do the same. When you get the job at the Met, I'll come and watch you onstage."

"That would be lovely. If I get it."

"You will," he replied gently. "You've worked very hard toward that goal. I'm proud of you," he added.

"Thanks."

"Stay out of trouble."

She looked up at him with twinkling eyes. "You wish. You're the one who needs that advice."

He looked over her head. "Better go. Stasia's getting antsy." Stasia was motioning frantically now, and Tony was glaring at both of them.

Odalie laughed. "I guess so. Call me once in a while, will you? Just so I know you're still alive," she added, and with only pretended humor. She was really worried.

"I will. What's your cell number?"

She gave him the new one. "I don't have yours," she said.

"I use burner phones," he replied easily. "Throwaways. Untraceable."

It brought home what sort of work he did, and the danger of it. "Can't you find a job that won't get you killed?" his sister asked worriedly.

"And what would be the fun of that?" he teased.

She glared at him.

He realized that she wasn't kidding. He hugged her again. "Thanks for caring, sprout."

"I always will. Take care of yourself as well."

"I'll do my best."

"And text me once in a while," she replied. "Please?"

"I will. I promise."

"So long."

"So long."

Tony was grumpy all the way to Stasia's apartment. In fact, all three of Big Ben's passengers were silent on the way back.

"Thanks so much for the ride, Tony," Stasia said as they climbed out of the limo.

"Yes, thanks," Odalie added and made a beeline to the front door to the apartment building, where she had to wait for Stasia with her key.

Tony glared after her. "You'd think she was chased by wolves," he muttered.

She cleared her throat. Tony was really livid. Stasia was amused and had to hide it. "She probably has a reason you don't know about."

"She and your ex were having a good time together," he added coldly.

"She's fond of him," Stasia told him as she tried not to show her amusement. "He's very good-looking."

He looked down at her. "You could try your luck, again," he said.

She grinned. "No, thanks."

"You're howling with laughter, inside, where you think it doesn't show," he accused.

Stasia cleared her throat and forced the humor out of her expression. "No. Really," she emphasized.

He sighed. "Okay. Well, if you need me, you call."

"I will." She went on tiptoe and kissed his cheek. "Thanks."

He shrugged and smiled affectionately. "You're welcome. Sleep well."

"You, too."

She followed Stasia to the door, key in hand. Behind them, Tony stood at the back door of the limo, waiting until they were in the building before he left.

"What were you and Tony talking about?" Odalie asked, trying not to sound interested.

Stasia laughed softly in the elevator. "You," she said.

"Me?" Odalie cleared her throat. "Why?"

"He seems to be very antagonistic about Tanner."

Odalie just swallowed hard. "Does he really?" she asked in a higher-pitched tone. She frowned. "But he knows Tanner is my brother, doesn't he?" she added at once.

Stasia chuckled. "Actually, no, he doesn't."

Odalie was speechless.

The elevator stopped and let them out. They walked in silence to the door of Stasia's apartment, both lost in thought.

Stasia hadn't expected the encounter with Tanner. It had shaken her badly, and she hoped it hadn't been noticeable. All these years, she thought, and she was still under his spell. He looked at her and she melted inside. Pitiful, that helpless adoration for a man who couldn't see her. It seemed like a dream, that brief marriage that had been the culmination of all her dreams. Tanner, in her arms, wanting her with a desperation that hurt to remember. She'd loved him since she was in her teens. She still did.

The pain of it went through her like a knife. Deathless love, unwanted, unyielding, and there was nothing she could do about it. He had regrets, even more than she did. But there was nothing left of their relationship. Only ashes of a raging fire. But the ashes held a tiny flame, and it had come back to consume her. Tanner, she thought, her heart breaking. Tanner!

Odalie saw the torment. Once they were inside the apartment, she turned and hugged Stasia, who suddenly burst into tears.

"I thought you were holding it all in," Odalie said softly, rocking her. "Now, now. Life goes on. At least he isn't involved with anybody."

"He's always involved with somebody," Stasia moaned. "The only difference is that now I don't have to watch it."

"I think he was telling the truth," Odalie countered. "He never could tell a lie. And I don't think he came tonight because he wanted to see me. Well, not totally. He knows you work for Tony. Maybe he figured that you were coming, too." She hesitated. "It's been a long time since he's seen you."

Stasia drew in a long breath and went searching for a tissue to wipe her wet eyes. "He's like a virus that I can't cure," she said, blowing her nose. She went back to Odalie. "Thank you for being my best friend," she said, and forced a smile. "I don't know what I'd do without you."

"You'd drown in tears," Odalie teased. "Now go to bed and sleep. You're worn out, that's all. Everything will be brighter in the morning. You'll see."

"I guess you're right." She studied Odalie's beautiful face. "Tony was beside himself when you kissed Tanner," she added teasingly. "I've never seen him so miffed."

Odalie colored. "He was probably thinking about something. He hates me."

"Not really. He asked me to bring you."

She started. "He did?" she asked, her pretty light eyes wide as saucers.

"He did. And he's never heard you sing," she added. "When he does, he'll go nuts over you."

The flush got worse. "He hates me," she repeated.

Stasia hugged her gently. "He doesn't. You wait and see." She drew back. "His model wasn't there, didn't you notice?"

Odalie's delight was in her eyes. "I didn't."

"I'll bet she won't rebound, either. You should buy some really pretty clothes," she told Odalie. "I have a hunch that you and I are going to be going to a lot of parties pretty soon."

Odalie didn't reply. But she beamed.

"When are you coming home?" John asked Stasia. He'd called to ask how Odalie was doing, but he phoned after Odalie had gone to her voice class.

"I don't know, John," Stasia told him. "I need to be here a while longer to give Odalie moral support. She's very intense about this training, and she has an appointment, finally, to audition for the Met."

"Finally!" he exclaimed happily. "How did you talk her into it?"

"How do you know I did?" she teased.

"Because she'd never have done it without a lot of encouragement."

"I sort of prodded her," she confessed.

"Well, we're all grateful. She's got the talent."

"I know. She's sacrificed a lot for it, over the years."

There was a long pause. "She said Tanner was at some cocktail party you two attended," John added.

Stasia's heart jumped, just hearing his name. She took a breath. "Yes."

"Did he have anybody with him?" he asked, trying to sound nonchalant.

"No."

John hesitated. "I guess it was disturbing. You haven't seen him for years."

"Not since just before the divorce," Stasia agreed. "And it wasn't disturbing," she added curtly, lying through her teeth. "Not at all."

John heard the pained note in her voice and grimaced. He sighed. "I guess you aren't coming home anytime soon?" he added. "Maybe in November, for the cattlemen's ball?" he added, naming a yearly function in Branntville.

"It depends on my workload," she replied. "I'm doing private commissions in addition to my restoration. It takes up a lot of my time."

"Even dating time?" he probed.

"John, you know I don't date anyone," she returned quietly. "I've been married. I don't want to repeat that mistake, ever."

"You might fall in love," John persisted.

"Pigs might fly," she returned curtly. "And that's all I want to say about it."

There was another pause. "Sorry," he said.

"You're a lovely man," she replied after a few seconds. "But I don't feel that way about you, John, and it's never going to change. You have to accept it."

She could almost feel the tension between them.

"It's still Tanner, isn't it?" he asked.

She didn't reply.

"Okay, I'll quit. I'm working on a plan to expand our bloodline," he said. "We're adding several new bulls. I've been searching them out on the internet. Come fall, I'll be doing a lot of traveling to add new bulls to our livestock!"

She laughed, and the tension abated. "That sounds like fun."

"I love it. Nothing prettier than a purebred bull!"

"I gathered. Well, I have to get to bed. We start to work early at the gallery."

"How's your boss?"

"Oh, he's not really my boss. Sort of an overprotective would-be dad," she replied. "Tony didn't ever have kids with his late wife, so I'm sort of adopted." She laughed. "He's not as bad as his publicity."

"He's still a gang boss," he pointed out. "That's a job you don't quit, if you want to stay alive."

"And you've only met him once," she replied. "That doesn't mean you know him."

"Fair enough," he sighed. "I guess if he's looking after you, he has to be okay."

"He is. Nobody hassles me. He's very protective. So is Big Ben."

"Big Ben?"

"His bodyguard and chauffeur. If I ever have to go out at night, Big Ben comes in the limo and drives me."

He smiled to himself. "I like that."

"So do I. I feel like a treasured child."

"You are. Treasured, I mean, by all of us."

"Thanks, John. That's sweet."

"I am sweet," he argued. "I even go out of my way to protect rattlesnakes!"

"Excuse me?"

"See, there was this rattler that we found near the house. Big fella, lots of rattles, obviously very old. The men wanted to kill it, but I stopped them. We got the snake into a bag and I drove him to a deserted field and liberated him!"

"He might bite somebody!"

"Naw. He's a sweet snake. Didn't even strike at us when we put him in the bag."

"I have never heard of anybody in Texas who protected a rattler!"

"Now, you have," he said smugly.

"Can I ask why?" she asked suspiciously.

"I don't know," he confessed. "It just felt wrong to kill him. I mean, he wasn't bothering anybody, and he wasn't aggressive at all. When the guys called me out to the field where they found him, they were gathered around him in a circle and the snake was just lying there, looking at them."

"Odd."

"I know. Never saw anything like it, and I've killed plenty of snakes."

"Maybe it was a girl snake and it likes men," she said, tongue-in-cheek.

"There's a thought." He smiled.

"But you let it go, what if it bites somebody?"

"I guess I'd feel pretty bad," he admitted. "But I don't like killing anything. That's why we're running purebred beef."

She frowned. "I thought your dad had a cow-calf operation," she said.

"He used to," he said. "But when I got out of college, I persuaded him to change it over to breeding bulls. There's a lot more money in it. And I taught him about feeding less corn and more grass, and using the methane in cow manure for power. We've gone green." He chuckled. "Didn't win us many points with the vegans, but at least we don't run slaughter cattle anymore."

"You're a magician," she laughed. "I can't imagine your father doing that!"

"Neither could Mom," he said. "But he's happy to have me

taking over some of the responsibility for the ranch properties." He paused. "I'm looking after your father's place as well."

She grimaced. "Dad also had a cow-calf operation," she began.

"Not anymore. We're running purebred Santa Gertrudis on our place, purebred Angus on your dad's place and purebred Santa Gertrudis also on the place that was Tanner's."

"Oh, that's very nice!" she exclaimed.

He sighed. "I thought you might like it," he said softly. "I'm not keen on slaughtering anything."

"Not even rattlesnakes," she said amusedly.

"He was a very old snake, by the look of him. I put him out in a field full of rabbits."

She paused. "Any particular reason why?"

"He had no teeth."

She sat up on the sofa where she'd been sprawling. "He what?"

"Had no teeth. No fangs."

"How? Did you pull them?"

"No. That had apparently been done long ago, God knows by whom. I figured if he could get a rabbit—they swallow their food whole, you know—he could at least stay alive."

She sighed. "I see." She shook her head. "John, you are one of the nicest people I know."

"Might you consider coming home in time for the cattlemen's ball in November, then?"

"If I can," she said, emphasizing what she'd already told him.

"That's great," he said, and sounded as if he'd won a prize.

She laughed at his enthusiasm. "John," she added softly, "I won't change my mind. I hope you know that."

"Hey, a starving man is grateful for any crumbs," he pointed

out. "And it isn't as if I'm bounding from one woman to another."

"I guess not."

"So, I'll see you in November," he replied.

"Bye, John."

"Bye."

He hung up the phone and sat where he'd been, on the
arm of his armchair in the living room, just staring at his cell
phone.

His mother came up behind him and hugged him.

"You never give up, do you, sweetheart?" she teased in her
softly accented Texas voice.

"I never do," he admitted. He stood up and hugged her
back. "I keep hoping that she'll change her mind."

"I had a friend like that, in the dark days when your
father ran me off because he'd been told that we were related by blood," she reminded him. "He was a good man,
and kind, and I was fond of him. But it was always your
father, John," she added, her voice soft with love. "Even if
he'd never touched me for the rest of my life, it would have
been Cole. I loved him. I still do, breathlessly!"

"And he loves you," Cole teased, pulling her out of John's
arms and into his. He bent and kissed her hungrily.

They smiled at each other, wrapped in that all-consuming
love that had nurtured both of them for three decades.

"Love never wears out, does it?" John asked gently, smiling at his parents.

"Never," Cole agreed with a smile. "How about those
breeding bulls you've been looking at?" he added.

"I'm going to fly up to Montana tomorrow to have a look
at the bloodline and make a decision," John assured him.
"You want to come?"

Cole shook his head. "Not this time. I've got too much

work to do here. And don't you stay gone long," he added, shaking a finger at his son. "You have work to do here also."

John chuckled. "Sure. I think I'll go pack a bag and make a couple of appointments with Montana ranchers."

"Good idea."

Heather leaned against Cole after John left and laid her cheek against his broad chest. "It's still Stasia, you know," she whispered.

He kissed her forehead and held her close. "I know. It's a tragedy in the making. She still loves Tanner."

"I think it's mutual. She ran into him at a cocktail party. Odalie said it was like watching a fire kindle."

"On her part, I'm sure." He looked down at her. "What about on his part, though?" His face hardened. "He cost us our hopes for a grandchild." He hugged her. "I was looking forward to it so much," he confessed. "And I could never get over what he did to her. Bringing his damned mistress home with him so that she could ridicule Stasia and make her feel stupid, shaming Stasia in tabloids…!"

Heather reached up and put the tips of her fingers over his firm mouth. "My darling," she said gently, "that was five years ago. Are you really going to forbid our eldest child to ever come home again?"

"Yes, I am," Cole said bluntly, and his eyes were blazing. "If he ever gets his life together and straightens out his priorities… But that would be a long shot. He's been selfish for too long."

"My fault," Heather confessed. "I spoiled him."

His lips compressed.

She sighed. "He might have changed," she added. "If you won't speak to him, how would you know if he's different?"

"He's a hired assassin," he said curtly.

"Cole!"

"Well, it's the next best thing," he muttered. "He sells his services to the highest bidder. There's no honor in it!"

Heather knew better, but she loved her husband. So she just smiled and pressed closer into his arms. Someday, she didn't know how exactly, but someday she'd find a way to make peace with Tanner, for all of them. She had to!

TEN

Stasia finished the painting of the little girl and carried it to the address of the art museum patron who'd commissioned it.

The whole family, including the subject, gathered around to see it for the first time.

The little girl in the painting, Annika, laughed with joy and danced around, running to hug Stasia, who picked her up and kissed her chubby little cheek.

"It's magnificent," Annika's father exclaimed.

Her mother had tears in her eyes. "It is," she agreed.

Stasia just smiled. She'd never done anything that pleased her more, and the delight her clients showed just made it even more joyful.

"Thank you for my picture," Annika said. "It looks just like me!"

The child smelled like flowers, and beneath that was the smell of a small child, which was utterly delightful. Stasia fought tears. If she hadn't lost her child, she might have had a little girl like Annika. The thought had tormented her for years.

Annika wiggled finally and Stasia put her down, wiping her eyes unobtrusively. "You're very welcome," she said softly, smiling at the little girl.

Annika smiled from ear to ear while her parents enthused once more over the painting.

That night Odalie called her.

"How'd the meeting with your clients go?" she asked.

"It went great. They have friends with a little boy about Annika's age. The friends are going to see Annika's painting and, if they like it, they may want me to paint the little boy."

"Good for you! I'm so proud of you, Stasia," Odalie added gently. "You've come such a long way since you left Texas."

"But so have you," her friend replied with affection. "Voice lessons and auditioning for the Met. That's a very big deal."

Odalie laughed. "I guess it is. I was so homesick at first. I miss my family. Having you here helps a lot. You're family, too."

"That's nice of you to say so."

"You'd still really be family except for my idiot brother," she said with resignation.

"We all wound up in different circumstances." She paused. "I just wish Tanner had found some less dangerous profession to get into. He's already lost an eye."

"He lost everything," Odalie agreed. "But we all have a purpose, you know. Sometimes it takes an upheaval to point us toward it."

"That's comforting."

Odalie sighed. "I keep wondering what my purpose is. I

love singing, and I'd love to sing at the Met. But I have no life except for music."

"That's a purpose," Stasia pointed out.

There was a pause. "So it is. I'll stop complaining now and go to bed," she laughed.

"Good idea. I've had a long day, too. There's another cocktail party next week. Tony asked if I'd bring you," she added when Odalie hesitated.

"He did?"

Stasia noted the change in Odalie's voice. She couldn't quite hide her delight, despite her so-called antagonism for Stasia's benefactor.

"He did," Stasia replied warmly. "A good excuse to go hunting for another pretty dress, yes?"

"I'll go Saturday," came the reply. "There's a new boutique near where you live. Want to go with me? You might find something you like, too."

"I'd love it," she replied.

"I'll pick you up about nine."

Odalie said. "That way, we can both sleep late."

"Excellent thinking. I'll be ready."

Tanner was back in the apartment he was renting from a friend who went to Nice for a few months.

In the living room, there was a grand piano. Tanner's friend also played, and very well.

He sat down on the bench and positioned his long fingers on the keyboard. He began to play. It was the theme song from *Anastasia*. He was trying to reconcile his memory of Stasia with the woman she'd become. It was fascinating. She was poised, sophisticated. She was lovely.

He'd never been able to forget her. Their brief marriage was like a spring flowering in a heart covered with winter snow. He could still see her running toward him in a yellow sundress, barefoot, with flowers in her hair. She'd been so beautiful, radiant with her pregnancy, which he hadn't even known about.

Then he recalled Julienne's taunting words, the ridicule that had stripped the light from Stasia's face and turned it inside out to darkness. She'd run away. He'd had no idea that she'd fallen at the pool because of Julienne, that she'd lost the baby he hadn't known about. It wasn't until he and Julienne had returned that Cole and John had told him.

His father was terrible in a temper. All the children had minded when they were young, because Cole's anger was always evident in narrowed light eyes whose gaze was much worse than a whipping. Neither Cole nor Heather had ever used physical means to subdue rebellion. There had been time-outs and withholding of privileges. For the boys, not being able to play video games had been the worst punishment. For Odalie, it was no shopping. It had worked quite well.

Tanner often wondered what kind of father he'd be. He hadn't been around children often, but in his line of work he found himself in small foreign villages from time to time. His reaction to the children had surprised comrades, because he was fascinated with them. They seemed drawn to him. He enjoyed teaching them things about the world around them.

His own child had been lost through his selfishness. If only he hadn't brought Julienne home with him! If he'd gone home alone, how different things might have been.

But all of it was his own fault. Stasia's father hadn't helped, of course, with the will that had required them to marry to save the ranch. It hadn't been such a bad idea. Stasia was pretty and sweet and anyone could see that she'd loved Tanner breathlessly. Everybody knew. He knew. He hadn't encouraged her because he knew he wasn't going to be able to settle down and run a cattle ranch. Children had been impossible, or so he thought.

Now, with the loss of his child, he wished he could go back and change things. Stasia was beautiful, with maturity brightening her features. She said she wasn't involved with Tony, but that wasn't the impression he got at the party. Tony had been livid when Odalie kissed her brother.

His hands lifted from the keyboard. Odalie. He scowled. It began to make sense. It wasn't Stasia that Tony was possessive about; it was his sister. It was Odalie. And judging from the antagonism that positively radiated from Tony when he looked at Odalie, there was some powerful emotion there.

Odalie was old enough to know her own mind. Tony was much older, of course, but he'd seen marriages with even a twenty-year difference that worked extremely well. It wasn't the age, it was the compatibility. Common interests, nonaggressive personalities, mutual ideas on religion and politics, those made a successful marriage.

Not that he wanted to get married again. His heart jumped as he thought of Stasia. She didn't date anyone. Neither did he. His reason was guilt. What was hers? Could she still care, even a little? She was belligerent when he'd insinuated that Tony kept her. Odalie said that she wasn't involved with Tony. Now he understood. The big man had feelings for Tanner's sister!

That wouldn't go over well with Cole, he knew. His father was as straight as an arrow. He never broke the law, not in any way, and Tony was a notorious gang boss, even if he was mostly legit these days. Cole would be furious if Odalie set her sights on Tony.

Well, that was a worry he didn't have at the moment. He had other projects underway.

His cell phone rang. He looked at the screen. It was a

burner phone and only two people had the number. He pushed the button.

"Are you packed?" a deep voice asked.

It was his client. "Certainly."

"Okay. I need you to be on a plane to Manaus tonight. You'll be met on the concourse tomorrow."

"I'll be there. Where are we going?"

"You'll get all that information when you get here. Don't worry about gear. Everything will be provided. Your fee has been wired electronically to the account number you gave us."

"Do I need fake ID?" he asked.

There was the faintest pause. "No. Come as yourself. No disguises either."

"Very well. I'll see you then."

He hung up and went to pack. He traveled light, only a khaki bag with multiple compartments. He put in the usual clothing, but at the last minute he opened another bag and took out a photograph of his family. It was the only physical one he had, the rest being digital and on his regular cell phone. He had throwaway phones for missions, however, and he couldn't risk taking that with him. It stayed in the apartment he'd rented.

He looked around, checking to make sure he'd packed what he needed. He took the clip out of his .45 automatic and skinned the bullet out of the chamber. He packed both, in different compartments. If he'd been taking a regular flight, the handgun would have presented problems. But there would be a private plane waiting for him, because his employer worked for a top-secret federal agency. He smiled to himself as he checked the ankle gun he always carried, and the Ka-Bar knife in its shield at his waist. He was an expert in tae kwon do; he had a black belt in the martial art, and he was also practiced in judo and a few forms that were amalgamations of other martial arts. In other words, he could handle himself in dangerous situations.

He took the bag into the living room and set it on the couch. He was wearing khaki as well, slacks with pockets and a long jacket with even more pockets over a simple beige designer shirt.

He took out the cell phone and punched in a number and waited.

"Hello?" came a hesitant deep voice.

"It's me, John," he said to his brother.

"It's about time!" John exclaimed. "I didn't recognize the number. I usually don't answer the phone when that happens, but I had a feeling...how are you?"

"Off to a mission," he said. "I just wanted to say goodbye."

John sighed. "You've never done this before."

Tanner shrugged. "I had a feeling," he repeated quietly. "I just...well, you know."

"I do know. That's what makes it hard. I've only got one brother," he added with forced humor. "And even though you are a huge pain in the butt, I like having you around somewhere on the planet. So don't leave the world. Okay?"

"I'll do my best."

"Can you at least tell me where you're going?"

"The Amazon."

John grimaced. "That's a dangerous place."

"Every place is dangerous these days," Tanner replied. "You can get taken out in a riot, or some fool can shoot you when you're walking down the street or run you over with a car. We live in horrific times."

"Got a point," John conceded. "Is it a sanctioned job, at least?"

Tanner chuckled. "Yes. It's sanctioned."

John let out an audible breath. "Well, that's not much comfort, but it's better than the alternative."

"Not by much," his brother replied. "Look, I'm not expecting anything dramatic, but just in case...tell the family I love them."

"You're spooking me."

"Don't mean to," Tanner sighed. "But those are words we don't say enough. You never know which mission may be your last."

"I guess you're right." He paused. "Don't get killed."

"I'll do my best. I promise." He paused. "Dad still got it in for me?"

There was a hesitation.

"Never mind searching for the right words," Tanner said. "I know Dad as well as you do. He doesn't get over things."

"He doesn't. It's his only real fault except for that temper."

"I remember that temper so well," Tanner said. "He gets real quiet and then he just stares at you, with those eyes. It gives me chills even in memory."

"I know. I'd rather he hit me," John laughed.

"Mom doesn't see the temper. He's never mad at her, even when she does things like running the car through the back wall of the barn."

"That's a sweet memory," John said, grinning to himself. "She got all upset when Odalie was in trouble at school. Dad got into it and Odalie started crying. When Mom tried to comfort her, Dad gave her that look. She grabbed the car keys and said she was going for a drive, but what she did was take out part of the barn. Dad spent the rest of the day apologizing for upsetting her, and he bought her one of those big portable pianos she'd been hoping for, as a consolation gift. That's the only thing he's really afraid of—Mom crying. It's like her secret weapon."

"Always works, too!"

"Yes, it does. Can I ask what you're going to South America for?" John said.

"Sure. Go ahead."

"Okay. Why are you going to South America?"

"I said you could ask the question. Not that I'd answer it," Tanner chuckled.

John laughed, too. "I give up." He paused. "It wouldn't have anything to do with that agent who was recently promoted to head of the agency—the agent you used to work for? The one who was itching to get you into trouble?"

There was a long pause.

"All right, I know when I'm beaten. But you be careful. Mom will start bawling if anything happens to you, and Dad will bankrupt us buying her consolation gifts!"

"I get the picture. I'll do my best." He sighed. "Thanks for sticking with me, through wind and storm."

"You're my big brother. I love you," John said simply.

Tanner glanced around the room. "Same. You know Odalie's got feelings for that mob boss, don't you?"

"It's pretty obvious when she talks about him. She cusses. First time I've ever heard her do that. She avoids most men."

"Not that one. Stasia says he's okay, though. She likes him. He's sort of a father figure to her, and she's a daughter figure to him," John replied.

"I guess she knows what sort of person he is," came the quiet reply.

"She'd have to. She's known him for five years. Time enough to get the measure of the guy. You be careful in foreign parts."

"I will. Take care of our parents and Odalie."

"I will." He noticed that Tanner deliberately didn't add Stasia to the people he wanted his brother to watch over. "You left out Stasia."

The tone of the conversation changed abruptly. "Don't try to back her into a corner; not ever. She won't change her mind."

"You sound very sure of yourself," John muttered. "But are you? You don't want her. Why should it matter to you if I try my luck?"

There was an ominous silence. "I'll talk to you when I get back," he said tersely.

"Sure." Another pause. "Listen, Tanner," John began in an apologetic tone.

"So long."

Tanner hung up abruptly. John turned off his own phone and grimaced. Tanner was leaving the country for some dangerous job and John had upset him over Stasia. He felt bad about it. Of course Tanner was right, Stasia was never going to love John. He knew it. He was sorry he'd upset his brother, especially at a time like this.

He went back to work, nursing his regrets.

That night, Heather asked him if he'd heard from Tanner.

He didn't want to tell her, but he couldn't manage to lie. None of the Everett kids had ever done that. They were almost legendary for their inability to tell anything but the truth.

"Yes, I did," John said heavily.

"And something's wrong," Heather commented, grimacing. "I can always tell. I know when Tanner's upset or in trouble, God knows how."

"He's got a job in South America, somewhere in the Amazon," Tanner told her.

She closed her eyes. "The most dangerous place on earth!

Why there? Why not someplace safer?" she moaned. She looked at John. "He's already lost an eye!"

"I know." He sat down across from her in an armchair and leaned forward. "He says he can't live without a little risk. It's a way of life to him."

"And he's never coming home to live," Heather replied, the light going out of her pale eyes. "I know that, too. I just want him to be alive, wherever he is!"

"He phoned me to say goodbye. He wanted me to tell all of you that he loves you."

Tears stung her eyes. "Oh, dear."

"He's never done that before." John sighed. "I'd tell Dad, but we'd have a big blowup, and we don't need that."

"I'll tell your father," Heather promised.

"He'll be mad."

"He's been mad since Stasia lost our grandchild," she replied. "It really hurt him. He had all these dreams." She looked up. "We can't really count on Odalie to give them to us, because she's bent on a career in music, like I was before I married your father. And Tanner…well, that ship's sailed. And you, my darling, won't give up your own dreams."

"I can't."

She smiled. "I do understand. But Stasia is the sort of woman who loves once and forever."

He shrugged. He managed a faint smile. "Hope springs eternal?"

"It springs uselessly in this case." She studied him. "And Tanner hasn't mentioned her to you?"

He bit his lower lip and looked guilty.

Heather felt her stomach fall. "Come on. What happened?"

"He wanted me to take care of the others. I noticed that he didn't mention Stasia so I asked him about it. I said that he didn't want her, why did it matter to him if I tried my luck."

He looked down at his linked fingers. "He was angry. So was I. I started to apologize, but he hung up." He glanced at her set expression. "I hate having him mad at me, especially when he's going off on some dangerous mission. He wouldn't tell me what it was, just where it was. I'm sorry," he added when he saw the way Heather looked. "I shouldn't have said anything to him about Stasia. It's just...well, he doesn't even want her!"

"John," she said quietly, "if you'd let yourself listen to what you just said, it rather proves the opposite. Tanner still loves her."

John bit his lip. "I guess he does. But she doesn't know. They argued at the party, Odalie said. He thought Tony Garza was keeping Stasia and he was furious. So was she. She told him she paid her own way and stormed off, so that would have made things even harder for him." He grimaced. "I'm sorry. I'm so damned sorry! They can't help what they feel, but neither can I. It's like a fever that just consumes me!"

"That's how I feel for your father," Heather told him. "After three decades and more, the feeling hasn't lessened one bit. But it's a returned love, in my case. Yours is...different."

He shrugged. "I've done my best to fight it."

"I know you have, my darling. I'm so sorry."

"One day," he began with an earnest expression.

"One day, Tanner will find a way back to her," Heather said. "And she'll go to him. They love each other. They just don't know it yet. If you get in the way of that, there will be three miserable people. If you do stay out of the way, there will be just one—you. Sometimes we don't get the things in life that we want the most," she added softly. "In which case, we have to learn to accept the inevitable."

"I'll go insane," John said through his teeth.

She got to her feet. So did he. She hugged him. "John, the best cure is hard work. And believe me, I know."

He sighed and hugged her back. "I know you do. I'll try."

"Meanwhile, you might look at the eligible women around town."

He drew back. "There's Miss Raines who's fifty-five and smokes, there's Tina Dean, who thinks her dog is a reincarnated former boyfriend and she dresses him in the boyfriend's T-shirts and sits him at the dinner table…"

She burst out laughing. After a minute, so did he.

"Okay, it's a small town and there's not much of a selection. You should go to cattlemen's conventions and workshops. You might find a woman who loves cattle and animals and likes to plant things."

He smiled, indulging her. "And why would such a woman appeal to me?"

"Because women who love animals and like to plant things are the best people on earth. They're generally gentle and kind and nurturing. That's the sort of wife you need, to live on a ranch."

He made a face. "With my luck, I'll find a militant vegan who'll want to clothe all the cattle and teach them how to read."

She laughed. "Well, that's a possibility. But would such a person go to a cattlemen's convention?"

"Sure. Every time, we have a small crowd of protesters who say we're oppressing cattle and we should free them."

"Then you should tell them that we don't run slaughter cattle."

"You can't appease some people, Mom. Especially militant people who only see one side of any argument. No compromise."

"That's sad. Lack of tolerance is our biggest issue these days, and yes intolerance is rampant, despite all the admonitions to love each other and not offend anybody. We've killed free speech."

"Life goes on." He kissed her forehead. "I'll go out and help the men oppress the young bulls into the next pasture."

"Don't get trampled."

"Mom! I'm so sweet that the cattle run over each other trying to get to me so I'll pet them. Even Dad's prize bull!"

"Your father's prize bull will let total strangers pet him, and he follows your dad around like a dog. If anyone even breathed a word about eating him, your father would be on them like a duck on a june bug!"

John agreed. "And isn't that the truth? I'll see you later."

Heather stared after him with a worried frown. Tanner was going to be in danger. If only Cole would give a little, just a little, on the subject of his eldest child. It had wounded him that Tanner didn't try to change his mind, didn't argue about losing his livelihood. Cole could be inflexible, but he usually got very upset when any of his kids was mad at him. He'd break down if they apologized.

Tanner would never apologize, not for anything. No punishment touched him. Heather felt guilty about that, because she'd spoiled him when he was little. If she'd been less protective, things might have been different.

She wondered about Cole's blatant antagonism toward their eldest. It wasn't like him to be so unfeeling. Of course, it was the loss of his first grandchild that had triggered it. He'd had so many plans, looked forward to the child with great eagerness.

Perhaps they should have had another child, she thought. It was like empty nest syndrome that women had when a child left home. Cole was going through it as first one child, then two, found professions and went away. John was the only child left at home. Poor Cole. She wished she could change him, just a little. Later, she'd speak to him. It might help.

Tanner arrived at the airport in Manaus with his single bag and walked onto the concourse.

A man in plain clothes gave him the eye. The man was dressed in casual clothing and he looked insignificant. Probably an agent, Tanner told himself, because that was the sort of man usually chosen for the profession. Far from the flamboyant men portrayed in motion pictures, the real agents looked like any other moderate human, people you didn't really notice at all.

He didn't meet the man's eyes; he kept walking. If the man was an agent, and wanted to talk to him, they'd eventually speak. Meanwhile, it was safer not to react, in case he was wrong.

He moved through the crowded airport with his gaze straight ahead, his walk telling people he knew exactly where he was going. Actually, he had no idea. His client had promised that he'd be met at the airport, and the man usually kept his word.

As he walked, he considered what he really knew about his ex-boss. The man was highly political. He blew whichever way his higher-ups did. He was like a chameleon; he could change his personality and his appearance at the drop of a hat. Only once had Tanner had to call on him for help during an overseas mission. His boss had let him down badly at the time. Funny, remembering that now. Tanner had been blamed for another agent's incompetence, and it was only intervention from a senator he knew that had saved him. His boss had thrown him under the bus immediately with no questions asked. Now, that same ex-boss was suspected of being a double agent, and Tanner was here to get the goods on him. Drugs were involved, he knew. There was a militia in this part of the world that did nothing except protect the coca that was so lucrative in trade. Phillip James was up to his neck in it and Tanner knew, but black ops was entwined with that sort of black market trade for funding. People knew. Nobody blew the whistle. He frowned. If his boss was a double agent, why wouldn't he be hunted by a more visible agency? It didn't make sense. But, then, Tanner was paid to do a job, not reason why he was doing it.

He grimaced. Perhaps he should have refused the assignment. But that wasn't Tanner's style. Besides, he still had scores of his own to settle with James about the massacre in the Middle East. Tanner was the only person who had concrete evidence of the attack, including covert video from a cell phone that a now-deceased colleague had shot at the scene. It was in a bank, in a safe-deposit box, and nobody knew that Tanner had it. The problem was that James promised to make sure evidence connected Tanner with the atrocity. A high-level senator was on his list of supporters, and the man was bound to James by unknown bonds.

Someday, though, he was going to have to try to do something. As James acquired more and more political power, the chances were good that he'd escape punishment forever, and that would be unforgiveable. Some of the civilian victims had been little kids. Tanner groaned inwardly, remembering the horrible aftermath.

As he walked, he kept the ordinary man in sight with peripheral vision. Yes, the man was definitely following him.

He went through the door outside into the searing heat and deliberately stopped at an empty bench.

As he sat down, the other man joined him.

"Hello," the man said with a smile. "Mind if I share the

bench for a minute? I'm so out of breath I can't go much farther. Hot as hell, isn't it? And summer almost over."

Tanner's heart jumped. He knew the phrase. It was one
they used to verify the identity of a fellow agent.

The response was, "Yes, and winter is coming." The answering phrase was a tip of the hat to the series *Game of
Thrones*, which one of the higher-ups in his agency had been
obsessed with. There were several code words that referenced
the series.

He looked straight at the man. "Yes," he said, "and winter is coming."

The nondescript man chuckled. "That's a favorite series on
the beltway. I hear even Senator Johns is recording *House of the
Dragon*, so that he can binge-watch it whenever he has time."

"I like it, too," Tanner said.

"Oh, yeah, I like watching the dragons intimidate people.
I'd love a dragon," he added.

Tanner shook his head. "Not me. Imagine the cost of feeding him meat!"

The other man chuckled. "Well, now I see your point."

Several people walked by while Tanner stared at his phone
and his companion stared into space.

When they were clear once more, the nondescript man
spoke again. "I have a car waiting. Whenever you're ready.
Got any luggage?"

Tanner indicated the small bag at his feet. "I travel light,"
he explained. "Only carry-on bags."

The man nodded. "Sensible." He leaned closer. "Nothing
that could identify you…?"

"Are you nuts?" Tanner asked politely. "Listen, this isn't
my first ball game, if you get the message."

"Sure. Sorry. I was told to make sure." He got to his feet.

"Sure, I can give you a lift," he said deliberately as several people passed around them. "No problem."

"I appreciate it," Tanner replied with a smile, playing along.

"Okay, then, my ride's right over there."

His ride was a Jaguar convertible, which surprised Tanner. "You must have a nice budget," he remarked when they were inside, with the other man at the wheel, headed out of airport parking.

His companion cleared his throat and thought for a minute. "Well, we confiscate a lot of cars," he said finally. "This one belongs to my boss in Manaus. He loaned it to me with several warnings about hunting me down if I put a scratch on it."

Tanner laughed out loud. "I remember your boss," he said. He glanced at the driver. "And I always believed he meant it."

"Oh, yes," the other man agreed. "He followed a man across north Africa with two liters of water and a sturdy rope."

"I don't imagine that the object of his hunt fared well," he added.

"No. He didn't. But he was a turncoat, and you know the agency's position on people who spy for the enemy."

"I do indeed. That's why I'm here," he added curtly.

The other man glanced at him. "This is going to be tricky. There's a big meeting going down with some of the regional drug traffickers, and your ex-boss is coming in person to deal. You'll go in with a small group of agents and be transported to within a mile of the location. I hope your shots are current."

"They are," Tanner said. "What sort of evidence am I collecting?"

"The usual, and get film," he added grimly. "We want to bring him up before a Senate investigating committee. We have to have the goods."

"I'll make sure that we do." He scowled. "Why a group of agents?"

The man hesitated for a second. "The traffickers are heavily armed. You need backup."

"I see."

"Don't worry, they're good kids," he added.

Tanner frowned. "Kids?"

"Figure of speech!" the other man said quickly. "They'll have all the supplies you need, including weapons. You won't have to bring anything with you."

"Just my bag," Tanner said.

The man scowled. "No ID in that...?"

"Are you nuts?" he asked, exasperated. "I've been doing this since I was in my late teens."

"Sorry. I'm sorry. Just being cautious. This is one big mean fish we're trying to land. I really don't want to give him free bites at me," he added almost under his breath.

"I get it. No, there's no ID," he said. "And we'll pack out our trash. The authorities will never know we've been in the country."

"That's the idea."

"What about extraction?" Tanner asked.

"That's been arranged. The man leading your backup group will tell you all about it. No worries."

Tanner felt oddly uneasy. But then, he usually did on these black ops jobs. So he just nodded. "Where are we going?"

"To meet your colleagues," came the bland reply. "You're going to get details of your mission, in a place where we're not likely to be observed."

Warning bells were going off in Tanner's head. Something was wrong. He couldn't put his finger on it. This man didn't fit the profile of a gofer, and Tanner's ex-colleague, his client who'd paid for this op, was a fanatic when it came to protocol. This was far and away not the way the man did business. It was slipshod.

Tanner glanced at his companion, but the man seemed laid-back and unconcerned. Perhaps he was just tired, Tanner told himself. He was reading things into the contact that could be interpreted two ways. Just the same, he was aware of the pistol in his ankle holster. The other was in his bag but neither assembled nor loaded. In a pinch, he was a master of martial arts. It would be all right, he considered. Of course it would.

Two weeks later, a man arrived at Big Spur in a nonde-script automobile. Cole was out on the ranch, helping round up the bulls. Heather was in the kitchen cooking, and John was on the phone getting some information for Cole on new legislation. It was a sunny, lazy day.

John saw the newcomer as he exited the car and walked up onto the porch carrying a paper bag. He looked around him warily, as he paused and knocked on the front door.

John opened it. "Can I help you?" he asked, his light eyes as piercing and curious as his father's ever were.

"Are you one of the Everett family?" the man asked in a slow Texas drawl.

"Yes," John replied. The man looked jumpy, nervous. It disturbed John.

Before the man could speak, Heather, who'd heard the car drive up, came out of the kitchen and onto the porch wearing a white apron over her slacks and blouse.

John felt a chill run over him as he recognized what the man was pulling out of the paper bag.

Heather beat him to it. "That's Tanner's bag," she said unsteadily. "I gave it to him for Christmas two years ago, when you and I snuck into Dallas to see him." Her pale blue eyes went frantically to the stranger. "Why do you have it?" she asked abruptly.

John saw more than she did. He took the bag from the

man. There was dried blood on it. A lot of dried blood. He looked inside. There was a mangled photograph in the bag, wedged into a corner. It was a family snapshot of Cole and Heather, Odalie and Stasia. John had taken the photo last year and gave it to Tanner at a secret meeting.

He looked at the man with faint horror. "Why is there so much blood on the bag?" he asked in a husky tone.

Heather's face paled as the man looked from one to the other. He grimaced. "Well, that's the thing. We don't know. He's gone missing and the only clue we have is that bag. Tanner's ex-boss recognized the photo inside, so he knew it belonged to Tanner." He sighed. "I'm sorry to tell you that we think…we believe," he faltered, "that he was…killed."

ELEVEN

John caught his mother before she fell and put her gently onto one of the chaises on the porch. "Need a wet cloth?" he asked.

She shook her head. Her eyes went back to their visitor. "They're sure?" she asked, her voice breaking. "That my son was…was killed?"

The visitor drew in a long breath. "Yes. We're pretty certain. I'm so very sorry. I knew your son. We worked together on several classified actions. I'm not even sure who recruited him for this mission. It's all very hush-hush."

John was staring at the bag with eyes that didn't want to see. He choked back the emotion he felt. "Do they know who was responsible?" he asked with ice dripping from his voice.

The man shook his head. "There's an ongoing investigation, is all I can tell you." He put the bag on an empty rocking chair. "It's in a foreign place, so things are going slower than we like. But we won't quit." He sighed. "We wanted you to know. I'm sorry I had to be the one to tell you."

Heather sat up, rubbing at her wet eyes. "Thank you for that, at least." She looked at him with sad, pale eyes. "There's no hope that he could be…that his remains could be returned to us?" she faltered.

He shook his head. "It was a classified action. I can't even tell you exactly where it happened; just that it was overseas. Apparently there were no remains to be found. Just this, at the site where we arranged to pick him up." He drew in a long breath. "I wish I could give you hope. But there is none. Our jobs are extremely dangerous, sometimes fatal, but vital to the security of our nation. He gave his life in the line of duty, to save other lives."

John just nodded, his mind already going back to the last time he'd spoken to Tanner, when his brother had told him to give his love to the family. It was as if Tanner knew something lethal was about to happen.

"That is some consolation," Heather said, her voice unsteady. "But not much."

"Of course not," the visitor agreed. He forced a smile. "I lost my partner of twenty years a couple of months ago in a similar situation," he confided. "It wasn't easy for me, either."

"I'm sorry for your loss," John said.

"I'm equally sorry for yours." He handed John a card. "That's me." He indicated the name and two phone numbers. "I'm not supposed to do this. But the circumstances of this action…" He hesitated and his lips made a thin line. He took out his cell phone and powered it down. "The circumstances are suspicious," he said in an undertone. "If I can find out anything I'll send you a text on a burner phone. Our boss had it in for Tanner," he added coldly. "I think it was a setup. Tanner knew something damaging about the boss. There are some financial deals involved with this, and some nasty politics that I don't like."

"Thank you for being honest," John said.

"If you have any contacts with covert operatives," the man continued, "you might consider digging deeper. I don't dare. I'm on the boss's bad list, too. I questioned the mission after the fact. If you don't hear from me again, I might be on the wrong side of a mound of earth."

"Watch your back," John said.

"Easier said than done." He looked toward the bloodstained bag. "He was a good operative and a friend," he added curtly. "He didn't deserve this."

He turned his phone back on. "Damn," he muttered convincingly, "the cell reception is bad here, isn't it?" He glanced at John.

"Terrible," John confirmed, going along with the deception. "Sometimes we have to drive out to the main road just to make a call. Sorry."

"No problem." He nodded toward the bag. "Again, I'm sorry for your loss."

"Thank you," John replied, and the gratitude came also from Heather, whose face was covered with tears.

The man nodded at them, put down the bag he'd carried Tanner's kit in with a deliberate and meaningful glance at John before he walked back to his car and drove away.

John held Heather while she cried. He was choked himself. "I keep remembering that last phone call," he said, his voice hoarse.

"Me, too," she sobbed. "Oh, John, how can we live without him?"

There was a faint roar as one of the ranch trucks came into the yard and stopped at the front door. Cole got out, tall and rangy and not smiling. His silver eyes were flashing like lightning.

"One of the boys saw a car pull up here. Who was it?" He stopped on the porch. "Honey, what's wrong?" he asked abruptly, pulling Heather up from the chaise, close, and rocking her gently in his arms. "What is it?"

"It's Tanner," she began brokenly.

"Tanner," he ground out the name. "Damn him! He's not to set foot here. I mean it!"

John was livid. Of all the times to be obsessive. He turned to his father. "You can't bend an inch, can you?"

"I never have," Cole replied, turning piercing light eyes on him. "You know how I feel about your brother."

"Oh, yes, I do."

"What's the matter with you two?" Cole growled, looking from Heather's tearstained face to John's pale, strained one. "And what did that stranger want?"

"He brought us something," John said icily, and he picked up the bloodstained kit and slammed it into his father's chest. "Now you won't have to worry about us sneaking out to meet Tanner ever again. That should make you happy!"

He turned and stalked away, his heart breaking in his chest.

Cole still didn't get it. He let Heather go and studied the bloodstained bag with the photo of the family wedged inside. "Isn't this the bag you bought at the luggage store a few years ago?" he asked. "Why is there dried blood on it?"

"I bought it for Tanner, for Christmas," she said in a defeated tone. "He took it on some secret classified mission overseas. That's all that's left…of him." She started crying again.

Cole pulled her back into his arms with a harsh groan. He was staring over her shoulder, transfixed at the bag still held in one big hand. Clarity ensued. He took a short breath. "He's dead?" he ground out.

"Dead," Heather sobbed. "Dead and gone forever. There isn't even a…a body to bury." She broke down. "I'll never see my son again!"

Cole almost broke his teeth, they were clenched so tightly.

He eased Heather back down on the chaise. He took the bloody bag in both big hands and as he stared at it, he looked back at the mess he'd made of Tanner's life with his harsh treatment.

He'd been livid about the way Tanner had treated poor Stasia, and he'd grieved for the grandchild he'd lost. But he'd never considered Tanner's feelings. The man was his son. He wasn't a monster. Perhaps he'd grieved, too, but Cole wouldn't know, because he'd shut his son out of his life, out of his family's life.

He put the bag down and lifted Heather into his arms. "Come here to me, sweetheart," he said softly and sat down on the porch swing with her in his lap, holding her close and rocking the swing into motion.

"I'm sorry," he bit off in her ear, and it was one of only a handful of times he'd ever said the words in his whole life. His son was gone, dead, and he'd never see him again. His memory was full of his own harsh treatment of Tanner, his unjust treatment. He'd have liked to apologize, but it was years too late for that. Tanner was gone.

"Who was he working for?" he asked his wife.

She sniffed into the handkerchief he'd pressed into her hand and took a steadying breath as she sat up, still curled into Cole's lap, comforted by his warm strength. "One of the letter agencies, I assume. He would never say, not even to John."

"Maybe there's a mistake," he said huskily. "They make mistakes. It might not be the same bag…"

"It's the same bag," she interrupted. "Didn't you look inside?"

He drew the armchair with the bag closer and peered inside. His whole face clenched as he saw the family photo with everyone in it except John, who'd snapped the picture and given a paper copy of it to Tanner, who wouldn't risk having it on one of his throwaway phones, in case he was captured. You never carried personal things with you on a mission. Except that Tanner had a premonition about this mission and had said so to John. Maybe that was why he'd broken protocol with the photo. Still, it was odd that he'd have carried it with him on so dangerous a mission.

"The man said a strange thing," she told her husband.

"What?"

"He said that if we had any covert ties, we might want to dig deeper." She looked up. "I got the impression that he didn't think Tanner was, well, lost. He was careful to disable his phone before he said it. And he also said that Tanner's boss was mixed up in something both political and financial. Maybe something crooked, that Tanner knew or learned about."

Cole's pale eyes narrowed. "I don't have covert ties. But King Brannt does. I'll go see him."

She shook her head. "They've all gone to the Bahamas on vacation, even Morie and her husband and the baby. And Cort and his wife are expecting. It's a huge family affair."

"Damn." He drew in a breath. "There's another possibility. Stasia's employer is head of a crime syndicate in New Jersey." He held up a hand. "Yes, I know, he's a scoundrel, but I've heard Stasia talk about some people he knows in the Bahamas, people with covert ties. It's worth a try."

Heather nodded. She grimaced. "You'll have to tell Odalie," she wailed.

"I'll cross that bridge when I come to it," he replied gently. "Meanwhile, I have to go and pacify our son." He made a face. "I was pretty overbearing."

She leaned up and kissed him hungrily, smiling under the devouring lips that answered hers. "You're always overbearing," she teased. "But we all love you anyway. People argue. They get over it, my darling. That's life."

He hugged her close. "I had no life until I married you," he said huskily. "That's when my life began. You're it. All of it."

She smiled and curled into his chest. "You're all of mine, as well. I only hope our children will someday find the same happiness we have."

He nodded, smiled sadly and kissed her again.

John was loading bales of hay into the barn, the small, square bales that were meant for livestock close to the barn. The big, round bales, covered with plastic, stood in the far pastures where cattle would winter later in the year.

John looked up as his father came into the barn, bristling.

Cole just sighed and stuck his hands into the pockets of his jeans. "I come unarmed," he announced.

"Okay."

He joined his father at the barn door, his face taut with grief and misery.

"Heather said your visitor advised digging deeper. King Brannt collects mercenaries, but Stasia works for a crime boss—well, he says he's a retired crime boss—and he has a contact in the Bahamas who has covert ties."

John stared at him. "You think Tanner may still be alive?"

"I do." Cole nodded. "It's a long shot, but none of us will rest until we know for sure."

"Odalie talks about that crime boss all the time," John remarked. He made a face. "Stasia works for him. I don't like her that close to him. He's dangerous, and he has enemies."

"From what I hear of him, his enemies don't thrive. Some of them have turned up in bodies of water," he added facetiously.

"That man mentioned that Tanner had run afoul of a former boss, one who has financial and political ambitions. Maybe Tanner left that bag deliberately."

"Faked his death, you mean," John replied, feeling less morose.

"If he has an enemy that powerful, it might have been his only option," Cole continued. "We need to try and find him, if he's still alive," he added heavily. "I just don't know how to go about it."

"I'll fly up to New York and talk to Stasia," John said, his heart lifting. "I'll tell Odalie while I'm there..."

"Just tell Odalie he's missing," Cole said firmly. "Let's not send her over the deep end unless we have to. She loves Tanner."

"So do the rest of us," John replied. "I'll never accept that he's dead. He's canny and street-smart. And if he knew going in that his ex-boss had a reason to go after him...it may be because of something Tanner knows that the ex-boss doesn't want told."

"Exactly what I think," John said.

"Have the company jet take you up there," Cole said.

"You were going to fly Mom down to Corpus Christi for shrimp tonight, I thought," John replied.

"You certainly must think your brother is more important than a shrimp dinner," Cole chuckled.

"Well, yes. Although a good shrimp dinner does have its winning points."

"Your mother won't mind." He hesitated. "I've been unjust to Tanner. He has to be alive. I've got a lot to make up to him."

John clapped his father on the back. "He's an Everett. It will take more than a sneaky ex-boss to put him out of action."

Cole smiled. "Okay. Go call the pilot and get him over here. Spend the night if you have to."

John's eyes twinkled. "Maybe Stasia's got a spare room."

Cole glared at him.

John sighed. "Okay. Maybe my sister's got a spare room."

Cole grinned. "That's more like it."

John knocked at the door of Odalie's apartment late that night. It had taken some effort to get to New York, and there were the inevitable delays.

Odalie opened the door and gaped at her brother. "Why are you here?" she asked at once, inviting him in and closing the door behind him. "Something's happened! Something bad!" she exclaimed.

He sighed. She'd always had that premonition mindset, like Tanner. She was usually right, too. "Yes, something's wrong," he said. "Tanner has…gone missing."

She went pale. "Gone missing? He was going on some sort of mission. He's…dead?" Her pale eyes filled with tears.

"I don't think so," he returned. "Neither does Dad. But we need covert people to go in and look for him," he added.

Odalie sighed. "You could ask Stasia's boss," she said sourly. "He knows all sorts of scalawags including mercs." Her face tautened. "Birds of a feather, as they say."

"Ouch! You've really got it in for the guy, haven't you?"

She bit her lower lip. "He hates me," she said curtly. "He's always picking at me, finding fault. He invited me to the cocktail party Tanner was at, but it was an aside, and he made sure I knew that it was only because Stasia was my best friend. I can't stand the man!"

John cocked his head. Where there was smoke, there was fire. "We'll call Stasia and get her to run interference for us."

She sighed. "I guess she could talk him into it," she replied. "He treats her like a daughter," she added. "It's sort of sweet. He doesn't like most people, but he's the biggest fan Stasia has with her art."

"No romantic ties?" he persisted.

She studied him. "Stasia still loves Tanner, John," she told him honestly. "And she always will. Any other man would only be second-best, she says that."

"Does he know?" John asked quietly.

She smiled sadly. "No. He thinks he's killed any feelings she had for him."

John let out a long sigh.

Odalie reached up and kissed his chin. "I know that you have hopes," she said softly. "But there's fantasy, and then there's reality. You have to face the facts."

"Only at gunpoint," he muttered. "There's always hope."

She just smiled. "I have a nice spare bedroom, and I can cook breakfast in the morning and it won't bounce," she assured him. "Now, let's get you settled!"

Deep in the South American jungle, Tanner was fighting the pain of a bullet wound in his side. A friend was taking him to one of the Amazon villages, out of the way of any agents who might be hunting him. It was the safest place right now. The men of the village were accomplished hunters and trackers, and they were adept with poison darts. Very few foreigners were willing to risk death to approach them.

"How do you know about this village?" he asked his friend, Enrique Boas.

He laughed. "There was an incursion here in Barrera, when El General retook his country from the little madman, Sapara, who usurped it. My mother lives in the village. It was where an ex-merc saved my life," he added. "I was taking Carisse Carrington—well, Carisse Kantor, now—to meet with the mercenaries with Emilio Machado while they staged for the attack." He grimaced. "We were both shot. She was captured and tortured. I was wounded more seriously. An American ex-merc, an anthropologist who is now married to El General," he chuckled, "patched me up until the doctor came."

"That sounds like quite an adventure," Tanner remarked.

"The grandest adventure of my life. Miss Carrington helped two of her fellow prisoners escape and was able to give El General specific information that led to winning the battle."

"She must be one hell of a woman."

"That she is. Sadly, the doctor who treated us both is now dead, a victim of the usurper who took over Barrera. But then, the usurper, Sapara, is now also quite dead and unmourned."

Tanner was still holding a piece of cloth over the wound. The bleeding had slowed, but not stopped, and he was sick to his stomach. He slumped a little in the jeep.

"You are not doing well, my friend," Boas said worriedly. "It is not much farther. My mother is adept with herbs. As soon as we arrive, I will leave you and go to Barrera to ask for help. You will have to get out of the country as soon as possible. The man who sent you into the ambush will not believe you are dead, despite the evidence I left behind."

"I know," Tanner said coldly. "He was my colleague years ago when I went with the agency, and then through some really dirty tricks, he became my boss. I've seen some of the dirty tricks he pulled. I just never expected to be the victim of one. I should have known something was off about this mission. I feel like an idiot for letting myself be lured into an ambush. And for several deaths that the ambush caused," he added, wincing as the pain and the memory of the two young agents who were killed almost doubled him over. James was responsible for this, for even more deaths to cover up what he'd done last year in the Middle East. Tanner should have gone to the authorities. He never should have kept quiet, whatever the cost. He was only afraid for retribution that might involve his family, not for himself. Now it was too late. And more people had died.

Boas glanced at him as he turned onto another deeply rutted road. "You know something, don't you? Something dangerous to him."

Tanner nodded. "He's cost many innocent lives. If I live to tell it, he's going to be facing a congressional committee."

"Then you must certainly live," came the reply. "The entire camp was wiped out," he added coldly. "Two new recruits, who trusted that they would be safe, used only as camouflage to lure you into the trap. He has a great deal to answer for."

"That sounds personal," Tanner remarked.

"It is. One of the recruits was my cousin, a fine young man with a wife and new baby son." His jaw tautened. "No man should be allowed to get away with what amounted to a slaughter."

"I heard that," Tanner said. The wound was hurting now. He'd used some pain meds from his kit, but he'd only had a few and they were wearing off already. "Damn, it hurts," he groaned.

"El General will make sure that you get home safely," Boas told him. "He's quite fond of Americans. Especially mercs," he added with amusement.

The jeep bounced a little along the ruts, and Tanner stifled a moan. They were driving down long, dry dirt roads, because the rainy season hadn't come yet to the Amazon.

"Mercs?" he asked, suddenly interested.

"Yes. His ragtag army that defeated Sapara mostly consisted of them. One of those is a former Army officer who is now head of the military for El General. And he has some amazing connections," he went on. "His oldest son is a lieutenant of detectives in San Antonio, Texas. And his son's wife's father is head of the CIA."

Despite the seriousness of his situation, Tanner burst out laughing. "My God," he said with faint reverence. "What connections!"

"Yes. And I was thinking," he continued with a glance at the man beside him, "that the head of Barrera's military might be able to assist you in your circumstances. Especially when he knows that you, also, are from Texas."

Tanner let out a breath. He'd never dreamed that he might find any help at all. His nemesis was head of the super-secret agency to which he belonged, and none of the operatives would dare go against him. Two had mysteriously vanished on top-secret missions in the past six months, one of whom had given the photographic evidence of the Middle East village slaughter to Tanner; the man had apparently fallen, accidentally of course, out of a high-rise apartment window. It was rumored that the ex-boss, Phillip James, now had political ambitions and his part in that covert mission overseas, one which had almost been the subject of a would-be whistleblower's revelations, could put him in federal prison or give him the death penalty if the full circumstances of the incursion were known. Tanner, who'd participated in the mission, not the slaughter, was the only operative left who could tell exactly what had happened.

"I would be grateful for any help," Tanner said. "Or I might not live long enough to bring the scalawag to justice."

"Most certainly I will do what I can." Boas shook his head. "It is a miracle that I had a friend who was among the traffickers, or you would be dead. The murderer was quite surprised when I shot him."

"Yes, and just in time to save me from another bullet, which would have ended me," Tanner said grimly. "He even bragged about it. He said that I'd never make trouble for his boss, and he'd be going right up the ladder to power with him." His eye burned with fury. "Fat chance. He killed those young men, his supposed colleagues, in cold blood. And he laughed."

Tanner drew in a breath. His wound was hurting badly. He let out the breath, slowly, trying to force down the pain. "If you hadn't found me, I'd be dead by morning."

"The jungle was full of news about the ambush, which I already knew of from my contacts in the agency. When I knew that you were among the insurgents, I went looking for you. I heard the shots even as I followed the helicopter to your location. That you survived is a miracle in itself," his companion said curtly.

Tanner cursed roundly. "The two men with me were raw recruits. Good men with high principles, who had no idea what they were walking into. They were decoys, to make sure I thought the mission was legit, so that I wouldn't suspect treachery." His mouth tightened. "We were told that we were intercepting drug traffickers, one of whom was my ex-boss. We were going to catch him red-handed with the drugs, which would have put a very public end to his activities without having to bring up the massacre he participated in. Well, there were drug traffickers, who'd been told that we were there to shut them down. Ten of them, and they came out of nowhere right into the camp before daylight. I played dead while the boss's agent sent the traffickers and the helicopter away. Then he noticed that I wasn't dead, that I'd crawled away, when he came back into the camp. He hunted me down, so that he could kill me. I'd have disappeared and nobody would have said how or when or even where." He was furious. "Phillip James is going to pay for that, I promise you."

"It would be good to avenge my poor cousin. But, first things first. I will leave you with my mother and her people. They can tend that wound before it goes septic and kills you," Boas added. He shook his head. "Had you no medical supplies with you?"

"Not enough," Tanner said angrily. "Barely even a bandage. A small medical kit was issued to our unit. I'm sure that was arranged beforehand. We just had time to discover that our supplies weren't with us. And, in fact, that we had nobody in the group with even basic medical training except me, before the attack came, out of nowhere. Thanks to you, the whole point of the operation, to get me out of the way, failed. The killer couldn't have known that you were in the vicinity, that you even knew of the ambush."

"I know everything that happens in this area of the jungle. We have ways of finding out things." He shook his head. "You were meant to be a human sacrifice, to protect your ex-boss from discovery of his treachery," his companion said coldly. "Your government is mad."

"Not all of it," Tanner replied. "We have some good people, people with principles who would never sanction such an action. It's just that the black budget funds some bad people, and because it's so secret, there's no congressional oversight. It's a funded agency with no accountability."

"And so it goes, with most covert work, even in my country," the other man said. "When I was much younger, as you know, I worked for my own country's intelligence network."

"It was where we met, when I was here on a cooperative mission. And a stroke of great good fortune for me, too," he chuckled. "Because you knew about the mission, through your own agency, and came looking for survivors."

"It grieves me that I found only one."

"While the renegade agent sent his cronies away, I crawled away and hid under some undergrowth, along with a great huge python," he added. "But the killer came after me. I was too sick from my wound to even try for the pistol in my ankle holster."

"I trust the python had already fed recently?" came the amused reply.

"Yes, apparently, because it wasn't threatening me." He shook his head. "When I was in basic training—I trained as a sniper, you recall—they sent me to a Southern state where we practiced in the woods. My companion was a very angry copperhead who put me in the hospital. I had to lie perfectly still while he attacked me or lose my place in training. They found me with my rifle still in my hands, my leg so swollen that the seam in my pants came apart."

"I trust that they passed you, after such an experience?"

Tanner laughed out loud. "Oh, yes. It was almost worth the pain." He grimaced. "Having given the matter much consideration, I'd rather be shot than bitten. It's less painful and more easily cured. As a rule."

"My mother is adept at healing," he promised. "The bodies will be found," Boas added. "But the traffickers will not care. There will be nobody to tell your ex-boss that you are still alive. Especially since I left your bag, with the photo in it, for agents to find. It will seem that you have been seriously wounded and crawled away to die in the jungle."

Tanner grimaced. "I'll have to hope that I can get back to the States and into a safe house before James is informed that his man is dead, and especially before he has time to send somebody else to look for my body. When it isn't found, he'll never believe that I'm dead. He'll be afraid of what I know and he'll be out for blood. Without a doubt, he'll send professionals after me next time. No more elaborate charades like this one." He paused to take a breath. It hurt. "They'll notify my family that I'm dead, and I won't be able to reassure them without giving myself away and giving James a target," he said suddenly. "My poor mother and brother and sister!"

"Your father is not alive?"

His face hardened. "My father disowned me years ago. He was right. I was a spoiled brat with no sense of honor. But he's held the grudge ever since. We haven't spoken in years." He stared straight ahead. The memory hurt. "I doubt he'll even feel it."

"You wrong the man," his companion said softly. "Even an angry father will grieve the loss of a child."

"I'd have to see that to believe it. And you don't know my father. Really."

They'd reached the edge of the village. People came running to see the driver, who had many relatives in the village besides his little mother, who hugged him warmly when he was out of the vehicle.

He spoke in their tongue, telling them about Tanner and who he was and why his presence in the village must be kept a close secret. He also asked his mother to treat the wound in Tanner's side, to which she agreed at once.

"You will be safe here. I give you my word of honor. And I will make a call to Barrera." He smiled. "I think my comrade who commands the army will be very interested in your situation. He, too, has been the victim of a vindictive enemy. How he turned the tables on the man, a fellow officer, is a story in itself."

"I'll be grateful for any help," Tanner said quietly. He shook hands with his friend. "You watch your back. James has cohorts everywhere, even here."

Boas smiled. "Here, I have the advantage. I know dangerous people. Not even your boss will bother me."

"Thank you for saving my life."

"I haven't. Not yet. But I hope to, with help from some

friends." He smiled. "Rest. I'll be in touch very soon." He cocked his head. "You don't have a cell phone…?"

"No," he said angrily. "The agent who went with us, the one who killed my colleagues and shot me, said we had throwaway phones and communication equipment in our kit. A lie, but we trusted him." He shook his head. "I used to be smarter."

"Anyone can be betrayed," Boas said simply. "That's life."

Tanner smiled. "Yes. That's life."

So his friend's mother took care of Tanner through a vicious fever while she used native herbs to treat the wound and try to bring down the fever. She reminded him very much of Heather, his own sweet mother, who was so caring of her children.

He hoped that he'd see her again; her, and his siblings. He was certain that they thought he was dead, but he'd prove that he wasn't. If he got home again. Perhaps his comrade's friend in Barrera could help. That would truly be a miracle.

He also hoped that he would live long enough for help to arrive. He could tell by the expression in his benefactor's face that her treatment wasn't working. Here in the jungle, any wound could turn septic. From what he was seeing, he gathered that his already had. He hoped Boas would hurry…

Odalie was quiet as they drove to her singing lesson. "Sorry about this," she told her brother, "but I really can't afford to miss even one lesson. I've phoned Stasia. She's with a client right now but she's going to get Tony to come over with Big Ben to pick us up."

"Tony?"

"Tony Garza," she said.

"Oh." He knew the name. It was Garza who'd made Stasia's

career possible. She owed him a lot. So did John, for keeping her safe in New York City.

"And Big Ben?" he asked. "Sounds like a clock."

"He strikes like that big one," she explained. "You'll understand when you see him. Tony's a big guy, but Big Ben overtops him. He was a professional wrestler..."

"Big Ben!" he exclaimed, as he made the connection. "Hell, I used to watch him on television. He retired undefeated!"

"It's all fake," she teased. "It's like a story script and they're actors."

He gave her a blithe look. "The bruises are real."

"Well, of course," she had to admit. "And we're here."

Her voice teacher lived in a modest house in Brooklyn. His walls were soundproofed so that he didn't disturb the neighbors too much as his students practiced. He was elderly, with silver hair and a big smile.

"Welcome, welcome," he told Odalie. "My wonderful student! You will grace the Met!"

"If I pass the audition," she said, with a groan.

"Do not be absurd," her coach said firmly. "You certainly have the talent, my girl. What you need is confidence!"

"Just what I've been telling her for years," John said.

The coach had been staring at him covertly, because John didn't shed his Texas regalia because he was in an Eastern city. He was wearing hand-tooled boots and a top-of-the-line Stetson over his pale blond hair.

He caught the coach assessing him.

"Sorry," the elderly man, Blake Tennyson by name, said apologetically. "Was I staring?"

John just grinned. "No problem. I'm Odalie's brother. Nice to meet you."

"Blake Tennyson," the other man replied, shaking the outstretched hand firmly. "And the feeling is mutual. You do look like a cowboy," he chuckled.

"I am. I'm a rancher. We both," he nodded toward Odalie, "come from a small community in Texas."

"That part I could have guessed," their host said warmly. He turned to Odalie. "And now we will work on 'Un bel di,'" he said.

She groaned.

"You can hit that note you fear so much. You must have confidence!"

She sighed. "Confidence."

John bent and kissed her cheek. "I'll walk around to that department store we passed on the way here and be back in, how long?"

"An hour," Tennyson told him.

"An hour," John replied. "Sing pretty," he told his sister.

She sighed. "Well, I'll certainly try to."

Tony was on the phone in the back of the limo, with Stasia beside him and Big Ben at the wheel.

"I know that," he was telling his friend, Marcus Carrera. "We need somebody good. Really good, who can keep his mouth shut."

"There's a guy who lives in a neighboring country, near where Stasia's brother disappeared." There was a shocked exclamation from Tony. Marcus laughed. "Yeah, I have contacts of my own in Washington, DC," he said. "I know all about the mission that was betrayed."

"You know where Tanner was?" Tony asked, surprised, glancing at Stasia, who was all eyes.

"Yeah." Marcus named the country. "And that's just between you and me," he added firmly. "It was one of those black budget things. Tanner was told they were going to take out a drug operation in conjunction with three agents from the host country. It was a lie. They were dropped into the target zone without phones, with limited medical supplies. A squad of drug traffickers attacked the camp and killed the two agents. Tanner's ex-boss's man shot Tanner and thought he was dead. He sent his colleagues away and went back to make sure, noticed Tanner missing and tracked him. He was about to finish him off when one of Tanner's old friends ended him. James must have been nuts to pull off such a stupid stunt. It was a total snafu," he added. "I guess he thought somebody might suspect him if Tanner suddenly died in this country from an attack."

"How the hell did they get their phones away from them?" Tony asked.

"They told them burner phones were in the supplies they were being dropped with."

Tony shook his head. "What a sorry thing to do."

"Two green recruits were put into the unit, along with your friend's brother," Marcus continued. "It seems that the brother knows something pretty bad about a botched mission in the Middle East, where several civilians were butchered. And I mean, butchered. A whistleblower came forward, but he only got a little of the information out before he fell out of a window in a hospital."

"How convenient," Tony said.

"Hey, we've done a few convenient things ourselves," he chuckled. "Might not want to share that with your friend," he added.

Tony glanced at Stasia and laughed softly. "I agree," he told Marcus.

"Anyway, I'll get in touch with the guy and get back to you," he said. "He was military intelligence in the army, and now he's head of the military in Barrera. His boss, El General,

Emilio Machado, has a son in Texas who's a lieutenant of detectives in San Antonio and the guy's wife's father is head of the CIA. How's that for connections?" he added on a laugh.

"It sounds like he could solve this problem all by himself," Tony replied.

"And he might. I'll get back to you as soon as I can." He paused. "We still don't know if her brother is alive, though," he added very quietly. "Every man in that unit was reported dead. There's no trace of paperwork that authorized the mission. You get my meaning?"

"There's somebody high up, like the brother's ex-boss who now heads that secret agency, who wanted to get rid of one guy and he sacrificed two green recruits to make it look like a sudden attack by drug cartel insurgents," Tony said.

"Exactly." He paused. "It's been my experience that when something like this is planned that well, it usually succeeds."

Tony grimaced. "Well, we'll see. Hope is the last thing we give up, you know," he added, glancing at Stasia with a reassuring smile that he hoped looked genuine.

"So it is. But it's better to face the pain head-on," Marcus replied.

"Only when we have to," Tony said.

"Whatever. I'll call you." He hung up.

"Well, we have hope," Tony assured her.

She sat back against the seat. It had almost brought her to her knees when Odalie phoned her the night before with the news about Tanner. After an agonizing night she'd gone to work, her misery so visible that Tony took her into the office and wormed the whole story out of her.

He'd promised help. She hadn't quite believed him until they were in the limo, on the way to pick up Odalie and her brother at the voice coach's home in Brooklyn. But what she'd overheard gave her real hope.

"Can I share any of that with Odalie?" she asked Tony, because she knew Odalie and John were beside themselves with worry.

Tony grimaced. "Well, some of it," he said.

"Which part?"

He chuckled. "I'll tell you while we get where we're going," he promised. He glanced at her. "Why do we have to pick her up?" he added. "Can't she call a cab?"

"Now, Tony," she said. "She's not so bad."

He glared at her. "Neither are roaches."

She burst out laughing.

TWELVE

I t was the middle of the night. General Winslow Grange's dark eyes were on a computer screen, not on his pretty blonde wife's sleeping figure in the bed beside him. Just as well she was finally asleep, he thought, because their little boy, John, had been teething and it had been a very long night for both of them. Only when she'd given up her objections and used the medicine the doctor had prescribed did the toddler finally sleep so that his weary parents could.

Except that a soft beep from Winslow's cell phone had diverted his attention from his pillow. A colleague of his was asking for help in a very secretive matter.

Intrigued, he picked up the phone and began to answer the plea for help. In the veritable middle of his reply to his colleague, there was another soft ping, this one from Marcus Carrera, a reformed gangster who was married to a girl from Jacobsville, Texas, where Grange had lived before the incursion to liberate Barrera.

He laughed softly to himself as he read the email. Amazing. Carrera and Winslow's former colleague were both asking for help for the same Big Spur, Texas, family, at the same time. It was a story he'd eventually tell again and again; leaving out all the names, of course, because you didn't talk about anybody's black ops missions if you wanted to do well. Even in a foreign country like Barrera!

He sent two emails, closed the computer, curled his sleeping wife into his arms, pulled the sheet over them and went to sleep.

It was blazing hot in New York City, even with the air-conditioning on. Tony wasn't about to sit in a parked car with the engine running on the street. So he got out with Stasia.

"I love Brooklyn," she told him, smiling. "I think it's the most beautiful part of New York City."

"It's okay, I guess," he conceded, walking beside her to the little house on the corner. "This is where she studies?" he wondered aloud. "I thought she'd be in a high-rise, or at least a bigger house."

"Her voice teacher lives a very modest life," she told him as they reached the door. "He's a widower. He says he doesn't want to rattle around in a house made for a family."

Tony thought of his own enormous houses in New York and New Jersey and just smiled.

Instead of knocking, Stasia opened the door and put her finger to her lips so Tony knew to be quiet.

He stopped just inside the door, not even aware of Stasia closing it as he heard the most powerful notes of "Un bel di" being sung with such fervor that chills ran through him. It was from his favorite Puccini opera, *Madame Butterfly*. It was, in fact, his favorite aria. He had dozens of recordings of it, from just about any known opera star.

But this, this was beyond anything he'd experienced in his life. He closed his eyes, in ecstasy, as the highest note was reached, held and then slowly, exquisitely, fell away into a profound silence.

Tony's eyes opened. He was spellbound. "I have to have that recording," he murmured half under his breath. "I've never heard anything so beautiful in all my life!"

Stasia was looking at him with amusement. He wondered why.

Voices broke into the silence. A man's voice, saying, "I told you that you had the range, but you didn't believe me."

A woman's laugh. "I do now," she said.

"You keep practicing that," the man continued. "But rest your voice, too. Be careful with it."

"Of course."

They both came into the room and stopped. The voice teacher's eyebrows rose.

"Sorry; it's too hot to stand outside, Mr. Tennyson," she apologized.

"Besides, we would have missed that rendition of 'Un bel di,'" Tony said with a smile. "Can you tell me which artist recorded it? I don't recognize the voice."

"But that was Miss Everett," Tennyson said, surprised. "She is my student."

Tony gaped at Odalie, who gave him a cool, haughty gaze.

"She…?" he exclaimed.

Stasia hid a smile. "We need to go. Are you ready, Odalie?"

"Yes, I am. Thank you again, Mr. Tennyson. Thank you very much!"

"I shall see you in two days," he replied, smiling.

The door opened, and one of the foremost opera stars in the city came in, wrapped in a cool couture dress, her black hair in a complicated braid, just graying at the temples.

"Miss O'Brien," Tony greeted her.

"Mr. Garza," she purred, extending a hand.

He lifted it to his lips and kissed it. "I hope to hear you in *Turandot* soon."

"As you will. Now you must excuse me. I cannot keep dear Mr. Tennyson waiting." She gave him a coquettish smile and went to greet the voice coach, who dismissed the rest of his visitors with a smile and led Miss O'Brien to the back of the house.

"That was Kiri O'Brien," Odalie exclaimed when they were walking toward the limo. "I have all the recordings of operas she's been in. She's the best, the absolute best, and I actually got to see her up close!"

"I never imagined I'd see you starstruck," Stasia teased.

"I'm always starstruck when I'm here," Odalie sighed.

Just as they reached the limo, John strolled around the corner, grinning as he joined them. "Talk about perfect timing!" he exclaimed.

"You couldn't have done it better," Stasia said with a smile. She glanced at Tony, who looked thunderous. "Tony, this is Odalie's brother, John. And John, this is my boss, Tony Garza."

Tony was stunned. He shook hands with John, shooting an odd glance toward Odalie, but he didn't say anything. Stasia hid a smile.

"How about dinner?" Tony asked. "I usually spend Friday nights at Antonio's. He's my cousin," he added.

"He's the best cook I've found so far," Stasia agreed. "He makes the most delicious pasta! It's almost as good as Tony's lasagna," she added with a smile at her boss.

"Thanks. I like his calamari," Tony said.

"And the desserts!" Stasia sighed.

John was watching her as if he'd found the *Mona Lisa*. "It sounds great," he said.

"Is it a dressy sort of place?" Odalie asked worriedly.

"It is," Stasia said. "You'll need to pull out something witchy," she teased.

Odalie laughed. "Okay, if you don't mind dropping us off at my apartment and coming back for us," she added, talking to Tony's tie.

"Sure. No problem," he said stiffly.

"We've found a contact, by the way, for Tanner," Stasia said as they piled into the limo.

"Who?" Odalie asked at once.

"Where?" John wanted to know.

"A man who heads up the armed forces in Barrera," Stasia said. "He's very close to where Tanner disappeared, or so we're told. We think he'll agree to help."

Odalie turned away as tears brightened her eyes. "If we can just find him alive," she whispered.

"It will be all right," Stasia said, trying to sound convincing. She was as worried as Odalie and John. She was just better at concealing it. "We'll get him out."

"If he's still alive," John said heavily. "Dad was really upset. He said he was sorry for the way he'd treated Tanner. Mom... well, Mom just went to pieces."

"I can only imagine how she felt," Stasia said. "She doesn't play favorites really, but Tanner's still her favorite." She laughed softly.

"I think the firstborn always is...oh, gosh, Stasia, I'm sorry! I'm so sorry! I didn't think..."

Stasia pressed her hand over Odalie's. "It was a long time ago," she said softly. "I don't think about it much."

It was a lie, and they both knew it. Tony, who didn't know about Stasia's miscarriage, was all at sea.

"His mother writes songs for the hard rock group Desperado," Stasia told Tony with a smile. "In fact, she's up to two Grammys now."

Tony was impressed. "She must be very talented."

"She is," John said. "She wanted to study opera, but she didn't want to leave Texas. In the end, she gave it all up to marry Dad. She said it was the best decision she'd ever made in her life." He shook his head. "When you see the two of them together, it's like they've just started dating. They've been married over thirty years, but it doesn't seem like it. I hope I can make a marriage like theirs one day." He tried not to look at Stasia as he said it.

"Everybody does," Stasia said, and her heart broke inside her at the memory of Tanner, of how much she'd loved him. Almost all her life. "But we don't all get the brass ring, you know. Some of us settle for great careers." She grinned as she said that.

Tony chuckled. "You'd know."

"And I wouldn't have any of it except for you, Tony," Stasia said gently. "I'll never forget that."

"Aw, I didn't do anything. I just pointed you in the right direction. You had the talent to go anywhere you wanted to go."

"Didn't somebody say you lived in New Jersey?" John asked abruptly.

Tony nodded. "Yeah, I do. But I do a lot of business in the city here with my gallery and museum. And during opera season, this is the only place to be."

"Opera, again," John groaned, glancing at Odalie. "It's all I've heard for fifteen years! Opera!"

"You never had to listen," Odalie chided.

"I did spend a lot of time out in the barn with the bulls," John said accusingly. "Except when I was in the military."

"That's right, he joined the service to get away from your piano practice and voice lessons," Stasia teased.

John brightened. He smiled at Stasia with his whole heart and she ground her teeth together and asked Tony about a project he was putting together for teenage boys in the New Jersey neighborhood where he lived.

Tony warmed to his subject.

"You really think rough juvenile delinquents from the back streets of New York will be interested in the arts?" John asked quietly.

"Look at me," Tony invited. "They don't come much rougher than I was. There was a similar outreach program in Jersey, just about the time I decided to drop out of school and go to work for my old man." He sighed. "Somebody put on a recording of 'Un bel di,' and I had to leave the room."

"You didn't like it?" John asked.

"I was almost in tears," Tony corrected. "Up until then, it was hard rock. I'd never even heard classical music, much less opera. But once I discovered it, I was like a sponge. I couldn't get enough of it."

"I'll bet your father wasn't impressed," Stasia said, tongue-in-cheek.

Tony grimaced. "He knocked me around a bit," he conceded. "But he couldn't sway me. Ever since then, I've been into any opera I could find to watch. Well, with the exception of Rossini," he added darkly. "I hate Rossini."

"Me, too," Odalie murmured.

Tony raised an eyebrow. "You like Puccini."

"I love Puccini," she corrected. "Everything Puccini, from *Madame Butterfly* to *Turandot*. Plácido Domingo sings 'Nessun dorma' like an angel," she said in a husky tone.

"He does. But I prefer Pavarotti."

"It would be a very close competition," she conceded.

Tony was studying her closely. "I've never heard a voice like yours," he said, and for once, he wasn't antagonistic. "Clear as a bell, and you enunciate every single syllable. Do you speak Italian?"

"No, just Spanish," she replied.

"Spanish is just vulgate Latin," he replied. "You should be able to read some Italian, even without studying it."

"I've studied Italian a bit," she confessed. "I love languages."

"Also, German is good to learn. Opera has many tongues."

"I noticed," she said, and managed a smile. "That will go against me in auditions, that I don't speak the languages, I mean."

"Not the way you sing," Tony replied.

She flushed and couldn't meet his eyes. "Thanks," she said. It meant a lot, that he admired her voice, because he didn't like her. It meant he was honest about his opinion of her voice.

"Is that what you want to do with your life? Sing at the Met?" Tony asked.

"It's been the dream of my life," she replied. "I've given up everything for it. There's nothing in life I want more. Just that. To sing at the Met."

"Well, Mr. Tennyson thinks you have the talent, and I've always been your biggest cheering section," Stasia teased. It amused her, the way Tony was watching Odalie. He'd been antagonistic toward her from their first meeting. But after he heard her sing, his whole demeanor changed.

"You won't need a cheering section, with that voice," Tony said quietly. His dark eyes smoothed over her beautiful face.

Something in the way he looked at her made her flush. She cleared her throat and started talking to her brother about the ranch.

Tony smiled to himself. Amazing, he thought, that a woman of her age was so innocent. Because she was. He was experienced enough to know. He'd never liked clueless women before. This one was the exception. He was surprised to find that he found her very attractive, and not just because of her looks.

Stasia hadn't been forthcoming about Odalie because Tony changed the subject every time her name was mentioned. He'd have to change that around. He was interested in everything about the fledgling diva.

Tanner was delirious. The fever was raging and his wound was badly infected. He was aware of movement around him, of voices. But he was so sick that nothing much registered.

He felt the prick of a needle in his arm. The room he was in was white, very white. He frowned. Hadn't he been in a village?

He blinked. He looked up to a pair of dark eyes in a face stamped with authority. The man was dressed in a uniform. He looked military from the floor up, from combat boots to decorations on his chest.

"Tanner Everett, I presume." The clipped voice sounded vaguely amused. "I'm glad we were able to get you here in time. A few more hours and there would have been no hope of saving you."

Tanner tried to speak but his throat was too dry.

"You're in Barrera," the man said. "In Medina, in our finest hospital. I'm Winslow Grange. I'm in charge of the military here."

Tanner tried again. His voice sounded rusty. "Glad to meet you. And thanks."

Winslow just smiled. "You have some powerful friends," he mused.

"Not many," Tanner replied. "And my enemies outnumber them lately."

"Yes, I did some checking. Well, actually, my boss's son's father-in-law did some checking. You've almost been the victim of a rogue agent who allegedly killed two recruits in an attempt to bring you down and who was killed by another agent in the act of rescuing you." His eyes narrowed. "I gather that you have damaging information of some sort about someone very high up in politics in the States."

"I do," Tanner said. "The head of the agency in question was responsible for the slaughter of several civilians during an incursion in Iraq. I'm the only eyewitness left who's come forward. The other two fell from windows," he added meaningfully.

"Fell from windows. Mmm-hmm."

"I don't think anyone believed the official story, but the man has powerful friends."

"He has some very powerful enemies as well, and I'm about to turn them loose on him," Winslow told him. "I'm sure Enrique told you that one of those green recruits who was sacrificed was his cousin."

"He did," Tanner replied.

"He was also a cousin of the top man in our secret service," Winslow continued. "Who was extremely fond of him and is out for vengeance. Of course, we call it justice, not revenge."

"A rose by any other name," Tanner said, his voice even more hoarse now.

"Exactly," Winslow said. He glanced toward the door. "Are you up to a few visitors?" he added.

Tanner couldn't even manage a smile. "Probably not…"

"Oh, I think you'll change your mind when you see who they are," came the amused reply.

Tanner turned his head and there was his family. All of it. Cole, Heather, John and Odalie.

He fought tears. He was weak from his ordeal or he would

never have shown weakness in the first place. They gathered around him, the women first, hugging him as carefully as they could and wiping away tears.

"We thought you were dead," Heather sobbed. "A man came to see us with your bag that I gave you. It was covered in blood..." She had to stop because her voice was so choked.

"I'm a weed, Mom," he teased, hugging her. "The bag was supposed to throw everybody off the track and convince them that I was killed."

"It might have," Winslow Grange broke in, "except that Enrique knew about the operation and was in time to rescue you. The bag, of course, was sent to your family to make sure nobody went looking for you."

"The man who brought it was very kind," Heather said.

"And very helpful," John added, patting his brother on the shoulder and smiling. "He advised us—after he made sure his phone was shut off."

"Wise man," Winslow said, nodding. "I know who he is, and where he is. He'll be needing rescue pretty soon. There are plans to help him fall out of a window..."

"How do you know so much?" Odalie asked while she carefully hugged her brother.

Winslow chuckled. "My best friend is the father-in-law of President Machado's eldest son." He paused and pursed his lips. "He's head of the CIA."

"Nice connections," Tanner said weakly.

"Very." Winslow sobered. "One of our planes is going to transport you back to the States," he said. "You'll need to be low-key and you'll need some formidable protection until we can put together enough evidence to hang your former boss out to dry."

"When he finds out that his man missed, he'll be in his office in DC looking for ways to save himself," Tanner said.

His face hardened. "He'll need to save himself from me when I can get on my feet."

"Now, now," Winslow said. "We didn't save you so that you can put your own head back in a noose."

"Exactly." Cole moved closer to the bed and shook his son's hand. "I've made a lot of bad mistakes," he added quietly, his pale eyes searching his son's face. "I hope I can make up for them."

"You're just human, Dad," Tanner replied. "And most of the bad mistakes were mine. I was a damned fool. I destroyed Stasia's life."

"No, you didn't." The voice came from the doorway. Tanner looked, and there she was.

"You came with them?" he asked huskily, his eyes absolutely eating her.

Behind them, John was grinding his teeth. Stasia's feelings were on display, tears of joy running down her pale cheeks as she slid her hand into Tanner's.

"Yes," Stasia said, forcing a smile. "You scared us all to death."

He searched her eyes, his face giving nothing away. "I had no idea I was walking into a trap," he said. "I had two green recruits." He winced. "They were slaughtered and left in the jungle. I'd managed to crawl away into the jungle and hide while the rogue agent leading the attack was sending his drug trafficking friends away. I was lucky that the python keeping me company had fed recently and wasn't interested in trying to eat me." He managed a chuckle, but he wasn't letting go of Stasia's hand.

She wiped at her wet eyes with the other one. "They'll be after him, won't they?" Stasia asked Winslow, her dark eyes full of worry.

"Yes," Winslow replied, pulling no punches. "And with

everything they've got. From what you've told me, your ex-boss," he added to Tanner, "stands to go to federal prison for the rest of his life."

"Which makes him desperate," Tanner agreed. "I know where there's a safe house," he began.

"Forget it," Winslow replied. "He'll know where it is."

"You're coming home with us," Cole said quietly. "I have three men on the payroll who originally came from federal agencies. They were high-paid mercs, from Jacobsville. King Brannt got in touch with Eb Scott for me."

"He was at our wedding," Tanner reminded Stasia. "I didn't introduce him."

"I wouldn't have expected you to," Stasia said. "It was more or less a shotgun wedding, thanks to my overprotective dad."

"He had no idea that you'd grow up to be a famous artist," Tanner replied and managed a smile for her.

She shrugged. "Not so famous. But I love the work I do as a restorer."

"I like your friend Tony," Tanner told her.

"Speaking of whom," Cole interrupted, "he's loaned us a couple of big guys." He chuckled. "They're mostly pretending to be supervisors. Guys had never seen a horse in their lives. But I was grateful for the muscle. We can't have too much, under the circumstances."

"The more the merrier," Winslow agreed. "You're safe here, but it's going to be a different story when you go home."

"I've had years of practice taking care of myself," Tanner replied.

"And you're damned good at it," Winslow told him. "But in your present condition, you're not up to speed."

"He'll be fine," Cole assured the military man with a smile. "We've got the ranch wired for bear."

"And we can all shoot guns," Heather said, smiling at her

son. "Even Odalie," she added, and Odalie grinned. She'd been in skeet shooting competitions not so many years ago.

"Some of us can," Cole mused, and gave his wife a long, meaningful look.

Heather flushed. "It was an old truck and it wouldn't crank half the time anyway!" she protested.

Winslow's eyebrows were raised in a silent question.

Cole chuckled. "When we were first married, I thought she needed to learn to shoot a gun. So I gave her a .410 and pointed her toward the target. She turned to ask me a question and the gun went off. Bullet hit the engine block of an old pickup truck I used to drive." He shook his head. "I decided she was safer in front of a piano than behind a gun."

"You just didn't want the competition," Heather said with a grin at her husband.

He pulled her close with a long sigh. "Trucks can be fixed. People, not so much."

"Riley was going to quit anyway," Heather reminded Cole, her cheek resting on his broad chest.

"Well, being in the truck when the gun went off pretty much made the decision for him." He looked over at Winslow with an amused smile. "None of us liked the guy, but I didn't have a concrete reason to fire him."

"He tried to have me prosecuted for attempted murder, however," Heather recalled.

"Yes, but we have great attorneys."

She nodded. "We do, indeed." She looked past Cole to her eldest child. "Tanner was a much better shot than I'll ever be."

"Good thing, too, considering my line of work," Tanner told her with a warm smile.

"Yes, but mercenary work is more dangerous than most kinds," Cole replied.

"That was a sideline, like security jobs," Tanner said. He

studied his family, and Stasia. "I work for the government," he added quietly. "For a letter agency that's relatively unknown."

Cole frowned. "You never said."

Tanner gave him a long-suffering look. "I didn't exactly have a chance to."

Cole grimaced. "I know. My fault."

Tanner sighed. "We're all only human," he said quietly. "Even you, Dad."

Cole shrugged. "Point taken."

"Are you coming home with us?" Tanner asked Stasia.

"My job," she began.

Tanner's hand curled around hers. "You're a soft target, honey."

"A what?" she asked, stammering a little because the feel of Tanner's big, warm hand around hers was making her weak.

Tanner knew it and had to keep a poker face. He was hoping for second chances. Hoping hard. "A soft target," he repeated. "If my ex-boss can't get to me, he'll go for anybody connected to me. Especially people I care about."

"Oh." She didn't know what else to say.

"Which means that you'll be safer at Big Spur than in New York," Cole added. He smiled warmly at Stasia. "It's a big house," he reminded her. "Plenty of room."

Tanner's fingers were caressing hers. "I'll worry if you try to go back to work. A lot," he emphasized. "I've been shot," he added, contriving to look as weak as possible. "Somebody will have to look after me."

"You can afford a private nurse," she began.

"I don't want a private nurse," he returned. "Bullet wounds really hurt," he said huskily.

She ground her teeth. "Tanner…!"

"A poor wounded man, in terrible pain, people trying to off him," he continued.

"You're not poor," she retorted.

"I'm wounded," he persisted. "In terrible pain. People are trying to kill me." He looked up at her pointedly.

"Oh, all right," she said, exasperated.

He smiled and brought her fingers to his lips. "That's my girl."

Fever shot through her at the touch of his mouth on her skin. It had been years since he'd touched her. Memories came flooding back of their one night together, a feast of erotic sensation that she'd spent years trying to forget.

Tanner read all that in her face. He felt joy like a balloon swelling inside him. She still cared. It was impossible for her to hide it. At least he hadn't managed to kill all her feelings for him. It would be a long recovery. Proximity would be his greatest ally.

John drew in a breath. It was obvious that his brother and the love of his life still had some residual interest in each other. But he wasn't about to give up hope. There was a chance, even if it was a small one, that Stasia might only be feeling sorry for her ex-husband.

"I'll get back to work. The doctor is going to release you in an hour," Winslow said, smiling. "There's plenty of room in the plane, so you can all go together."

"Thanks, General Grange," Cole said, extending a hand. "We owe you."

Grange shook the hand. "Your son has friends he didn't know about," was all he had to say. "And he's lucky that he did."

"Thank Enrique Boas and President Machado for me," Tanner told Winslow. "And I'll never forget what you've done."

"I had a lot of help," Winslow said. "But you're welcome." The smile faded. "Don't let your guard down. If any tidbits of information come my way, I'll be in touch."

"Thank you," Heather told Winslow, reaching up to kiss his cheek. "If you didn't already have parents, I'd adopt you," she teased.

"I'd be proud," he replied, smiling. "You're pretty famous, Mrs. Everett."

She shrugged and smiled back. "I've been fortunate." She looked at her husband with love that radiated like a beacon. "In my marriage and my career."

Cole winked at her. "That works both ways."

"Thanks again," Tanner said, shaking Winslow's hand. "If I can ever do anything for you, I will."

"I'll keep that in mind. Take care."

Tanner was still holding Stasia's hand. He looked up into her soft eyes and sighed. "That I will," he said huskily.

Two days later, lying in bed in his old room at the Everett ranch house, Tanner was eating a bowl of chicken noodle soup that Stasia had made for him. She was sitting in the chair beside his bed, just watching him.

"John's crazy about you, you know," he said between bites.

"I know." She made a face. "He's such a good person. But I don't want to get mixed up with anybody."

He looked at her over his soup bowl. "Even me?" he asked softly.

She flushed and lowered her eyes.

"We got off to a bad start," he told her as he finished the soup and put the bowl and spoon on the bedside table. "I was spoiled and aimless at that point in my life. I didn't know what I wanted. I made a mess of both our lives, not to mention the grief I caused my family."

"You paid a higher price for it than we did."

"No. I didn't." He leaned back against the pillows and looked at her quietly. "You paid the price." He drew in a breath, shifted and grimaced as the stitches pulled. "Do you ever think about the baby?" he added softly. "Whether it would have favored you or me? If it would have been a boy or a girl?"

It was a painful question. Her face mirrored her inner turmoil. "I think about it all the time," she said. "It was the worst day of my life, when I lost it."

He averted his gaze. It all came back, Julienne's taunting, her very presence in the home that should have been Stasia's, the accident, the anger in Cole's and John's eyes, the banishment. "If I live to be a hundred, I'll never forgive myself for bringing Julienne to the house with me."

"You loved her."

"The hell I did," he replied curtly. "She was good in bed. That was all she had going for her. She was cruel and arrogant and she looked down on everybody."

"She lasted a long time."

"Because she wasn't important to me," he said surprisingly. "I didn't want ties. That's why I brought her home with me that day."

She blinked. "Excuse me?"

"I wanted you," he said softly. "More than anything. But you meant white picket fences and children. Ties."

She was frowning. "I don't understand."

"Julienne was my shield," he said simply. He drew in a breath. He hadn't wanted to tell her the truth, but he'd caused her so much pain already, he thought she was entitled to it. "Stasia, if I hadn't brought her with me," he said in a gentle, husky tone, "I'd never have been able to leave you."

THIRTEEN

S tasia just stared at him blankly. She could hardly believe what she was hearing.

"But," she faltered, "you didn't want me. You hated the whole idea of getting married. You went away with Julienne…"

"I was confused," he replied, his gaze sliding over her like caressing hands. "I knew how you felt about me. I didn't want any part of it, or so I told myself. After the wedding, I planned to leave and go back to Julienne. But I dragged my feet."

She leaned forward, fascinated.

He drew in a long breath. "But it didn't go the way I planned," he continued. He searched her face quietly. "I'd wanted you for a long time. I tried to deny it. I knew I had nothing to offer you at that point in my life, and I was resentful at the will that forced us to marry. But I honestly couldn't resist you." His teeth clenched and he averted his face as he relived the beautiful passion of that long night. "I never thought I could succumb to a woman that completely, so that I was obsessed with her. But I did, that night." He registered the shock in her eyes. "The next morning I was ashamed of what I'd done and desperate to get away from you." He laughed shortly. "I didn't realize how hungry I was for you until I was back with Julienne and I couldn't bring myself to even touch her."

Stasia caught her breath. That was something she hadn't known.

"Surprised?" he asked with a faint smile. "So was I. That was why I brought Julienne with me when I came home. I thought just the sight of her would set you off and you'd leave." He groaned softly. "But I provoked a tragedy." He shook his head. "I never meant you to be hurt," he said. "I fed my father and John a pack of lies about not wanting the baby after Minnie spilled the beans, but I didn't mean it, I swear I didn't! Oh, God, when they told me what happened to you; nothing ever hurt so much! I knew that nobody would speak to me if I called to find out how you were. I called your attorney. He was kind enough to check and tell me that you were going to be all right."

"I didn't know that you'd called."

"I'm not that coldhearted," he replied. "Not even after all the years I've spent doing covert ops."

"None of us knew that you were working for the government," she said, leaning forward. "We thought you were a mercenary."

"That was my cover. I'd been doing jobs for the government for many years, under the man who's now trying to kill me. He always did love bucking the rules, but the ones he broke in Iraq will see him hanged," he added coldly. "He massacred civilians. And he's not going to get away with it. I held off starting anything because I was afraid for all of you, making you targets. But the fat's in the fire now and it doesn't matter anymore."

"If he heads that agency you work for, he has political power," she worried. "He could send legitimate agents to arrest you."

"He'd have to go through my dad," he mused. "That's something even I wouldn't want to try."

She smiled. "I know. I like your dad."

"He and Mom have been like your family since your father died," he said. "I'm sorry that I made things so hard for you, honey," he added softly, loving the way she flushed when he used the endearment. "If I could go back and change things, I would."

"Life goes on," she said simply. "When I was little, my mother always said that it's the bad experiences that really shape us as people. It's how we react to things, not the things themselves, that turn us into the people we become."

His eye narrowed. "You never spoke of your mother."

"It was too painful. I found her, you know."

He nodded. "We found her," he added. "And I held you while you cried," he reminded her.

She smiled sadly. "You were always there, during the worst times of my life."

"Except when you lost the baby," he said heavily. "And that's the one time I should have been there. God, what a mess I made of things! I'm so damned sorry, Stasia!"

She bit her lower lip. It was painful, that memory. "Your mother was wonderful to me. She told me that she'd almost lost you. She spent a lot of time in bed, and you had some pretty bad illnesses when you were very small."

"I was always sick," he said. "Amazing, that I grew up to be so healthy."

Heather stuck her head around the door. "Dessert?" she asked.

He asked, "What kind?"

"German chocolate cake," she replied softly.

"My very favorite."

Heather laughed. "I remembered. Stasia?"

She smiled but shook her head. "Thanks, but I don't really like sweets."

"There are dill pickles in the fridge," Heather teased.

"I love dill pickles!" Stasia enthused.

"I remembered that, too." She took the bowl and spoon. "I'll be back with cake," she promised.

"If you come back without it, I'll lock the door," Tanner promised.

Heather laughed as she left.

Stasia was grinning, too.

"I don't know anything about your life after I left," Tanner said. "How did you end up doing restoration work?"

It was a subject that she warmed to. These were good memories. Tony had found a place for her at a famous art school in New York, and even paid for her tuition. He'd found her a nice apartment and paid for it despite her objections. When she graduated, he'd gotten her hired to work at the art gallery and museum he owned.

"He's like a second father," she explained to Tanner. "He's always been there for me. I honestly don't know what I'd have done without him. Dad had bankrupted the ranch and I didn't even know."

"I should have found a kinder way to break it to you," he said with remorse.

"There is no kind way to do that," she replied. "I like my bad news straight up," she added. "No sugarcoating."

"That's the way I am as well," he replied.

She studied him hungrily. "I'm so glad you weren't killed! You need to send somebody with a bat to talk to your ex-boss," she added with some heat in her tone.

"He'll be taken care of," he assured her.

"I liked General Grange," she remarked.

"So did I. He has some powerful connections."

"So do we, apparently." She laughed. "General Grange mentioned that he'd had two requests for help for you, from two really strange sources. One would be Tony, I imagine," she said.

"The other was Marcus Carrera, who's been a friend of mine for several years," he told her with an amused smile. He studied her with quiet affection. "Your boss has some powerful connections of his own."

"Yes, he does. He always paints himself as a bad man, but he's really not. I mean, he ran with gangs and did some frightful things, even before he was a crime boss. But he's got a good heart," she added doggedly.

He stared at her, admiring the beauty that he'd overlooked for so many years. It delighted him that Stasia had chosen to take leave from her job to take care of him. Not that his mother wasn't helping. Odalie had gone back to New York, after Tony's promise to look after her while she continued her studies and prepared for her Metropolitan Opera audition.

"I think my sister has a case on your boss," Tanner said.

"I think so, too. And Tony's very much interested in her since he heard her sing. He loves opera."

"He's still a gang boss, you know," he replied with a sigh. "That's not the best recommendation for her future."

"Odalie's tough, though," she told him. "Not in a mean way, or an overbearing way, but she stands up to people."

He laughed. "She was a scrapper by the time she got to high school. But when she was in grammar school, John and

I were constantly fighting her battles for her. She was a beautiful child." His voice trailed away, and Stasia knew he was thinking about the child she'd lost.

Her eyes slid over him covetously. After all the years, all the pain, there had been nobody else in her heart. She'd loved Tanner for most of her life. She wondered if she'd ever be able to be just friends. Because he wasn't looking toward her for a partner, and she knew it. His taste ran to experienced women. That tag would never fit Stasia. In her midtwenties, she'd only ever been intimate with one man—her ex-husband.

"What are you thinking?" he asked quietly.

She flushed.

He laughed, very softly.

His face was oddly flushed, and she didn't think it was the repartee between them. She got up, frowning.

"What is it?" he asked.

She put her hand on his forehead and frowned. "Tanner, you're burning up!" She pulled the sheet aside and unbuttoned his pajama jacket, trying not to remember how it had felt to be held against that broad, hair-roughened chest in the dark.

Sure enough, the wound was red and ugly-looking, and there was something resembling pus between the stitches.

"I'm calling the doctor right now," she said, and left the room.

She found Heather in the kitchen, putting cake on a plate.

Heather took one look at her face and knew something was wrong. "What is it?"

"Who's your doctor?" Stasia asked urgently. "Tanner's wound is infected."

"Oh, dear God," Heather burst out.

"It's okay," Stasia said, hugging her. "Honest. He just needs a good antibiotic. He's not dying."

Heather hugged her back and then stood apart. "Sorry. I worry."

"Of course you do," Stasia said gently. "The doctor?"

"Sorry. I'll get the number for you. His name is Gunther Markham," she said. "He's just started in the practice. Our doctor retired."

She looked in the telephone directory and wrote the number on a pad by the phone. "That's it right there."

"Thanks."

Stasia phoned the office, explained the problem and arranged a televisit. Tanner was in no condition to be sitting in a doctor's waiting room for God knew how long.

He was just finishing the last bite of cake while Heather hovered when Stasia got back to his bedroom.

"That was delicious, Mom," he said with a weak smile.

Stasia walked in. "I got you a televisit," she told him. "In…" She looked at the watch she wore, one he'd given her for Christmas years ago. It was very expensive—in fact she'd protested at the time, to no avail—and it still worked like a charm. "In half an hour," she finished. "He's going to work you in."

"That watch," Tanner remarked as he studied it.

"It's one you gave me for Christmas one year," she explained.

He stared at her. "And you still wear it."

"Well, these never go out of style," she said defensively.

But he knew why she wore it. And she knew that he knew; it was in that faint, arrogant smile that he sent her way.

She didn't take him up on it, because Heather was sitting by the bed.

"I'm all right," Tanner assured his mother. "I've had wounds before. Plenty of them. This is nothing more than an inconvenience," he added softly.

Heather took a long breath. "I'm going to die one day of worry about all of you," she accused.

He chuckled. "No, you aren't. You're the strongest one of us."

She made a face at him.

"He's right. The doctor will send antibiotics to the pharmacy and he'll be fine," Stasia told his mother.

"How did it get infected, though?" Heather worried.

"We were in a jungle," he pointed out. "And we had to travel through it to the airport. It doesn't take much to cause infection. In fact, Grange worried about that before we got on the plane."

"Anybody who's been in battles in the jungle knows about the risk of infection," Stasia said softly. "Apparently even a scratch can kill you if it isn't treated."

"Exactly. And how did you know that?" he asked Stasia.

"I read books about mercenaries and jungle combat," she said, surprising him.

His eyebrows went up.

"Well, not about normal mercenaries…"

Now Tanner was intrigued. "Well?" he prompted.

"I love the *Alien vs. Predator* movies and books," she confessed. "I've got them all, even the comic books." She flushed. She hadn't shared that hobby with anyone.

Tanner burst out laughing.

Stasia was puzzled.

Heather glanced at her and grinned. "He has them all, too, boxed up in his closet," she said. "He's been crazy about them for years."

Stasia's eyes softened. Amazing, she thought, how little

she actually knew about the man to whom she'd been briefly married.

"There's a new series, by Tim Lebbon," he said.

She nodded. "*The Rage War.* A three-book trilogy, where the predators and the humans unite to fight a bunch of lunatic humans bent on conquest. It's my very favorite. I wish they'd make a movie about those!"

"So do I," he said.

"But my favorite older books are the ones by Steve Perry, about Machiko Noguchi…"

"A little Japanese woman who lived and hunted with the predators," he interrupted, and laughed at her expression. "I know. She's terrific. That would make a hell of a movie."

"It would. I've hoped for years that they'd do one, but it never happens. They use elements of her story, but it's always a different heroine than the one in the books and comics."

He nodded. He shook his head. "Amazing, that we have that in common and never knew it."

"Yes, it is."

"The predators." Heather shook her own head. "I like murder mysteries."

"Different strokes for different folks, as you used to say, Mom," he said.

His cell phone rang. He picked it up. "It's the doctor's office," he explained, and answered it. It was the nurse, going over his meds and symptoms. She sent him a link to the video chat. A few minutes later, the doctor came on.

Stasia had taken a photo of the wound, which Tanner had shared with the nurse. The doctor had seen it. He asked a few questions, assured Tanner that he'd be fine, and prescribed a powerful antibiotic.

"If you need anything, or your wound doesn't start to heal, you get back to me, okay?" the doctor asked pleasantly.

"Will do. Thanks."

"All in a day's work," the doctor replied with a smile, and hung up.

"I'll send somebody to the pharmacy the minute it's ready," Heather said. "I'll see which one of the boys is around the house," she added, talking to herself.

"I feel better now," Stasia said. "That wound looks really bad."

"It will heal. It just needs some antibiotics." He smiled at her. "I've got plenty of scars from other wounds."

A reminder of the dangerous work he did. She withdrew into herself. She knew that he'd never be able to settle for life on a Texas ranch. It was what he was insinuating, with the reference to other wounds.

He watched her go away mentally while she sat by his bed. He knew from her expression that she was unsettled, and he could guess why. He considered how a woman might feel if she was married to a man in some dangerous profession, forced to sit at home and worry and wait, hoping he'd come home alive. It was a staggering thought, one he'd never entertained before.

He frowned.

She got up, smiling vacantly. "I'll leave you alone for a little while. I need to check on some things at work," she added.

Now he was the one who went away without leaving. It was a reminder that she didn't live on a Texas ranch anymore either. She had a profession and a good job in New York that she wouldn't easily give up. It was disturbing to him to think about that.

Their jobs were going to be a major obstacle if he thought about anything permanent. He frowned. Where had that thought come from? He wasn't seriously considering a future with her, or was he?

He hadn't been intimate with a woman for a long time. He wasn't really interested in women. His job was dangerous, and subject to huge adrenaline rushes. It was probably why he wasn't interested. On the other hand, when he looked at Stasia, his blood ran hot through his veins. Amazing, that after all the years in between, she still made him hungrier than he'd ever been in his life. That was surprising. He had some serious thinking to do.

Stasia called New York to check on the status of her latest project at work. They were managing well without her, came the gentle reply, and how was her ex-husband? Apparently Tony had made them aware of why she was absent.

Next, she called Tony.

"How is he?" was his first question.

"His wound's infected," she said. "We had to get the doctor today."

"The trip to the airport through the jungle, I imagine," Tony replied with a smile in his voice. "I had a bodyguard not so long ago who'd been with a group in South America. He almost lost a leg because of an insect bite that went septic."

"We learn something new every day," she laughed. "How are you?"

It was a loaded question. He drew in a breath. "Your friend has some very odd ideas about me," he commented, keeping the emotion out of his tone.

"What sort of odd ideas?" she wondered aloud.

"I think she's watched too many reruns of *The Godfather* trilogy," he muttered. "She keeps asking me about how to dispose of bodies."

Stasia laughed. "Maybe she's got one that she needs to get rid of."

"More like, she's got me in mind," he grumbled.

"So you're still fighting."

"Look, it's not me starting the fights," Tony said defensively. "She starts sprouting horns the minute I open my mouth!"

"You scare her," Stasia said simply.

"You got that backward," he huffed. "She scares me! I just defend myself."

Stasia knew better, but she didn't push it. "How's it going, with the Met audition?"

"Aw, she's got herself convinced that she'll faint or fall into the orchestra pit when she walks on the stage," he muttered. "No self-confidence."

"That doesn't sound like the Odalie I know," Stasia replied.

"She's just a walking bundle of nerves," he repeated. "If she doesn't straighten up and get her head on straight, she'll never make it to the audition, much less through it."

"You might work on instilling a little self-confidence in her," she suggested.

"I told you, she starts fights!"

"Don't take the bait," she advised.

"What?"

"Don't let her provoke you. Change the subject."

"How?"

"You know how to change the subject," she teased. "You say, 'Bang! Speaking of guns…'"

"Hey, now that's not funny. She's got this thing about guns, too. She shudders every time Big Ben's piece shows in his shoulder holster."

"It is funny, when you know the truth," Stasia told him calmly. "She's a Triple A shooter."

There was a pause. "Excuse me?"

"She's a Triple A shooter. Skeet. She used to win district and even state competitions. She was in line to go to the World Skeet Shooting Competition in San Antonio, Texas, but she got sick and missed her chance." She paused. "She's not afraid of guns, Tony. In fact, she can shoot anything from a .12 gauge to a .45 double-action Ruger Vaquero."

"Well, I'll be damned," he said softly.

"Now you know," she replied. She grimaced. She probably shouldn't have told him that, but it might make things a little easier for the pair of them. They were attracted to each other, but Tony was fighting it as hard as Odalie was.

"Why?" he asked.

"Distraction."

"Distraction?"

"I'll let you work on figuring that out. I have to go and see about Tanner." She hesitated. "There's a little problem here."

"Which is?" He was suddenly all business.

"Really can't talk about it," she said, worried about the line being tapped. Considering who Tanner's adversary was, it was a real concern.

"Just a sec."

She heard him calling something to Big Ben. He came back on the line. "Ten to one your ex-husband's got a burner phone."

"A what?"

"Go ask him. I'll wait."

She went back into the bedroom with her cell phone in one hand. Tanner was more flushed than ever.

"Did your mother find somebody to pick up the prescription?" she asked.

"Don't know," he said on a breath. "She hasn't come back yet."

"Tony wants to know if you have a burner phone," she said, frowning, because the terminology was new to her.

He smiled. "Look in my top drawer, there." His head indicated the big Mediterranean dresser against the wall opposite the bed.

She opened it. There were four phones in it. She glanced at him.

"They're called burner phones because they're throwaways. The line can't be traced to an address," he explained. "Drug lords use them. So do people in other professions."

Of which his was obviously one. She took one out and handed it to him.

"Give Tony this number," he said, and called it out to her.

She gave it to Tony.

"Hang up your phone. I'll call him right back," Tony said and hung up.

The throwaway phone rang. Tanner answered it.

"Okay, tell me what's going on," Tony told him.

Tanner glanced at Stasia. "He wants to know what's going on," he said. She just nodded.

He sighed. "My ex-boss was responsible for a massacre of civilians in Iraq during a black ops incursion," he told Tony. "I'm on his hit list. He sacrificed two green agents to get to me in South America. I got lucky or I'd be dead. I understand that I have you and Marcus Carrera to thank for that," he added with a smile in his voice.

"All in a day's work," Tony said. "I like fair play. Who is this guy?"

"Name's Phillip James," he said quietly. "I worked for him undercover for several years. He seemed to be an honest, dedicated agent when he started out. Then he got money-hungry and power-hungry and he discovered drugs. Then he pulled some shady strings and got promoted to head of the agency."

"Yeah. That happens. The money is real good and they like the power that goes with it. He wouldn't be the first nice guy who succumbed. He's with your agency?" he added and named it.

"He is." Tanner shifted in the bed. He was feeling pretty sick. "He's dangerous."

"So am I," Tony said very softly. "I'll make a couple of phone calls. Any witnesses to this massacre besides you?"

"Half a village," Tanner told him on a heavy sigh, "but most of them are dead. The rest are too intimidated to talk."

"Name of the village?"

He told him. He laughed. "Don't tell me you've got somebody over there?"

"I've got somebody everywhere," Tony said, and it wasn't a brag. "Any evidence besides eyewitnesses?"

"Hell, yes," Tanner replied. "I've got a recording that was made by a colleague who died accidentally on purpose. It's in a safe place."

"When did this happen?"

"Last year," Tanner told him. "I wanted to expose him, but he made some threats against my family. I held back. But now, he'll be out for blood when he discovers that I'm not dead, and he'll do his best to make me that way. So I've got no reason to hold back. I want to nail him to the wall."

"I'll help," Tony replied. "Watch your back in the meantime, and I mean watch it. Get everybody close to where you are and arm them. A cornered snake will strike."

"I heard that," Tanner said. "Thanks."

"No problem." Tony hung up.

Stasia went close to the bed, bent and put a hand on his forehead. She grimaced. "Tanner, you're burning up."

"I noticed." He tossed the phone aside and drew her face down to his. "Pay no attention," he whispered. "It's just the fever, making me delirious. I have no idea...what I'm doing..."

He drew her face to his and his lips moved on her soft

mouth in a slow, tender exploration that made her catch her breath. It had been so long. Forever!

His long fingers spread against her cheek as he tilted her head and his mouth became insistent. But after a minute he groaned and lay back against the pillows, grimacing. "Damn!" he whispered, and his hand went to the pajama top above the wound.

She was disconcerted, but her nursing instincts came back all at once. "I'm going to find your mother," she said.

"Send Craig Danvers in here, will you?" he asked, naming one of the cowboys who was formerly a federal agent. "Tell him to bring his gun."

"Tanner!" she exclaimed, horrified.

"It's just a precaution," he said gently. He smiled. "Tony's idea."

She relaxed, just a little. "Okay. I'll track him down."

He smiled at her, still tingling from the hungry contact with her mouth.

She left him, trying not to show how affected she was. She found Heather just coming in the back door.

"I can't find anybody," she moaned. "They're all helping round up the yearlings to ship to their markets!"

"Do you have phone numbers?" Stasia asked.

Heather rolled her eyes. "Of course. Duh!"

She pulled out her cell phone. "I'll see who's available…"

"Can you find Craig Danvers?" Stasia asked. "Tanner wants to talk to him."

"Yes. Just a sec." She punched in numbers. It took four rings before a deep voice came on the line. "Hi, Craig? Tanner wants to see you right now. Yes." She paused. "He's not doing well. The wound's infected. I can't find anybody to send to town to get his meds. I'd go, but I need to be here when Cole gets back. He's running an errand for me." She nodded, as if he could see her. "Yes, that's fine. Thanks. I'll go back out and see if one of the boys has come in for lunch. Sure. Thanks!"

She hung up. "He's coming right back. Stasia, will you step out back and see…?"

"Of course I will."

She went out the back door and toward the bunkhouse just as a man in slacks and a pullover T-shirt came around the house.

"Oh, hi," Stasia called to him. "Could I get you to run into Branntville to the City Pharmacy and pick up a prescription for Tanner? It's on Cole's credit card, all you have to do is pick it up. I've already called to tell them we're sending someone."

"My pleasure," he replied with a smile. "I'll go right now." He turned and went back the way he'd come.

Stasia went back inside, a little puzzled by the cowboy's apparel. He didn't look like a working cowboy. But then, when they had a day off, most of them wore casual clothes. It was just that this man wasn't wearing boots or a hat, and that was odd, on this ranch. But she put it out of her mind. She was getting paranoid, and she had a good excuse for it. Besides, she didn't know most of Cole's cowboys. It had been a long time since she'd lived on the ranch after her miscarriage.

She went back into the house. "I found one of the men. He's going right to the pharmacy."

"Oh, thank goodness," Heather said. She grimaced. "I'm not much help. I'm sorry."

Stasia hugged her. "He's very tough," she pointed out. "And he's a survivor."

"He's missing an eye," Heather said under her breath, her blue eyes meeting Stasia's dark ones.

"Nobody's lucky all the time," Stasia said, reassuring her. "But he's still alive, you know."

Heather drew in a long breath. "Yes. He's still alive."

Stasia smiled. Heather smiled back.

The cowboy was back in less than half an hour with a prescription bag. He handed it to Stasia, who'd heard him drive up.

Not a vehicle she'd seen before, she thought as she went to meet him. A sedan, not a truck. But maybe he used a ranch truck when he worked. She smiled as he gave her the bag.

"Thanks very much," she told him.

"No sweat. Hope he gets better soon." He smiled and walked back to his car.

Stasia went into the bedroom with the prescription bag and pulled out not one, but two prescriptions.

She frowned. The antibiotic was straightforward. But there was a jar of cream as well. It had a prescription label that looked unlike the label on the bottle.

She noticed that there was a slight film on one side of the jar, as if it had already been opened. There would have been no reason for someone to do that.

"What's wrong?" Tanner asked, because she looked worried.

"Did the doctor mention sending some cream for the wound?" she asked.

"No."

She took out her phone, realized she didn't have the doctor's number and went to get it from Heather again, because she hadn't written it down.

"What's wrong?" Heather asked.

"I'm paranoid, that's all," Stasia said, but she was already punching in numbers. "Yes, this is Stasia Everett," she said, using her married name because she'd never had it changed back after the divorce. "I'm calling about a prescription that Dr. Markham sent to the pharmacy for Tanner Everett? Did he send a cream along with an antibiotic? Yes, I'll wait."

She glanced at Heather, who was biting her lower lip.

The doctor came on the line. "No," he said without preamble, "I didn't prescribe a cream. It's not necessary. The wound will heal better without a covering. Just give the antibiotic."

"Thank you. I will."

She hung up, without telling the doctor her reason for the question. She looked at Heather and then at the jar of cream.

"Could you call the sheriff's department and ask them to send their investigator out here right away?" Stasia asked quietly.

Heather let out a breath. "You think something's wrong," she said.

Stasia nodded. "The man I sent to the pharmacy was in street clothes driving a sedan. I don't think he works here. And this," she said, nodding toward the smear on the outside of the jar, "wasn't prescribed by the doctor. I'd bet real money that it's something to make the wound worse."

"I'll call right now," Heather said.

Stasia went back into the bedroom. Tanner had taken the first of the antibiotic capsules. He stared at her. "Don't tell me the doctor never prescribed a cream."

"Exactly."

He smiled tenderly. "Nice instincts," he said.

She shrugged. "I thought maybe I was just being paranoid. But it seemed the thing to do, to ask the doctor if he'd actually prescribed a cream. And he hadn't."

"Well, that pretty much answers the question about whether or not my ex-boss knows I'm still alive," he said heavily. "Too many people knew that I was in the hospital in Manaus. Any half-decent agent could have pumped a worker for information in an innocent way." He lay back against the pillows. "I expected maybe a sniper or an explosive package. I didn't expect a lethal prescription."

"Neither did I." She looked worried.

"Hey," he said gently. "I've survived any number of ambushes. Case in point," he added, indicating the eye patch.

"Yes, you're tougher than folded metal," she said with a faint smile. "But nobody's invulnerable."

"I'm working on that," he assured her.

She pulled in a long breath, her eyes on the jar.

"You might put that on the dresser," he advised. "And don't touch any of what's inside it. I have a very bad feeling about what it might be."

She put it down on the dresser very carefully, and only after pulling a tissue from a box to set the jar on.

"Now go wash your hands," he said. "No way am I risking you," he added softly.

She turned away quickly, so that he wouldn't see the blush that flamed on her cheeks. And he didn't let on that he'd seen it anyway.

FOURTEEN

The sheriff's investigator, Paul Simmons, was from Los Angeles originally. He was small and dark, wore glasses, and seemed very good at his job.

He had an evidence bag for the jar of cream. He spent several minutes questioning Heather and Tanner and Stasia.

Stasia was able to give him a good description of the man and the sedan he drove.

"Mr. Everett," he addressed Tanner, "does anyone you know have a reason to want to cause you harm?"

"I'm a federal agent," Tanner replied quietly. "Quite a number of people have reason to want me dead. Most recently a man who caused many deaths in a country overseas during a classified action," he added.

The investigator cocked his head. "And you can't go into specifics."

"Not unless your security clearance is the equal of my own," Tanner returned with a faint smile.

"Surprisingly, it probably is," the man replied. "I was military intelligence in the Middle East during Desert Storm."

Tanner laughed. "Small world."

Simmons smiled. "Yes, it is. I won't press you for details, but I want to get this to the state crime lab and have it analyzed," he replied. "I'm fairly certain of the outcome."

"So am I," Tanner replied. He shook his head. "I'll never understand how honest people can become so corrupt."

"Money and power," the other man said sadly. "Even the best of people can be tempted."

"That is unfortunately true," Tanner agreed.

"I'll get this to the proper people," the investigator said. "Meanwhile, I'd suggest some armed protection…"

"Armed protection, reporting for duty," Craig Danvers said as he came in the door, a pistol at his hip.

Tanner smiled. "This is Madman Craig Danvers," he introduced the tall, blond man to his two companions. "I won't tell you why he got the nickname, and neither will he. Suffice it to say that it's well-deserved."

"Thanks very much for making me sound like a psychopath," Craig told his friend with a sardonic smile.

"It's not that sort of nickname," Tanner amended. "He can shoot straight and he isn't afraid of anything on earth, except…"

Craig held up a hand. "And we won't mention that, now will we? Or I might slip up and mention your own nickname."

Tanner just grinned. "Fair enough. Have a seat."

"What's up?" Craig asked, all business.

"Poison cream for my wound," Tanner said simply. "But the would-be assassin didn't count on my personal guardian angel," he added with a warm smile at Stasia.

"I don't trust people," she said defensively.

"Wise precaution," Craig said. "That's how I stay alive on the highway when I'm driving," he added, crossing his legs after he sat down in the chair beside Tanner's bed. "I assume that every other driver on the road is hell-bent on killing me. Works like a charm."

They all laughed.

"Well, I'll get this to the crime lab," Simmons said, indicating the evidence bag. "I'll let you know what we find. Watch your back."

"I always do," Tanner said.

"How did you think of poison?" Craig asked Stasia.

"The label on the jar wasn't quite right, and there was a smear of cream on the jar, just at the lid. I didn't think any pharmacist would let something that sloppy out of his sight."

"Exactly," Tanner replied.

"Besides, the so-called cowboy was wearing street clothes without boots or a hat." She sighed. "This is Texas, you know. Boots and cowboy hats are sort of the state uniform for ranch workers." She grinned.

She was staring pointedly at Craig, who was wearing expensive leather boots and a wide-brimmed Stetson with its trademark buckle headband.

"I was born in Fort Worth," he said. "I'd never be able to call myself a Texan if I didn't have the appropriate gear," he told them. "Besides, I work on a ranch."

"My ex-boss is trying the easy approach, but when he realizes that it isn't working, he may go looking for soft targets," he told the other man, looking pointedly at Stasia's pretty face.

"We've got that covered," Craig assured him. "And I've put a man on the top story with a top-of-the-line sniper rifle."

"Good idea," Tanner said. "You've got somebody watching my mother as well?"

"Yes. And your brother. We haven't told him that," he said with an amused smile. "We don't have the insurance."

"John would tell you that he could take care of himself. And certainly he can, under normal circumstances. But these aren't," Tanner said grimly.

"Not to worry," Craig told him. "We've got you covered like tar paper."

"That helps," came the reply. Tanner stretched and grimaced. "I feel rough."

"You need some Tylenol for the fever," Stasia said worriedly. "And if you aren't better by tomorrow, I'm calling the doctor again."

"Worrywart," Tanner teased softly.

She just smiled and went to ask Heather if she had a bottle of Tylenol.

Late that day, just after dark, Tanner was restless. Stasia hadn't left him all day. She was worried. She knew that he could handle himself when he was sound of body, but that wasn't the case right now. Even having armed people around didn't ease her mind. Tanner's ex-boss was desperate and, apparently, inventive.

"Will you stop fretting?" he asked after she'd straightened the covers four times and rearranged the things on his bedside table again.

She grimaced. "I'm sorry. It's just worrying, that's all."

He held out a hand. She went to him and sat down on the edge of the bed. "You haven't slept," he said softly.

She started to deny it, but she was fairly certain that her bloodshot eyes and dark circles would give her away. She grimaced. "No. I haven't."

"Neither have I, except for cat naps," he replied. He reached up, despite the wound, and levered her over onto the bed next to him.

"The wound…!" she protested.

He leaned over her. "The wound doesn't hurt. Well, not much, anyway. Come here." He drew her gently to him and pulled up the comforter over both of them. "We're well protected. Any assassin who comes near the house will leave in a shoebox. Okay?"

She drew in a steadying breath. It was heavenly to be so close to him. Even after all the grief of the years between, he was still the only man she'd ever loved. She was certain that her attraction showed. She couldn't control her fluttery heartbeat or her uneven breathing.

He ran his finger down her flushed cheek. "I'm not in any condition for what you're nervous about," he whispered, and his lips touched her eyelids tenderly. "Besides. The door's wide open."

"Oh. Well, yes," she faltered, because those lips were making her giddy.

"You taste like cotton candy," he whispered as his mouth slid down her nose onto her soft, parted lips. "And you go to my head like whisky…"

His mouth opened hers without force, with gentle persuasion that left her limp and shivery in his arms as he held her.

"I'd forgotten how good this was," he whispered gruffly. "I spent years trying to forget that one night we had together. I was never able to do it."

She drew in a shaky breath. "Me, neither," she confessed.

His mouth grew slowly insistent. "Have you ever thought… that we might try again?" he whispered.

Her eyes opened and found his one eye piercingly blue. "Again?"

"Yes." His fingers spread on her cheek. "I'm getting older," he said. "Dodging bullets was exciting when I was in my early twenties. But I'm slowing down. Eventually, I'll become a liability to anyone who hires me."

"You're addicted to adrenaline rushes," she accused sadly.

He drew in a long breath. "Yes, I am. But doing black ops is a pretty lethal way to satisfy them."

"You worked as a bodyguard, too," she said. "I heard about the woman you were guarding in Chicago."

He smiled. "She married her boss," he chuckled. "And he'll be on his knees in no time. She's more than a match for his outbursts of temper. Besides," he added with a grin, "her grandmother is mixed up with a high-ranking member of the mob from Detroit. Apparently he's now sharing territory with the outfit in Chicago as well. Tony knows those guys," he added.

She sighed. "Tony knows everybody," she said. "And I mean, everybody. He has contacts in some of the strangest places on earth, and he has a lot of political power as well. I've seen him use it a time or two. Besides all that, he's wealthy—and not from any criminal enterprises. He made his fortune buying and selling art. He's very good at it."

"Something you'd know about," he said, searching her eyes. "No romantic interest there?"

"With Tony?" She laughed softly. "No. Daughterly, certainly. He's practically adopted me. I don't know how I'd have managed if he hadn't come along…" She grimaced. "Sorry," she added when he looked hunted.

"I caused a tragedy and just walked away, is that what you think?" he asked quietly. "It wasn't like that. I was haunted, by what I'd done, by what I'd been. I spent a lot of lonely nights thinking about you, thinking about ways to get back to you, to make up for what happened."

"It was a long time ago," she began.

"It was yesterday, sweetheart," he said in a breathlessly tender tone. "Just yesterday. The pain never stopped. I put myself at risk, hoping that I'd catch a bullet just to get away from it." He drew in a breath. "All I managed was to lose an eye and accumulate a few scars." He smiled sadly. "You can't die when you want to."

She touched her fingers to his chiseled mouth, loving the feel of it. "I never wanted you to die. I wasn't that vindictive. I was just sad."

"About the baby," he whispered. He kissed her hungrily. "So was I. Sad, guilt-ridden, eaten up with memories of my own selfishness."

"You've changed, though," she replied.

"So have you," he replied. "We're older. Wiser. And I've learned things about life that I'd never have managed here. I needed to grow up and face the fact that the world didn't revolve around me and the things I thought I was entitled to. I cringe when I remember how spoiled I was."

"You had irrational spurts of kindness," she whispered with a smile.

"Such as?"

"You were always there when I was in trouble, or in pain. When I found my mother," she added, wincing at the memory. "When Dad died."

He smoothed down her tangled long blond hair. "At least I did the right thing a time or two," he conceded. "But I hurt you more than I ever hurt anyone else."

She didn't say what she was thinking, that he'd hurt his father and mother more.

"Dad was livid that last day I was here," Tanner said. "I didn't realize how much he and Mom were looking forward to the baby." He sighed. "I didn't even know."

"I was going to tell you, when…" She broke off.

He brought her soft palm to his lips and kissed it fervently. "When I screwed up everything. If I could just take back that one day!"

"You aren't the only person who needed to learn things," she said. "I was a real wimp in those days. Instead of running away like a spanked child, I should have slapped Julienne until her teeth rattled and ordered her out of our house."

"You'd do that if it was happening now," he said. "But it won't happen again. Not ever, and that's a solemn promise. I don't have women, Stasia," he whispered, nuzzling his nose against hers. "I can't. Not after you."

She was shocked.

He drew her closer and pillowed her cheek on his shoulder. "I suppose those wild rushes of adrenaline compensated," he mused. "It's been a wild few years."

"Yes." She was content, just to lie in his arms and feel his strength, feel him breathing. It was like the last time they'd been together, in his bedroom. It was the closest to heaven she'd been in all the years between. She closed her eyes. "I'm sleepy," she said softly.

He chuckled softly. "Me, too."

And it was the last thing they said for a long time, because they both fell asleep. All the sleepless nights finally caught up with them.

Heather, pausing at the open door to ask if they wanted anything from the kitchen, just stopped and stared at them with a loving smile.

She'd hoped and prayed that one day they might find each other again. Stasia had been notoriously disinterested in any other men. Heather didn't know about her son, but she imagined it was the same with him. He and Stasia were different people, but they had a history. Now if they could just manage to get past it!

While she was studying the sleeping duo, John came down the hall. Heather put her finger to her lips.

John paused beside her and saw Stasia held close in Tanner's arms. And for the first time, he realized that he'd been living in a fool's paradise. It didn't take a mind reader to know how things stood with his older brother and the woman he loved. Obviously Stasia wasn't holding grudges or hatred for the man who'd caused her miscarriage. On the contrary, she looked sublimely happy where she was.

Tanner was less easily read, but he was intense in all his feelings. He loved his ex-wife. As far as John knew, he'd never been unfaithful, despite the divorce. His face fell as he stared at them.

"I'm so sorry," Heather said softly, because she could feel the pain that emanated from him.

He looked down at her and drew in a long breath. "Well, at least I'm sure now that I was daydreaming." He glanced back toward the two oblivious people in the bed. "When Tanner's safe again, I'm going to go up to Wyoming and look at some of those seed bulls Dad's interested in. I may stay for a few weeks."

Heather hugged him. "I think that might be a very good idea. But not yet," she added firmly.

He smiled and kissed her forehead. "No worries. We're getting the yearlings ready to ship. If I tried to leave, Dad would send one of the men to drag me back."

"You know, he probably would," she replied with a smile.

Cole came in an hour later, worn out and sweaty despite the cool weather. Heather heard the sound of his boots and motioned to him.

Curious, he took her hand and let her lead him down the long hall to Tanner's room, where the door stood ajar.

He glanced inside. "Well," he said.

She pressed close against his side. "I think we might get grandkids after all," she whispered.

He bent and picked her up in his arms, carried her into the living room and sat down with her in his lap.

He kissed her hungrily, feeling the surge of pleasure as she kissed him back with equal hunger.

"Thirty years, and we still burn each other alive," he whispered against her soft lips.

She smiled and sighed. "I know. But it was a rocky road to get here," she said.

"Very." He rubbed his cheek against hers. "From time to time, I wish I could go back and make that witch Tessa pay for the lies she told, for what she did to us."

She smoothed the frown from between his pale eyes. "She wrote me a letter."

"When?" he asked, infuriated.

She put her fingers against his lips. "She has cancer, Cole. It's terminal. She wanted to apologize for what she did. She said she wanted to clear her conscience before the end."

"Cancer." He relaxed a little. "It's almost unforgiveable."

"Nothing is unforgiveable. You believed her, and your mother had just died and couldn't contradict that rumor—which she certainly would have."

"Yes. She said in her will that she hoped we'd end up together," he said. "It was mostly my fault," he said after a minute. "I believed Tessa." He grimaced. "It didn't help when I asked our housekeeper at the time about Dad and your mother, and she answered in a way that made me think she'd seen something that confirmed what Tessa told me."

"It was forever ago," Heather said. "The important thing is that we finally got rid of all the rumors and found out the truth. Your father loved your mother. He would never have been unfaithful to her. Never. Any more than you'd be un-faithful to me, or vice versa."

He smiled and his blue eyes were soft with love. "Have I mentioned today that I love you madly?"

She laughed, a gurgle of pure joy. "At least twice. Have I told you that I love you madly, too?"

"At least twice." He wrapped her up tight. "But it bears repeating," he teased, and bent to her mouth.

And neither of them said anything else for several sweet, passionate minutes.

In New York, Tony was using one of the burner phones he'd had Big Ben bring to him. He was talking to a very well-known senator in Washington, DC. He was asking hard questions as well.

"Tony, you know I can't share classified information with you. And this isn't a dedicated line!" the politician was complaining.

"I could share what I know with that television reporter you didn't want to talk to after the Senate hearings," Tony said easily.

There was a long pause. "You wouldn't…"

Tony just chuckled. "And you know that I would," he contradicted. "Listen, this kid's like the daughter I never had," he said, serious now, "and her husband has been targeted by that yellow snake you're trying to protect."

"I'm not trying to protect him," the man argued. "It's not that!"

"Oh, I get it," Tony replied. "He's got something on you, right?"

The man cleared his throat. He was afraid to admit that on an open line.

"You got a burner phone?"

"A what? No!"

"Get one of your flunkies to go out to an electronics store and buy you a couple. Then call me back."

"I've got a hearing today…" came the weak protest.

"I have the reporter on speed dial," Tony said casually.

"All right!" The man sounded hoarse now. "Okay," he said on a heavy breath. "I'll send somebody right out."

"Call me back. Write down this number."

"Of course. Yes, of course, I will." He hung up.

Tony pursed his lips. The man had guilt lathered all over him, and Tony had no plans to expose him. But if he spooked his congressional contact, so much the better. He wasn't going to let Stasia down.

Meanwhile, Winslow Grange was on the phone with his best friend, the head of the CIA, David Cassaway.

"Some people are doing a big business in burner phones lately," Cassaway mused.

"In a society as corrupt as ours, it pays," Winslow agreed. "Which is why we're both using them," he added.

"Point taken," Cassaway conceded. "What can I do for you?"

"I just helped rescue an agent who worked for one of the top-secret agencies in DC," he replied. "Apparently, the new head of the agency, his ex-boss, sacrificed two green recruits to make it look like an ambush in an Amazon covert pursuit of drug traffickers."

"That would be Phillip James," Cassaway said curtly. "He started out in my agency, but he had a friend, a pretty shady one, who coaxed him away from us. He was a good kid, fresh out of college, brilliant in mathematics, good at tactics. And then his buddy got hold of him. There's big money in this game if you know how to play it, and the buddy did. So

Phillip learned the ropes and started buying four-thousand-dollar suits and driving Ferraris."

"Somebody must have noticed," Winslow pointed out.

"In this political climate, it's best to mind your own business. Amazing how many people accidentally fall out of high windows or shoot themselves in the back of the head," he added.

"I heard that."

"So, Phillip started gathering information of the blackmailable kind on all the people in power. But he took a little too much of his own product overseas and went nuts in a camp full of civilians. There were twelve deaths—most of them children. It was covered up, of course," he said quietly. "Can't have the government involved in anything of that sort. So he walked."

"No prosecution?"

Cassaway laughed mirthlessly. "I told you, he has something on everybody in town. They didn't dare prosecute him. The agent who witnessed it, Tanner Everett, had proof. But James threatened him with the lives of his family if he talked."

"Damn!"

"See what I mean? The only way to get rid of a man that corrupt is by using corrupt means."

"So. Do you know of any plans to do that?"

"Not at the moment. And even if I did, I wouldn't say so anywhere in town. Even on a secure line."

"I get it."

"I think your victim is safe for the foreseeable future, however," he added. "His people are filthy rich and his father is a power in local politics. He could make waves. So the word is that the perp is being allowed to retain his position as long as he doesn't rock anybody's boat by trying to kill anybody else."

"That's sick."

"Hey, welcome to my world!"

Winslow drew in a breath. "Well, I guess that's something. I don't know the gentleman in question. I'm doing a favor for a friend. Two friends," he amended.

"Yes. Your friends have spent some time in front of congressional committees over the years," he pointed out.

"But never convicted."

"True enough. Between them, they have just enough clout to keep our bad boy away from Tanner Everett's door. For now, anyway."

"I hate seeing someone get away with attempted murder," Winslow said. "Especially someone who's killed civilians and offed two green agents."

"You don't feel any worse about it than I do. If it was my agency, it would be handled. Under the circumstances, however, there's no way to cross agency lines to do anything. I will keep my eyes open, however. And I'd advise the Everett man to watch his back. James is drug-happy and power-happy. It's a bad combination that can lead to irrational decisions. Mostly deadly ones."

"I see where you're coming from."

"Besides, there's always the hope that he'll cross someone meaner and even less forgiving than he is," Cassaway sighed.

"That has been known to happen."

"It has. Especially with your two acquaintances involved." He paused. "Wasn't a body found in a backwater of New Jersey in an oil drum a few years back…?"

"I know nothing," Winslow said facetiously.

"Good thing. You might find yourself in front of a congressional committee," he chuckled.

"Well, thanks anyway. Knowing what you're up against is a little protection, at least."

"It may not seem like it, but mean people do eventually get called to account."

"So they say. Just between you and me, that happens a lot here in Barrera."

"Lucky devil. Come on over sometime and play chess with me."

"I'll do that. How're your granddaughters?"

"Growing more beautiful by the day, just like their mother," he replied. "And Gwen's pregnant again. Rick's hoping for at least one boy. Not that he doesn't love his two girls."

"I'm happy to just have one kid," Winslow said. "We'd have liked more, but it wasn't in the cards. Still, I can look forward to grandkids one day!"

"Of course you can. That's one of the few perks of growing old. Take care."

Winslow hung up and hesitated for a few seconds before he pulled out another phone and dialed a number in Texas.

Tanner answered the phone, temporarily alone in his bedroom. It was one of the throwaway phones, so he had a pretty good idea of who was calling.

"Winslow or Tony," he mused as he picked up.

"Winslow," came the amused reply. "I have good news and bad news."

"Bad first."

"Your ex-boss isn't going to be prosecuted for trying to off you," came the reply. "I'm damned sorry."

"Me, too, but it's what I expected. What's the good news?"

"I lied."

"That's what I thought."

"My contact in DC said to watch your back. Your ex-boss is now an addict and he's power-mad as well. He could make an irrational choice that would put you in danger. The one thing that might save you is that your dad is rich and he's a political powerhouse in Texas."

"That's what I've heard. He's already had somebody here trying to poison me."

"What? When?" Winslow asked.

Tanner explained.

"Damn!" he muttered. "He didn't lose any time, did he?"

"No. And I guarantee the perp will be out of the country by the time our sheriff's investigator can finger him for attempted murder," Tanner said.

"I've been talking to another friend," Winslow said. "There's not much he can do. I hope you've got protection, not just for yourself, but for your family as well."

"I don't like having my family in harm's way!"

"I can understand that. But I live with it, too. I'm not the most popular person in Barrera. Sapara had friends," he added, referring to the usurper who'd almost taken over General Machado's country and ruined it before Grange, leading a ragtag army with the general in front, had taken the country back.

"We do what we must," Tanner said. "Next time you're in town, give me a call. We'll have a rematch on that last chess game."

"Are you retiring?"

"I believe I am," Tanner said. "My ex-wife seems willing to give me a second chance. So does my dad. I think I'll go back into the cattle ranching business. At least, I should collect fewer bullet holes."

"Bulls have horns," Winslow, who also had a ranch in Texas, advised.

Tanner chuckled. "So they do. Anyway, thanks for the assist."

"Wish I had better news. If I hear anything, I'll give you a call."

"Okay. Thanks."

"My pleasure."

He'd just put the phone down when Stasia came in with two cups of black coffee. She handed him one with a smile and sat down on the bed beside him.

"Business?" she asked, trying to sound nonchalant.

He put the mug on the bedside table. "Sort of. My ex-boss isn't going to be prosecuted."

"Damn!"

"On the other hand, I have friends." He slid his hand into hers. "How would you feel about marrying an ex-fed with a few scars and raising kids and hell in Texas?"

Her coffee sloshed. She put the cup down. "What?" she asked softly.

"We could get married again," he said. "But this time it wouldn't be at gunpoint. Dad says he'll give me back the ranch if I plan to stay here. If we got married," he mused, studying her flushed face, "he might be convinced that I planned to stay. And if we had a couple of kids, that would really help convince him. Right?"

She just nodded, spellbound.

"So?" he asked, smiling. "You can have a nice new set of rings. I'll even let you pick them out."

"You're serious?"

"Oh, I'm serious," he said huskily, drawing her down to him. "And if you need convincing…"

FIFTEEN

The antibiotic worked quickly. Within a week, Tanner was back on his feet and relearning the ranching business.

"I feel bad about John," Tanner told his dad as they studied two bull yearlings in the barn. "I know he had hopes."

"And he knew they weren't realistic," Cole replied. "Stasia's loved you her whole life. It wasn't likely that she'd change her mind, no matter how bad things got."

"I've put her through a lot," Tanner said quietly. "I've put all of you through it. I was a spoiled kid. God bless Mom, she did her best, but…"

"But I gave in when I shouldn't have," Cole finished for him. "You didn't turn out so bad. You just had to come to grips with reality. I'm sorry it cost you so much," he added, noting the eye patch.

"I found my feet, though," Tanner replied. "It took a few

hard knocks, but I learned a lot about life and people. And I made some really interesting contacts."

"Like our friend Tony," Cole mused.

"I think Odalie's got a case on him," Tanner said. He turned to his dad. "He's mostly legit, but he's done some pretty bad things in his time. You can still mention his name in Jersey and turn people's faces pale."

"On the other hand, he's taken good care of Odalie. And especially of Stasia. What about her job?" Cole asked.

"We're talking about that. She loves New York, and she still wants to paint, but she's never really liked living in the city. She's a country girl. She wants to talk to Tony before she decides."

"Is she going back to New York?"

"No. Actually, Odalie wants to come down for the yearling sale and barbeque, but I'm no more comfortable than you are about letting her travel alone." He grimaced. "Nobody's really safe with my ex-boss still on the loose. She's nervous about coming."

"I don't want her coming down here alone," Cole agreed.

"I knew you wouldn't. Stasia talked to Odalie. She's going to call Tony and ask if he'll bring her down Friday night in the jet."

"We can introduce him to cattle culture," Cole chuckled.

"And barbeque," Tanner added with a grin.

Meanwhile, Tony's contact in the nation's capital had sent out for two burner phones and called Tony back on his own throwaway.

"Okay, here's the deal," Tony said, and there was menace in the very softness of his voice. "I want your boy off my baby girl's ex-husband and his family. Or else. He isn't the only man who can make people disappear. And I know lots of better ways than a gun."

There was an audible swallowing sound. "Yes, but what he's got on me..." he began.

"He can't use it," Tony said. "The evidence has already been erased."

"What?! How?!"

"I know lots of guys who owe me favors," Tony said simply. "But I mean what I said. You rein that yellow coward in and keep him out of Texas."

There was a sigh. "Well, since you've been kind enough to save my bacon, I guess I can intimidate him enough to put a burr under his saddle."

"Just what I was thinking. Remind him of who I am. And tell him that I'm not intimidated by congressional committees. He doesn't want to be the guy who tries to bring me up against one. You get my drift?"

"Oh, yes, I do."

"I thought you might. I'll be in touch."

"I'll keep the wolf away from your girl's door."

"Good man. See how nice it feels, being on the right side of the law?"

"And you'd know?" came the mock exclamation.

"I would right now," Tony replied. "See you."

Odalie called him later that day. He'd had a row with his mistress, who couldn't understand why he wasn't interested in her lately.

"You're never around when I call!" she complained. "You're always off somewhere with that painter!"

"She's an artist. She's my family," he added coldly.

"Oh, all right, the artist. When are you going to take me

to the ballet?" she coaxed. "I bought a new dress and everything."

"It will have to wait. I've got several deals in the fire right now. I'll call you."

"But, Tony…!"

"I've got a call," he interrupted, noting the number. "I'll talk to you later." He hung up and pressed the other button. "Yeah?" he asked curtly.

Odalie was nervous enough about even asking her best friend's adopted father for a favor in the first place. And he certainly didn't sound welcoming. "Tony?" she asked and her voice reflected her discomfort.

"Sorry," he said, changing his tone. "I've been arguing with somebody. What do you need?"

Odalie hated her own cowardice. She wasn't afraid of people normally. But Tony made her blood run hot. He was the only man who ever really had. She'd had a mild crush on Cort Brannt, who was now married to her former enemy and now friend, Maddie Lane. And Cort had been more a habit than a love interest.

"I need to ask a favor," she said after a minute. "Stasia hasn't called you…?"

"No." He lowered his voice. "So, is this favor for you or Stasia?"

"Me. Her. Both of us," she stammered.

Her nervousness amused him. They'd been sparring for several months. But lately she got all tongue-tied and flushed around him. It was flattering. She was beautiful. Besides that, she sang opera with a genius. The only real problem was that she was from Texas high society, and she was only twenty-four. Tony was a mob boss in Jersey and he was thirty-seven. The years and the backgrounds were wrong. But then, it never hurt to look at the menu, even if the delicacies were off limits.

"And what would this favor be?" he persisted.

"I want to go home for a few days, but Dad and Tanner don't want me to fly to Texas by myself," she muttered. "Neither does Stasia or the rest of my family. John's gone missing, Tanner's still recovering from his wound, Stasia's taking care of him, and both my parents are up to their ears preparing for the yearling sale and barbeque this weekend. It's sort of an occasion on the Big Spur."

"So you need a ride, huh?" he asked, cutting through the static.

"Actually, I need somebody to go with me. They think I'll get killed on the way to the airport, I guess," she muttered.

He laughed softly. That deep voice made little ripples against her skin. He was the sexiest man she'd ever known.

"When do you want to go?" he asked.

"Friday. Tomorrow. The sale starts the day after and runs through the weekend." She hesitated. "Dad says you're welcome to stay for it. It's really great barbeque and the house is huge. Plenty of room for guests. You can take Big Ben along, he can have a room as well. If you'd like to, I mean. I guess it doesn't sound like much to somebody as sophisticated as you," she added hesitantly.

She made him feel ten feet tall. Sophisticated. He was a poor kid from the ghetto who'd hit it big, thanks to his family connections. He'd fought all his life for respectability. He never expected to find it from a debutante.

"I like barbeque," he said.

She let out the breath that had caught in her throat. "Then, if you'd like to, I can get tickets…"

"I've got my own jet," he reminded her. "And my own pilot. What time?"

"Could we go about five?" she asked. "I've got one more voice lesson this week…"

"Five's fine. I'll pick you up at your place."

"Okay." She sounded breathless. "Thanks!"

He chuckled. "No problem."

She hung up, already planning what she was going to wear. It had been a very long time since she'd been excited about dressing up for anyone, except for Cort Brannt. And Cort had been a suitor for several years before he discovered Maddie. Not that she'd felt that way about Cort. His attentions had flattered her. They hadn't been returned. She'd avoided entanglements since she knew she wanted a career in opera.

This was...different. She felt as if she'd taken an unexpected step off a cliff. She didn't understand why Tony affected her this way.

But then, it was better not to worry about things, she decided. Not yet, anyway.

Tony knocked on her door at five sharp on Friday afternoon. She opened the door, breathless, wearing a pale blue midi-length belted cotton dress with short sleeves and a flaring skirt. Her long pale blond hair was around her shoulders, held back from her face with a scarf that matched the dress. She wore low-heeled shoes in a matching color.

It was like a body blow, he thought, just to look at her. She was truly beautiful. The dress accentuated a perfect figure. She wore little makeup, too, not the thick eye shadow and emphatic vivid red lipstick that his mistress favored. No. Odalie looked as natural as a country girl on a leisurely walk. He wanted her. And hated himself for it.

"Ready to go?" he asked, averting his eyes to her suitcase on wheels.

"Yes," she said.

He looked pretty good too, in a designer polo shirt, a burgundy color that suited his olive complexion, with dark slacks.

It was autumn, but not cold enough today for even a sweater.

He motioned for Big Ben, who came in, smiled and nodded at Odalie, and took her suitcase out to the car.

She locked up the apartment, fumbling a little with the key.

"I really appreciate the ride," she said after an uncomfortable silence on the way to the airport.

He murmured something noncommittal, his eyes on the city out the back seat window beside him.

She took a slow breath, trying to calm her heartbeat. It was very obvious that he was only doing a favor for Stasia by flying Odalie down to Texas. And it looked as if it was killing him to share a car with her.

Her own eyes slid around to the city passing by as they went toward the airport. It was going to be, she thought with resignation, a very long trip. Perhaps she should have asked her father or Tanner to just send one of the cowboys up to escort her—maybe Craig, with his background in law enforcement.

Tony's aircraft was a twin-engine Cessna, white and big and modern-looking. The pilot met them as they went up the steps into a spacious cabin. There was white furniture, plush and comfortable-looking, along with a table and what looked like a refrigerator. In the very back was a bathroom.

Odalie's dad, Cole Everett, had a twin-engine Cessna of his own, but John had taken it somewhere in the northwest to look at cattle.

"Sit anywhere you want," Tony said. "If you need something to drink, just say so. We've got everything from soft drinks to champagne."

"Thanks," she said, perching on the very edge of a seat near the front.

Ben came in with her suitcase, which he stowed in a compartment. He checked around the cabin, nodded at Tony and went to sit in the back of the plane with his cell phone. He put earbuds in and concentrated on the screen.

"He loves video games," Tony said when he noticed her gaze on his bodyguard.

"So does my brother," she replied.

"Tanner?"

"No. John. He and a neighbor used to play together all the time. I think John has every console game ever made."

Tony just nodded. He went up front to speak to the pilot and came back shortly afterwards.

"Buckle up," he said, taking a seat a few feet away.

She fastened the belt and leaned back, uneasy. She got motion sickness just from riding in cars, much less airplanes. She usually took a pill for it, but she'd been so excited about going with Tony on the long trip that she'd forgotten to take it. God forbid that she should start throwing up. She hesitated to even ask for an airsick bag, if he had such a thing. She swallowed, hard, and closed her eyes.

Takeoff took a few minutes, but she did all right until they were airborne. Then she sat back, seat belt unfastened, pale and getting more nauseous by the minute.

Tony noticed, although she hadn't expected him to. He came to stand over her. "Do you have anything to take for it?" he asked gently.

She looked up at him, and nodded.

"What do you want to drink?"

"Any sort of soft drink that doesn't have caffeine," she replied. "I'm already nervous…" She ground her teeth at that involuntary admission.

He didn't say anything. He got a ginger ale from the fridge and handed it to her after she'd retrieved a pill from the tube of anti-nausea medicine in her purse.

"Thanks," she managed after she'd swallowed it. She looked at him. "How did you know?"

He smiled, and it wasn't a mocking one, either. "I used to have a bodyguard, Beppo, who worked with Big Ben. He couldn't even ride in a car without throwing up. I know the signs."

She gave him a wan smile in return. "It's been the curse of my existence. I always rode in the back seat when I went anywhere with my family, and I always had to take medicine for it." She swallowed, hard, again. "I'm so sorry…"

"For what?" he asked, searching her face. "You can't help being sick."

He had large dark eyes, and they were devastating at close range. Her heart was trying to work its way out of her chest, or it felt like it. She couldn't look away. It was like free fall.

She took another swallow of the drink, but her hand was unsteady. He took it from her and put it in a recessed holder.

Then, to her surprise, he scooped her up and sat back down with her in his lap, her cheek pillowed on his broad chest.

"Go to sleep," he said softly, at her temple. "It will help."

She almost shivered with pleasure. It was so unexpected. He'd been distant, almost irritated by her since he'd arrived at her apartment. Here he was, being unexpectedly kind. She'd never had such a reaction to a man. She'd had dates in high school, but only with boys who were strictly friends. She hadn't wanted any relationship to threaten her dreams of an opera career.

But lying in Tony's strong arms was doing things to her. She hadn't realized just how vulnerable she was.

He shook her gently. "Relax," he whispered. "I'm not going to hurt you."

She met his eyes. "I know that," she faltered.

He pushed a stray lock of hair away from her mouth and

stared at it for a long moment before his eyes slid back up to capture hers. He scowled, as if he was as puzzled as she was about their suddenly charged proximity.

"You act like a green girl," he said abruptly. "But that would be hard to believe. A woman as pretty as you are, I imagine your dad had to beat the boys away from your door."

"No. He didn't." She looked down, to where her small hand was resting on his broad chest. In the opening at his throat, thick curly black hair peeked out. It was sexy. He was sexy. He smelled of soap and expensive cologne and the nearness was intoxicating.

"Why?" he asked.

She drew a breath and felt her small breasts brush against him. She felt alive, as she'd never felt before. "I wanted to sing opera," she said. "Since I was in grammar school. Mom taught me piano and she had a voice coach for me, when she realized that I had the ability to sing. There was never anything I wanted more than to someday sing at the Met," she added, alluding to the Metropolitan Opera in New York City. "I've studied voice for years. In fact, I studied in Italy until a few months ago." She drew in a breath. "I was a horrible person," she blurted out. "Snobbish and selfish and... well, not very nice. Then I ran over a girl who was my worst enemy in school and suddenly I was needed. Not because I was pretty or could sing or was rich, but because she was hurt and needed help." She laughed softly. "It changed me. She's my best friend now, next to Stasia."

"You ran over her?"

"Yes. I was driving Cort Brannt's Jaguar. I took my eyes off the road and Maddie ran out in front of me to get her pet rooster out of the way. I hit them both." She closed her eyes and grimaced. "Nothing ever hurt so much. I'd been mean to her all through high school. I almost got her killed. Then, to do that…" She looked up at him. "It was a horrible experience, but it turned my life around. I'm not the same person I used to be."

He traced the outline of her high cheekbone with the tip of his finger. "Neither am I," he said. "I like to think I'm a little better than I used to be," he amended. "I'll never be the man my mother prayed I'd be. She knew what I was doing. She never approved."

"My brother said people were scared of you, where you come from."

"They are." His face tautened. "I had it rough as a kid. My father was mostly a butcher. He had territory in Jersey, and he kept it through intimidation. My mother tried to soften his influence, but she really couldn't. He was in too deep to get out, even if he'd wanted to, and he didn't." He drew in a breath. "You grow up in the family. It becomes more important to you than blood. After a while, you don't care about anything outside it."

She'd heard tales about Tony. Probably they were all true. She was surprised that it didn't really bother her. He might be terrifying to other men. But he was gentle with Stasia. And with herself.

"Stasia said you were married once."

He laughed hollowly. "For five years. She was the daughter of an underboss in the family. She was sweet and gentle and shy. We'd been married just a year when they diagnosed her with cancer. We both fought it. I sent her to the Mayo Clinic for treatment. She had the best doctors, home nursing." He grimaced. "All that couldn't save her. They'd operate, she'd get better, they'd say they got it all. And it would come back. Every damned time."

"I'm sorry. That would have been rough."

"Hell on earth," he said, and there was something dark and

cold in his eyes. "I buried her and said never again. Women have been disposable ever since."

She understood what he was saying. He didn't want to risk losing someone else that he loved. It depressed her, and she didn't understand why.

She wanted to talk to him, but the nausea medicine began to work. She yawned and her face nuzzled against his chest. "I'm so sleepy," she whispered.

He gathered her up closer, enjoying the soft warmth of her body, the faint scent of flowers that clung to her skin. "Go to sleep," he said.

It was the last thing she remembered.

Tanner was watching one of the ranch hands work a new filly in the corral on a leading rein. All around the ranch, there was activity because the sale was the next day. A tent was being set up with tables and chairs, and the equipment for making barbeque was placed nearby.

In the barn, the cattle that would be sold were being buffed up to look their best. It was going to be a long day.

Stasia joined him at the fence, looking young and sweet and pretty in jeans and a knit shirt with her hair in a ponytail.

"You look pretty," he said softly, and bent to brush his mouth over hers. "I've missed you," he added gruffly.

She slid against him and linked her arms around his neck. "I've missed you, too. It's been a long few years."

He nodded. He bent and kissed her again, harder. "Dad and I have been talking about the ranch property. He wants me to take it over again."

She looked up at him worriedly. "But you don't really want to be a rancher," she said sadly.

"We've already talked about that," he said, smiling.

"Yes, but you were hurt and not quite yourself at the time," she replied.

He smoothed back her hair. "I am now," he replied. His face was serious. "I've risked my life for years. Maybe it will be hard at first, not having those emotional highs I used to get from adrenaline rushes. But sooner or later, I'd land in a life-or-death situation that I couldn't come out of. It almost happened overseas." He drew in a long breath. "People died because a madman wanted me dead, because of what I knew. I'll have to live with that guilt."

She put her fingers over his chiseled mouth. "Tanner, people die because it's their time to die. In a firefight, in a car crash, in a lake drowning. It's the way things are."

He smiled. "You and that rock-hard fatalistic outlook."

She wrinkled her nose. "It's kept me sane. Especially since…" She stopped. She didn't want to drag up the past.

He held her close. "Especially since the baby," he said at her forehead. "That's another burden I'll have to live with." He drew away. "But we can still have children. The difference is that now I'm ready for them. I wasn't before."

"I'm not sure that I was either," she confessed. "I wasn't quite mature. Not the way I am now. I've seen the world."

"So have I. Now I think I can be happy just seeing cattle and long horizons," he added with a smile.

"What about that idiot who's after you?" she worried.

"One day at a time," he replied. "Now, let's talk about something nice. When do you want to get married?"

She just stared at him.

"My vote would be for as soon as we can get a license," he added, searching her dark eyes hungrily. "We can be married in church. But this time, it will be with all the bells and whistles, and I won't be leaving town the next day."

Her hands flattened on his chest. "Are you sure?" she asked.

He nodded. "I've never been more sure about anything in my life," he told her huskily.

She sighed. "Okay, then," she replied, smiling up at him.

He framed her face in his hands and kissed her hungrily. She kissed him back. After a few minutes they became aware of an odd silence around them.

Tanner lifted his head.

The fence was lined with cowboys, including his father.

"Nine out of ten?" Cole asked the others.

"At least," one of the wranglers agreed.

"Naw, ten out of ten," another cowboy said.

Tanner threw up his hands. "Is there no privacy in the world? I'm proposing marriage here!"

"Oh!" The wrangler jumped down, doffed his hat and bowed. "Excuse us! You two just go right back to what you were doing, and we'll work on prettying up some more cattle for the sale!"

They all scattered except for Cole, who jumped down, still laughing, to join them.

"You remind me of your mother and I when we agreed to marry," he commented. "Best damned day of my life."

"Best day of hers, too, to hear her tell it," Tanner chuckled.

"We had a rocky road to the altar," Cole replied, sobering. "Just like the two of you. But things worked out nicely for us over the years. Your mother almost died having you, and you were born with jaundice. It's why your mother was so protective of you."

"She still is," Tanner said, and he smiled.

"Yes, but probably we should have had more time-outs when you were little," Cole said firmly.

Tanner said, "It wouldn't have helped. I was incorrigible. I still am."

Cole put a big hand on his shoulder. "I overreacted. I'm sorry, for the lost years," he said solemnly.

"I'm sorry for them, too," Tanner said.

"However," he added heavily, "now that it looks like we might actually get grandkids," he mused, watching Stasia's involuntary blush, "I think that a great healing may be underway already."

Tanner smiled. "I want kids a lot. We both do." He drew her close. "She's a fatalist. I guess there may be something in that after all."

Cole nodded. "I think so, too." He turned to walk back to the house with them. "Now. About the ranch…"

"I knew that you had a hard time, having Tanner," Stasia told Heather later. "But I didn't know about him being born with jaundice."

"He was our first child. We were nervous anyway, and then I had to have the C-section. Cole almost went crazy. It scared him to death. Then to have Tanner born sick…" She shook her head. "Those were dark days."

"I think I'm beginning to understand why Cole reacted so violently to what happened to me."

Heather nodded. "I wish he'd been a little less vicious. It made it harder on Tanner."

"It did. But he grew from the experience, don't you think?" Stasia asked. She smiled. "He's very different from the man I fell in love with. Different, but better. Less brittle."

"Less spoiled," Heather agreed, smiling.

"I hope that Tanner and I have a marriage like yours," she said.

Heather just sighed. "We've been so lucky, even with our tragedies. We may be older, but we're both as much in love now as we used to be…why are you laughing?"

Stasia flushed. "Well, Tanner told me that when they were kids, they had to be very careful about which doors they opened, because you and Cole…well…" She broke off.

Heather burst out laughing as well. "I'm sorry to tell you that it's true. We were less cautious than we should have been, but too much in love to be sensible, even after three children!"

"I hope we can have at least two," Stasia said. "I hated being an only child."

"So did I. So did Cole," Heather replied. "We were both only children, and it was a lonely life."

"If John and Odalie both marry, this place will be over-flowing with grandchildren," Stasia mentioned.

"I don't know about John. He's used to being a bachelor." She didn't add that he was mourning Stasia. No need to open more wounds.

"And Odalie swears it's an opera career she wants, not marriage," Stasia agreed. "But she has a real attraction to Tony. I think it may be mutual. They're always at each other's throats."

"One violent emotion can mask another," Heather agreed. "Well, we'll have to wait and see. But meanwhile, we have a wedding to plan. I'm so happy!"

"So am I!" Stasia hugged her. "So now you'll be Mom again, but for good this time."

"Roll on the day!" Heather enthused and hugged her back.

When Odalie woke up, Tony was sitting in the cockpit with the pilot. She sat up and wondered if she'd dreamed having Tony hold her while she slept. When he came back into the cabin, she was sure it was a dream, because he was polite, but distant all over again.

"Are we almost there?" she asked, muffling a yawn.

"Ten minutes, more or less. Want to call your folks? We're

going to land at the airport in Branntville. My pilot has another passenger to pick up in Miami and transport back to Jersey," he said.

"We have a landing strip at Big Spur," Odalie said. "Dad has a twin-engine Cessna."

Tony shook his head. "He'll need to file a flight plan for Miami."

"Okay. I'll call Dad the minute we land," she said.

She did.

"Is Tony going to stay?" Cole asked.

She turned and looked up at Tony. "Dad wants to know if you and Ben are going to stay for the barbeque?"

Her expression was involuntarily hopeful. He saw that, but he still hesitated.

"Barbeque? And won't there be dancing?" Ben asked, joining them. "Does Mercedes still work there?" he added and cleared his throat. "She danced with me when we flew down with Stasia at Christmas and there was that party…"

"Party?" Odalie asked, surprised.

"You were in Italy," Tony said.

"Yes," she sighed. "I couldn't get home in time, there was that weather that closed airports…"

Tony just nodded.

"Are you? Going to stay, I mean?" she asked again.

Tony looked down at her and knew he wasn't going to leave, but he hated himself for it. She deserved better. He was all wrong for her. He didn't need to get involved with her, for her own good.

"Yeah," he heard himself saying. "We'll stay until Monday, if that's okay with your folks."

Odalie tried to hide her delight and couldn't. "Dad, he says they'll both stay. Okay. I'll tell him. You will? Yes. Thanks!"

"He'll meet us at the airport with the car," she said.

He nodded and sighed, as he wondered why he couldn't do the sensible thing. It was going to be a disaster. He just knew it.

SIXTEEN

Supper was a boisterous affair. Odalie had wondered about how Tony and Ben would fit in with the family, but they joined it seamlessly. Apparently they'd stayed overnight at Christmas, when she hadn't been able to get home, because Heather had already told them they'd be in the guest rooms they'd occupied during their last visit.

They were eating Heather's delicious banana pudding when Tony asked a question. "I'm curious about who you were named for," he said, nodding toward Odalie.

Heather laughed. "That was my idea. I was in a used bookstore and I found a historical novel by an American author, Frank Yerby, called *The Foxes of Harrow*. I didn't realize until later how very famous it was. They even made a movie of it back in the 1940s starring Rex Harrison and Maureen O'Hara. The heroine's name was Odalie. I loved the book, and the character. So when we had a little girl, I thought it was perfect."

Tony smiled. "My mother liked novels, too. But she liked movie stars more. Her favorite one was Anthony Quinn."

"And she named you for him," Heather guessed with a smile.

He nodded. "This pudding is wonderful," he said. "I can make lasagna and spaghetti, but I can't do sweets."

"He tried once," Big Ben interjected. He made a horrible face.

"Yeah, well nobody said you had to eat it," he muttered.

They all laughed.

In the evening, they all moved onto the front porch and sat down in rocking chairs while Cole and Heather shared the love seat.

"It's peaceful here," Tony said. "My grandfather had a little farm in upstate New York. I used to spend summers there when I was a kid."

"Did he have cattle?" Cole asked.

"No. Well, he kept a milk cow. But he had horses to help him with the heavy work. Percherons. I've always loved big horses." He laughed. "I stopped trying to ride when I grew up. I'm too big for most mounts."

"Oh, we've got a nice Belgian that would fit you," Cole said. "He was a rescue. Previous owner went to jail for the way he treated him," he added coldly.

"Good enough for him," Tony said. "A man who'll mistreat a helpless animal will do the same thing to people." He hesitated and looked around him in the dusk light at the other people. "Well, I guess that sounds hypocritical, coming from me. But I never hurt anything helpless, and I never would. Mean people, however, sometimes get mean treatment."

Cole chuckled. "That happens in Texas, too."

"We might go riding on Sunday," Heather said, curling up

next to Cole. "If we're still able to walk by then," she added on a groan. "I've been in the kitchen for two days making cakes and pies and breads."

"Homemade bread?" Tony asked.

"Oh, yes."

He sighed. "I haven't had homemade bread since my mother died. She used to make it."

"Well, you're welcome to all you can eat here," Heather murmured. "I made plenty."

"I'll take you up on that," he assured her.

Tanner and Stasia walked back to her room after the others had all turned in for the night. "Isn't it amazing how well Tony fits in here?" he asked softly.

"Yes, it is," she replied. "He's had a hard life, and a tragic one. His father used to beat him when he was a child. He almost killed him once, but his mother saved him. He said it was a relief when the old man was targeted by an enemy boss. Tony was sure he'd have killed the man himself when he was older, because of the way he treated his poor mother. He must have been some kind of maniac."

"I was lucky. My father loved me," Stasia added.

"Both my parents loved me. Too much," he added with a smile.

"You can never love a child too much," she argued.

He drew her close. "I don't think so," he said. "We'll love our kids."

"I wonder which one of us they'll favor," she said. "Your coloring is like Cole's and mine is like your mother's except I've got dark eyes."

He chuckled. "They'll probably be a mixture, like me and Odalie and John." His arms contracted. "I'm just sorry for the one we lost."

She pressed close. "But the next one will be fine," she said. "I know it."

"Me, too."

He bent and kissed her hungrily, twice. "I got the license today," he whispered, "while I was in town. If you wanted to, we could be married on Monday."

"Monday!" She hadn't thought about dates, about the future, about anything.

He brushed his lips over hers. "Monday. Church, minister, I do...?"

"But, wedding gown, invitations, all that?"

He kissed her harder. "I can't sleep with you until we're married, and I'm dying," he groaned as he gathered her close. "If I have to wait for all the trimmings, I'll just kill myself."

"Noooo," she moaned, and kissed him back.

"Then, Monday."

She drew back for a few seconds, looked at his strained expression, grimaced and said, "Monday."

They told the others at breakfast.

Heather gasped. "But the invitations, her gown, the reception...!"

Stasia patted her hand. "Monday. At the church." She looked at Tony, who was chuckling silently. "Will you stay?"

"Why not? I love weddings," he said.

She smiled at him.

The barbeque and sale was a riotous celebration, because of the upcoming wedding. Since many of the guests were neighbors, they were told and passed on the verbal invitations to their families. Stasia was guessing that the church would be overflowing.

While she and Heather brought out the food that had been

stored inside, Cole's head wrangler was doing his famous bar-
bequed ribs and baked beans on a huge gas grill. Cattlemen
stood around and talked while they waited for the lunch to
be served. Most of the yearlings were already sold, and an
agent for a packinghouse had just made an offer for the ones
that weren't.

"This is my kind of sale," Heather said when Cole told her.
She glanced over at Tony, who was standing by the makeshift
dance floor the cowboys had constructed with lumber and
lights. The band was already playing and one or two couples
were trying out the floor.

"Why don't you go and ask Tony to dance?" she asked
Odalie.

Odalie flushed. "You need me to help with the food," she
said quickly.

"We don't," Stasia said with twinkling eyes. "Go on. He
doesn't bite."

She grimaced but prodded by two pairs of hands and secretive smiles, she started toward the band.

"Do you see how nervous she is? Odalie, of all people!"
Stasia exclaimed. "She's always the calm person in any emergency, and she's almost falling over herself."

"Tony's very attractive," Heather said. "And Odalie may
discover that a career, however sought after, isn't as satisfy-
ing as a family."

"You found that out, didn't you?" Stasia asked.

"I certainly did. I was famous, in my day," she said. "I was
rich and I had wonderful clothes and audiences adored me.
And at night, I went home to a lonely apartment. What I have
now is so much more valuable than what I had."

Stasia was looking at Tanner, who seemed to sense her
stare and turned to smile at her. She smiled back and flushed.

"I'm so happy about the two of you," Heather added. "And so sorry for the way things happened, before."

"It was a bad time," Stasia agreed. "But we're going to make it this time. Wait and see."

Heather smiled. "No surprise, there."

Tony was glowering at the dancers, one of whom was Big Ben, with darkly beautiful little Mercedes in his arms, doing a two-step. Neither of them was really good at it, but they looked good together. Tony felt lonelier than he had in years.

He sipped the beer he'd been given, although he'd have preferred a good malt liquor. The barbeque smelled good. So did that homemade bread.

He was aware of a faint floral scent and turned to find a nervous Odalie standing beside him.

"Mom said that Mercedes talked about him all the time after Christmas," she murmured, indicating the couple on the dance floor.

"Yeah. He talked about her, too." He shook his head. "They're very different. But they aren't."

"I know what you mean."

She really wanted to ask him to dance, but she was suddenly awkward and tongue-tied.

He raised an eyebrow. "You want to dance?" he asked.

Her eyes widened. "Can you? Dance, I mean?" she blurted out, and then flushed, because it sounded sarcastic. "I didn't mean it like that," she faltered.

He just laughed. He sat his beer bottle on a nearby table and caught her hand in his. He led her onto the dance floor and into a slow two-step. But almost before they got started, the music stopped and started again. This time, it was a cha-cha.

"Finally. Something I like," he said, and he whirled her around. She followed his steps easily, melting into the rhythm.

"You're good at this," he teased.

"So are you," she said, her eyes sparkling.

"Oh, I've always loved to dance," he replied. "I can do most of the Latin dances. Not the tango, however," he added with a grimace.

"I can't do that one either," she told him. "It's too complicated. But I love Latin music!"

"Me, too. Latin, classical, opera, hard rock," he added with a grin.

"Hard rock?"

He nodded.

She sighed.

"I'll bet that doesn't mix with opera."

She laughed softly. "I like Twisted Sister and Bon Jovi and Def Leppard and Van Halen," she confessed. "Not to mention Fleetwood Mac."

"What?" He actually stopped dancing for a few seconds.

"Mom taught me to appreciate all sorts of music, even things like throat singing and ethnic groups from all over the world," she explained as he moved back into the rhythm.

"And here I thought you'd be a musical snob," he teased.

"Not me. Who taught you to dance?" she wondered.

His face tautened a little. "My wife," he said after a few seconds. "She could do all the dances."

"I'm so sorry," she said gently.

He saw the real empathy in her soft blue eyes, and he got briefly lost in them. "It was a long time ago. The memory stings from time to time."

"Yes, but it's not right to forget people we loved even if it hurts."

He nodded.

The Latin rhythm faded, to be replaced by another slow bluesy tune. Tony's arm pulled her closer than necessary and she felt his breath in her hair.

"You're full of surprises," he murmured deeply. "Just when I think I've got you figured out, you throw me a curve."

"People are complicated," she said, feeling breathless and lighter than air and nervous all at once.

His big hand spread on her back as he moved her gracefully to the rhythm. "Just what I was thinking," he said.

She thought she felt his lips in her hair. Probably she was imagining it, because she was feeling a desperate attraction to him that she was fighting with all her might. It was impossible. He hadn't even liked her before. It was a sweet piece of music and they were dancing, it was probably just the atmosphere that was trying to melt her into his powerful body. He was nothing like her. He came from a dark, dangerous world, and she was a hothouse orchid. It would never work.

She told herself that. But her heart wouldn't slow down and her breathing was almost frantic. At least he wouldn't notice, she thought.

But he did. He was much older than she was and very experienced. It touched him, that attraction, because she was a green girl and he was the kind of man her mother had probably warned her about when she was younger.

It bothered him most of all because he wanted her, suddenly and violently enough that if he didn't put some space between them, she was going to find it out for herself pretty quickly. He moved back just a little and looked down into her wide, fascinated blue eyes. He managed a smile. "How much longer until we eat?" he asked. "I'm getting hungry." And he was; just not for food.

She drew away with a self-conscious little laugh. She was almost relieved that he'd stopped dancing, because she was feeling more and more like dragging him into a dark corner, and that would never do. She must be feeling the effects of the music, she told herself.

"Let's go ask," she said, and turned to go back to where Heather and Stasia were uncovering huge containers of food and putting serving spoons in them.

Tony followed along behind her, relieved.

The meal was festive and very obviously enjoyed by all the guests. The Everetts sat with the Brannt family—or most of it. King Brannt and his wife, Shelby, with their son Cort and his wife, Odalie's friend Maddie. Morie Brannt Kirk lived in Wyoming with her husband and son, and they couldn't make it to the barbeque because their little boy had a cold.

"I haven't seen Morie in over a year," Odalie told Maddie and Cort. "I'm sorry the baby is sick, but I would love to talk to her."

"She'll be down for Christmas," Cort said with a grin. "I hope you will, too."

"I'll do my best," she promised.

Tony was staring at Shelby Brannt and frowning. "I'm sorry to stare," he told her, smiling, "but I have this feeling that I've seen you before."

"If you looked at magazine covers a few decades ago, you have," King said. "Shelby was a top model. But she also looks like her late mother."

"I do," Shelby said, smiling back. "My mother was Maria Cane, the actress. Her old movies still show up on the classic television channels."

"That's where I've seen your face," Tony replied. "My mother adored her movies."

"Small world," King said, his eyes soft and loving on his wife's face.

"Small, indeed," Shelby agreed. "Are you from New York, Mr. Garza?" she asked.

"Just Tony," he corrected. "No. I was born in New Jersey.

I still have property there. But I'm in New York a lot because I own a combination art gallery and museum. In fact, Stasia works for me." He glanced toward where she and Tanner were talking together. "Probably not for much longer, though," he chuckled.

"When's the Met audition?" Maddie asked Odalie. "I've tried to keep in touch but we've had a little excitement lately."

Odalie's eyes widened. "You mean…?"

Maddie smiled and her husband tangled his fingers in hers. "Yes. We're expecting. Exactly seven months from today!"

"Oh, I'm so happy for you!" Odalie said. "And so glad that things turned out the way they did. When I remember the things I did to you…"

"Stop that," Maddie said at once. "That was yesterday. This is today and we're best friends." She beamed. "And you have to be the baby's godmother."

"Oh, goodness," she exclaimed. "I'd be honored!"

"Told you so," Cort beamed. He scowled, looking around. "I haven't seen John yet. Where have you hidden him?"

"Dad sent him off to look at some breeding bulls," Odalie said. She frowned. "He never misses a sale, usually, but Dad said this was too important to wait."

"When he gets back tell him I've got the new Destiny 2 expansion for Xbox," Cort said.

She laughed. "I will. Then Maddie won't see you for a week."

"Oh, yes, I will," Maddie said, smirking. "He taught me how to play it!"

"Smart move," Odalie told him.

He grinned.

"You should show Tony the fairy I made of you," Maddie commented. "I don't usually brag about my work, but that was my finest piece."

"Yes, it was," Odalie said. She, like Tony, had finished her meal. "Would you like to see it? She's an amazing sculptor."

"I would indeed," he replied, interested.

Tony stood in the living room with the tiny fairy in his big hand and his expression was hard to read. He just shook his head as he compared it with Odalie.

"It's amazing," he said. "The fairy is identical to you."

"Maddie made it for me while she was recovering from the wreck. It's my greatest treasure," she added.

"I wish we could get her to do a couple of pieces for the gallery," he commented, handing the fairy back. "This is the sort of thing I collect myself. Unique art."

She looked up at him with wide, soft eyes. "I think she's the most talented person I know, next to Stasia. I'll ask her, if you want me to."

"Would you? I don't know if she'd feel comfortable coming to New York right now but we could plan an exhibit for next year, after the baby comes."

"That would be wonderful."

"By then, you may be looking forward to a season with the Met," he added with a smile, wondering why that stung even as he said it.

She just smiled. "I just might be, if I can work up enough courage for the audition."

"You have the talent," he said, studying her face. "You just need a little self-confidence."

She got lost in his eyes, dark and mysterious and piercing. She felt the world blur around her as he stared and she stared back in a silence that was bristling with electricity.

He moved a step closer, so that he could breathe in the fragrance that clung to her. "You'd better put her back up," he said, handing her the little fairy.

His hands closed around hers as she took it from him. She could feel his breath in her hair, feel the heat and strength of him so close. Her heart ran away. She could just barely get enough air to breathe.

She looked up into his eyes and felt as if she couldn't force herself to move away, not if the world erupted under her feet. He was looking at her with a similar expression, his jaw taut, his brows drawing together as they stared at each other blatantly in the tense silence broken only by the sound of music and laughter coming from outside.

It was like falling into fire, she thought dizzily, and she was afraid and hopeful all at once.

Neither of them spoke. It was like electricity binding them together. His eyes fell to her soft mouth and every trace of expression left his face, to be reflected only in eyes that burned like black coals.

She felt faint from the intensity of his gaze on her mouth. She looked at the chiseled perfection of his lips, and she wanted to feel them with a hunger that knocked the breath out of her. Insanity, she told herself while she could think. It was insanity. But he was looking at her mouth as if he'd die if he couldn't have it, and she was drowning in sensations she'd never felt in her life.

The tension was at flash point, when anything could have happened, when the front screen slammed and Tanner and Stasia walked in.

Like two people bound by a cord that suddenly snapped, Odalie turned away and put the little fairy carefully back on its shelf with hands that visibly trembled.

"We're ready for dessert. How about you two?" Tanner asked.

"I could eat some more of that banana pudding if there's any left," Tony said, and although his tone was jovial, he was stretched tighter than a cord. So was Odalie.

Tanner wondered amusedly what he and Stasia had interrupted.

★ ★ ★

The next day, Sunday, was spent lazing around the house and getting ready—or trying to get ready—for Monday's wedding.

Monday was the big day. Everybody dressed, and Tony and Ben packed to leave. Stasia wore a pretty white silk dress from her closet and carried a bouquet of white and pink roses that the florist had been kind enough to leave at the church for her.

The organist played the "Wedding March" and Stasia, on Cole's arm, came down the aisle. Tanner, in his best suit, waited for her at the altar, where the minister greeted her and then married them.

Tanner kissed her gently, feeling the ceremony much more deeply than the first time they'd married.

"This time, it's forever," he whispered tenderly.

She nodded, tears stinging her eyes. "Forever," she whispered back.

The reception was boisterous, and more cake was eaten. At last, the newlyweds went home to their own ranch. Tony and Ben wished the others goodbye and herded Odalie out the door before them, where one of the cowboys was waiting to drive them to the airport. Tony's Cessna was already there, waiting.

Minnie Martinez, wife of Juan, who was the ranch manager, had a small wedding cake ready for them on the table.

"It's beautiful, Minnie," Stasia enthused, hugging her. "Thank you!"

"I know you had one at the reception, but I thought this would be something just for the two of you," she added.

Tanner hugged her, too. "Thanks, Minnie. For more than just the cake. You, too, Juan," he told her husband, who was standing beside her.

"Be happy. And this time, you make it work," Minnie said, shaking a finger at them.

"We'll do that. I promise," Tanner assured her.

"We're off home," Juan said. "If you need us for anything, just call."

"Pancakes and sausage for breakfast in the morning?" Minnie asked as they were going out the door.

"And bacon," Tanner called after her. "A man can't live without bacon!"

"Absolutely!" Juan agreed.

They waved. And they were gone.

Tanner turned to his bride and sighed as he drank in her beauty. "And this man can't live without his beautiful wife," he said softly as he bent to kiss her. "You were the loveliest bride who ever walked down the hall."

She smiled under his lips. And very soon, she wasn't able to smile, or think, for a very long time.

She shivered in the delicious aftermath of a passionate lovemaking that had disheveled both the bed and its occupants.

"And I thought I knew something about men," she exhaled breathlessly. She glared at him. "You've been taking lessons!"

He chuckled, angling across her to kiss her swollen lips. "Lies," he murmured. "I haven't had a woman since you, that last night we spent together."

She froze. Absolutely froze. "That's...not possible," she faltered.

"It's very possible, when you combine an explosive wedding night with a guilty conscience," he said. "I didn't want Julienne. I couldn't touch her after I left you."

She was trying, and failing, to find words.

"You see, I wasn't ready to get married. But I wanted you to the point of madness, I just couldn't admit it, even to myself." He drew her against him and groaned softly as the flames of passion exploded again. "I had hell living with what I'd done. I went back into my old line of work so that I could exist without you. Danger was almost as good as a roll in the hay—which I never had." He lifted his head and looked into her drowning dark eyes. "All I wanted, all those years, was you. I lived in dreams."

Her eyes grew wet. "Me, too," she choked. "I told myself it was because I didn't want to risk losing anybody else, but that wasn't it. I loved you so much. I'd loved you for years. We got married and I was living in this beautiful fantasy. And then you came home with Julienne…"

He drew her close and rocked her. "I should have to be reminded of that every day for the rest of my life," he said huskily. "If I apologized every day, it wouldn't begin to make up for the grief I caused."

Her arms tightened around his neck. "It was a long time ago," she said on a long breath. "We can't go back and change a thing." She drew away and met his pale blue eye. "We have to go ahead."

He nodded. His gaze fell to her pretty breasts. He smiled and bent to rub his lips over them until she moaned. He eased her back down onto the bed and suckled her, hard, and she arched up and sobbed.

"Yes," he whispered. "Even when we're sated, it's still not enough. It will never be enough," he ground out as he moved into her. "I love you…!"

"You…what…?!" Her wild cry made him wild. He thrust down into her arching body, aching with need, groaning with each hard movement of his hips. He felt her body spasm and then, he was falling with her, falling into fire, burning with a fever that all the ice in the Arctic couldn't put out.

"Stasia," he ground out, shuddering. "Stasia, I can't…bear it…!"

He cried out as his body convulsed. She watched him, fascinated. She'd never seen him like that. He stilled finally and shuddered one last time. "Oh, my God," he moaned reverently.

"Are you all right?" she asked, worried.

He drew her to him, both of them still shivering with the remnants of fulfillment. "I had an orgasm," he said with wide-eyed incredulity. "I was beginning to think they were a myth!"

She laughed. "I could have told you they weren't. I had one, even the first time," she whispered. "But I was too shy to tell you."

"And now, not so shy," he teased. He brushed his mouth over her eyes. "I love you. More than my own life," he whispered.

She returned the tender caresses. "And I love you, more than mine."

He drew her close and just held her, without speaking.

"Tanner, what about that man who tried to kill you?" she worried.

"Tony says that's being taken care of," he said. "And I don't think Tony ever lies."

"He doesn't." She looked up at him. "When will we know?"

"Soon." He pulled her back down and drew a sheet over them. "This is where we begin, my darling," he whispered.

She smiled against his throat. "This is where we begin."

Tony phoned a few days later, to tell Tanner he had nothing to worry about. "It's handled. The guy's withdrawn into his own cave. He's still got his job temporarily. After the honeymoon, if you want, I know a senator who'll help you fricassee him. You can let me know later." He chuckled. "Little weasel wasn't as powerful as he thought he was," he added but without relating exactly how he'd vanquished James.

"I still need some recovery time before I open that can of worms, but I plan to. Those innocents shouldn't have died in vain."

"I hear you."

"I owe you one, Tony," Tanner replied. "Thanks. Thanks a million. I wasn't worried for myself," he added. "Just for the people I love."

"That's how they own you," Tony said unexpectedly. "Every soft target is an opportunity for any power-mad fool. I hate men like that."

"So do I, but I didn't have enough powerful friends to ask for help."

"Sure you did. You asked me." He chuckled softly. "But I didn't ask. You see, you can get a lot more with a smile and a gun, than you can with just a smile."

"I have a feeling you're not kidding."

"You're probably right. By the way, if Stasia wants to go on painting, she's got a ready market right here, and she'll get top dollar for her work. I'll even send her commissions, if that's okay with you."

"That's fine with me," Tanner replied warmly. "She's talented. I don't want her to give up anything she loves."

"That's the way it should be. Well, take care of yourselves. I'll be in touch if anything new comes up."

"You might think about coming down for Christmas," Tanner told him. "And Mercedes says you can bring Ben along," he added.

"I might do that."

"Thanks again."

"No problem."

Tanner found Stasia in the kitchen making coffee. She turned around into his arms.

"What did Tony say?"

"He got me off the hook. God knows how."

She grinned. "I have an idea how."

He kissed her nose. "Me, too, but we'll never share it."

Stasia laughed. "No. We never will."

"Well," he said after they had coffee and he was slanting his Stetson across his brow "I guess I'd better go out and talk to Juan about that new seed bull John sent home for Dad."

"Is John back?" she asked.

"Not yet. He's still looking for more breeding stock. But he says he'll be home for Christmas," he added with a smile.

"He's a nice man," she said softly, but the eyes she turned on her husband were brimming with love.

He saw that, and he smiled back. "I'll be home in time for supper."

"I'll have dinner on the table," she replied. She grimaced. "If I don't get lost in my work again. Sorry about last night."

He moved around the table and kissed her hungrily. "You can burn supper every night if I get the reception I had when we turned out the lights."

"Really?" she teased. She wiggled her eyebrows. "Nice to have weapons."

"You won't need them. Ever." He kissed her. "Paint something impressive."

"I'm painting you," she replied.

He was surprised. "Me?"

"My darling," she said, her eyes brimming with love, and finding a poignant response in his own, "you are the most impressive subject of my life. And this," she added softly, "is going to be the most exquisite painting I've ever done!"

And it was.

* * * * *

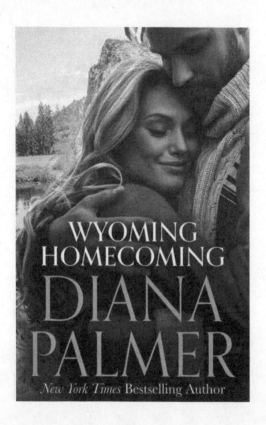

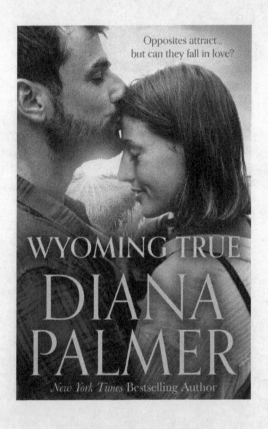